W9-BBI-165

Praise for the Gethsemane Brown Mystery Series

"The captivating southwestern Irish countryside adds a delightful element to this paranormal series launch. Gethsemane is an appealing protagonist who is doing the best she can against overwhelming odds."

– Library Journal (starred review)

"Gordon strikes a harmonious chord in this enchanting spellbinder of a mystery."

– Susan M. Boyer,
USA Today Bestselling Author of *Lowcountry Book Club*

"Charming debut."

– Kirkus Reviews

"A fantastic story with a great ghost, with bad timing. There are parts that are extremely comical, and Gethsemane is a fantastic character that you root for as the pressure continually builds for her to succeed...in more ways than one."

– Suspense Magazine

"Just when you think you've seen everything, here comes Gethsemane Brown, baton in one hand, bourbon in the other...There's charm to spare in this highly original debut."

– Catriona McPherson,
Agatha Award-Winning Author of *The Reek of Red Herrings*

"Gethsemane Brown is a fast-thinking, fast-talking dynamic sleuth (with a great wardrobe) who is more than a match for the unraveling murders and cover-ups, aided by her various– handsome–allies and her irascible ghost."

– Chloe Green,
Author of the Dallas O'Connor Mysteries

"In Gordon's Exceptional third mystery...her ghosts operate under a set of limitations, allowing her earthly protagonists to shine as they cleverly solve crimes. Fans of paranormal cozies will be enthralled."

– *Publishers Weekly* (starred review)

"For any fan who has become completely enraptured by the character of Gethsemane Brown, you will not only love the 'spirit' in this one, but you will also be thrilled to join up with Gethsemane on her third adventure...an all-out, fun-filled story."

– *Suspense Magazine*

"Gethsemane Brown is everything an amateur sleuth should be: smart, sassy, talented, and witty even when her back is against the wall."

– Cate Holahan,
Silver Falchion Award-Nominated Author of *The Widower's Wife*

"Erstwhile ghost conjurer and gifted concert violinist Gethsemane Brown returns in this thoroughly enjoyable follow-up to last year's *Murder in G Major*...With the help of a spectral sea captain she accidentally summoned, Gethsemane tries to unravel the mystery as the murderer places her squarely in the crosshairs."

– Daniel J. Hale,
Agatha Award-Winning Author

"In the latest adventures with Gethsemane, murder is once again thrust upon her and with determination and a goal, she does what needs to be done...The author does a great job in keeping this multi-plot tale intriguing...I like that the narrative put me in the middle of all the action capturing the essence that is Ireland. The character of Eamon adds a touch that makes this engagingly appealing series more endearing."

– *Dru's Book Musings*

The Gethsemane Brown Mystery Series
by Alexia Gordon

A Gethsemane Brown Mystery

EXECUTION IN E

ALEXIA GORDON

HENERY PRESS

Copyright

EXECUTION IN E
A Gethsemane Brown Mystery
Part of the Henery Press Mystery Collection

First Edition | March 2020

Henery Press, LLC
www.henerypress.com

All rights reserved. No part of this book may be used or reproduced in any manner whatsoever, including internet usage, without written permission from Henery Press, LLC, except in the case of brief quotations embodied in critical articles and reviews.

Copyright © 2020 by Alexia Gordon
Author photograph by Peter Larsen

This is a work of fiction. Any references to historical events, real people, or real locales are used fictitiously. Other names, characters, places, and incidents are the product of the author's imagination, and any resemblance to actual events or locales or persons, living or dead, is entirely coincidental.

Trade Paperback ISBN-13: 978-1-63511-515-4
Digital epub ISBN-13: 978-1-63511-516-1
Kindle ISBN-13: 978-1-63511-517-8
Hardcover ISBN-13: 978-1-63511-518-5

Printed in the United States of America

*To my parents, as always,
and to everyone who helped bring this, my 5th book, to fruition,
especially my agent, Paula Munier,
for convincing me to keep going.*

One

The afternoon sun shone bright over the village of Dunmullach in the southwest of Ireland. The fragrance of wildflowers—clover, honeysuckle, valerian—wafted on a gentle breeze over the cliffs of Carrick Point. Gethsemane Brown rested her elbows on a windowsill and gazed out the open window at the pastoral scene that surrounded Carraigfaire Cottage. The day reminded her of Edward MacDowell's "Summer Idyll."

Eamon McCarthy's mood, on the other hand, reminded her of Holst's "Mars: The Bringer of War."

"What the hell are they doing in my lighthouse?" Angry blue sparks punctuated the furious ghost's shouts. A deep blue aura surrounded him. "What's with the holy show?"

"Billy rented it to them for their wedding," Gethsemane said.

"Why the bloody hell didn't you stop him?" An anger-fueled blast of Eamon's leather-and-soap scent filled the cottage's interior.

Gethsemane leaned out the window and inhaled the fresh, green, salty smells of the cliffside. She counted to five and reminded herself that her spectral roommate's anger was really meant for his nephew, Billy McCarthy, who'd owned the cottage and lighthouse since Eamon's murder many years ago. "How the hell, bloody or otherwise, am I supposed to stop my landlord from renting out his own property?"

Another burst of sparks accompanied a string of swear words as blue as Eamon's aura.

"For the record," Gethsemane jerked a thumb in the direction of the century-old lighthouse that sat atop Carrick Point's promontory and dominated the landscape, "I don't want them here anymore than you do. Especially the groom."

"He's the fella you told me about? From the pub? The one Grennan's mot dissolved into screaming hysterics over?"

"'Screaming hysterics' overstates things. Verna got upset, sure, but I wouldn't call her hysterical. And she didn't scream." Seeing Ty Lismore walk into the Mad Rabbit with two of his groomsmen two weeks ago had sent Verna Cunningham, the Latin teacher at St. Brennan's Boys' School and Frankie Grennan's new girlfriend, running from the table in tears.

"What's between Miss Cunningham and the groom-to-be? A bad romance?"

"Chauvinist. You would assume—"

Eamon cut her off. "What else would send her running at the mere sight of him?"

"Um..." Nothing she could think of quickly enough to qualify as a comeback. "Give me a minute."

"Not a damn thing and you know it. Except maybe she's a fugitive murderer and he's the garda hot on her trail."

"You've been spending too much time with me, if that's the alternative you came up with." She and Eamon had solved several murders together since she landed in Dunmullach almost a year ago, starting with his and his wife, Orla's. "Yes, he probably broke her heart. But that's a guess because, other than telling us his name, Verna won't talk about him. At all. She's more closed mouth about Lismore than Frankie is about Yseult." Frankie, math teacher at St. Brennan's and Gethsemane's close friend, loathed speaking about his ex-wife, Yseult, a fugitive thief and con artist. Even mention of her name sent him into a funk he wouldn't emerge from for days.

"This Lismore fella sounds like a true wanker." A blue orb materialized and hovered in front of Eamon. It sizzled and popped with destructive energy. "I could do Miss Cunningham a favor and—"

Gethsemane cut him off. "Put it away."

"Why?"

"Because you can't blast every gobshite and wanker who darkens your day. For one thing, hitting people in the head with balls of energy is rude. For another, how would I explain it to Inspector Sutton?" She shuddered. She'd endured several run-ins with the head of the Dunmullach Garda homicide unit, encounters that usually involved her doing her best to convince the inspector that neither she nor her friends had killed anyone. He wasn't a fan.

"What if I just spook them? Move the furniture, levitate a few objects?"

"I thought you didn't do parlor tricks. They're beneath you. Isn't that what you told me when we first met and I asked you to prove you were a ghost?"

Eamon grinned and shrugged. An amused green tinged the edges of his still-blue aura. "Desperate times. The thought of that gang of bollocks making a bags of my lighthouse by festooning it with gewgaws and furbelows is making me spin in my grave. Literally."

"Rest easy. They're not festooning anything. Billy said the wedding's not until October. They're here now to do some planning and take some pre-wedding photos."

"Can we at least go see what they're up to? I promise to behave."

"If you don't want me to see your fingers crossed behind your back," she pointed to his semi-transparent hand visible through his semi-transparent torso, "you should dial up your density."

"D'you know how much energy it takes to manifest one of these orbs? I can't do it and fully materialize at the same time."

Gethsemane ducked as the blue projectile buzzed past her head. "All the more reason to put it away."

The orb vanished and Eamon filled in until he appeared solid. "Lighthouse?"

She nodded. "I admit to morbid curiosity about the woman who captured the heart of the man who, I assume, trampled on Verna's. Billy seemed impressed. Her name's Sunny Markham; she's American, a social media influencer, and an heiress."

"Social media influencer? That's an actual job description?"

Gethsemane snort-laughed. "She's young, rich, and beautiful. People want to be her but can't, so they settle for wearing what she wears, eating what she eats, traveling where she travels, you get the idea."

"How do they know all that?"

"She posts a carefully curated selection of photos on social media of herself living a fabulous life."

"Are you sure I can't use an orb?"

"I'm sure. Let's go. Maybe I can suss out some intel for Frankie so he'll know what he's up against."

"Race you." Eamon dematerialized.

Two

"What took you so long?" Eamon materialized next to Gethsemane as she crested Carrick Point.

"Allow me to point out that the abilities to dematerialize and translocate through the ether give you an unfair advantage." She stopped a few yards short of the lighthouse. "Oh, my."

A small crowd clustered around its base. Ty Lismore, looking as cold-blooded as he had at the pub, leaned against the tower, one foot propped against the stones behind him. The artful messiness of his brown hair contrasted with the severity of his ice-blue eyes. The two groomsmen who had accompanied him to the pub the day he brought Verna's past back to haunt her stood on either side of him, as they had when Gethsemane first saw them two weeks ago. The blond with the scar, Theophilus Derringer, flanked Ty's right and the handsome Asian, Brian Nishi, his left. All three men wore identical outfits—dark gray linen, modern-fit suits with white shirts open at the collar. Gethsemane's tailor grandfather would have approved. Theophilus looked uncomfortable, like a kid borrowing an older brother's suit for a special occasion. Brian looked as if he'd been born wearing sartorial splendor. Ty looked...like he had a mean streak no bespoke suit could disguise.

Gethsemane thought she recognized the fourth man in the

group, handsome and lean with curly dark hair that reminded her of Eamon's. She'd seen him around the village once or twice over the past week. She'd taken him for a tourist. He hunkered behind a camera on a tripod and snapped photos of the trio. Three women watched over his shoulder. Supermodel tall and supermodel thin, with flawless hair and makeup, they stood as if posing while the one in the center—a willowy, redhead in a barely-there, moss green, silk slip dress—barked instructions at the photographer. Gethsemane smoothed the pleats of her robin's egg-blue, linen sundress as she watched, feeling underdressed in comparison.

"Get some shots of Ty with just Brian and some with just Theo," the redhead said in a geographically-indistinct American accent. She sounded like a news anchor. "Get some shots of Ty by himself. And hurry. This light'll fade soon. I want to catch the sun reflecting off the tower's stone. And get both close-up and medium shots. I want to see all of the boys' faces in frame but still get as much of the lighthouse as possible. This needs to be Insta-perfect. I'm an influencer. My followers and sponsors expect my posts to be perfect. I don't have a lot of time to spend filtering before I post, so I need you to get it right first try. I've got endorsements riding on this."

The other two women, each in a dress similar to the redhead's but in different colors, clustered around her, smartphones ready. The porcelain-skinned brunette in salmon pink flashed a grin at the mahogany-skinned beauty in ivory. The redhead, as if radar had warned her of dissension in the ranks, whipped around to glare at them. The brunette's smile vanished. She and the other woman arranged their faces into expressions of rapt attention. The redhead turned back to the photographer and barked more orders.

"The blushing bride?" Eamon jerked a thumb at the redhead.

"The raging bridezilla," Gethsemane whispered. "I almost feel sorry for Ty. Almost."

"I thought you said they weren't festooning my lighthouse." Eamon pointed to several silk organza swags that framed the lighthouse door and draped the porch railings.

"I misspoke. Why don't you go tell her to take it down?" A grin played on her lips.

"You're funny today, darlin'. Must be the summer air. Even if yon bure could see me—which I doubt because I doubt she sees or hears anything besides her own self-interest—I'd have as much luck convincing her to change her ways as I'd have convincing the devil to give up brimstone."

The redhead looked away from the photographer and noticed Gethsemane. Her entourage followed her gaze. She broke off mid-command and spun, arms swept wide. "Gethsemane Brown! Impeccable timing. Your ears *must* be burning." Her newscaster accent morphed into a high-pitched, little-girl tone that reminded Gethsemane of the creepy children's choruses that sang nursery rhymes in horror films. "Ty and I were discussing wedding music *just* this morning, weren't we, Ty?" She didn't wait for him to answer. "Of *course*, you'll perform at mine. Ours. It'll be perfect."

"Insta-perfect," Eamon whispered in Gethsemane's ear.

Gethsemane ignored him. "I don't think we've met. You must be the bride-elect." She offered her hand.

The redhead ignored it. "But, of *course*, I know who you are. Mummy took me to see you perform Mahler with the Chicago Symphony, oh, *ages* ago when I was *just* a little girl. Baroness Von Meck sat with us in our box—you know Baroness von Meck, I'm sure, she's *such* a big supporter of the symphony—and fed us *all* the delicious gossip. So, anyway, of *course* you'll perform at our wedding. If you don't, my wedding won't be perfect and that's *just* not acceptable."

"Well-played." Eamon materialized with a smirk and an amused green aura. "In a few run-on sentences she managed to point out that she's younger than you, richer than you, more well-connected than you, and to suggest that the success of her wedding depends entirely on you doing what she wants. Well-played, indeed."

No one except Gethsemane appeared to hear or see Eamon. Most people couldn't. She, a reformed skeptic, had never seen nor heard a ghost before meeting him. The origin of her new-found ability eluded her. If any of her relatives or ancestors possessed it, her uber-rational scientist mother forbade anyone from saying so. Now, a small part of her wished the others could see him. Then she could tell him to shut up out loud.

Instead, she favored the socialite with the smile she reserved for deep-pocketed donors whose personalities were as dreadful as their bank accounts were large. "Ms. Sunny Markham, isn't it? I think that's what Billy said your name was."

"Of the Newport Markhams," one of Sunny's attendants offered.

Sunny tilted her head back and sniffed dismissively.

"Miss Markham," Gethsemane continued, "as delighted as I am to meet a fan, I'm afraid I'll have to decline your offer. I don't do weddings."

"But you must, you simply *must*. How could I settle for some local *amateur* when the winner of the Strasburg Medal and the Fleischer Prize is standing in front of me? I can't even *conceive* of anyone else performing. I. Can't. Even. You have to do it." The little-girl tone faded and a hint of coldness crept into Sunny's voice. "I always get what I want." She turned to her fiancé. "Don't I, Ty?"

Ty half-smiled. "Yes, love." He kissed her cheek. "Always."

Not this time. "Your wedding is in October. Michaelmas term will be in full swing then. As music director at St.

Brennan's, I oversee the entire department as well as carry primary responsibility for the Honors Orchestra. We've got a heavy performance schedule and we have to defend our title in the All-County. I wouldn't have time or energy to devote the attention to delivering the high-caliber performance that your wedding deserves. You still have time to find someone else. Perhaps Andrea Bocelli is available."

Sunny pouted. "Ty, make her change her mind." She pushed him forward toward Gethsemane.

Ty grinned, superficial charm radiating from him like summer heat shimmering on hot asphalt. "We would, of course, make your participation in our wedding worth your while. Although, I'm sure a music directorship at a," his oily smile grew wider, "boys' school pays quite well, Sunny and I could do you a bit better." He sounded like a BBC reporter. Had he and Sunny attended the same school of elocution?

Gethsemane dialed up the wattage on her own smile. "Thank you for your generosity but, no."

Sunny narrowed her eyes and her voice grew colder. "Nothing is more important than my wedding."

Her attendants and the groomsmen stepped back. The women huddled closer together as if sheltering against a storm. Ty cleared his throat.

The photographer stepped between Sunny and Gethsemane. "Sunny, sweet, if you want these photos to be hashtag-no filter, we really need to get on with the shoot before the light changes. Think of your sponsors." He put an arm around Sunny's shoulder and steered her toward the lighthouse. "Excuse us, won't you?" he said over his shoulder to Gethsemane.

Sunny looked from Gethsemane to the photographer then giggled. The little-girl voice returned. "My wedding will be the event of the century," she said as the photographer led her away.

"Everyone who matters will be there. You *wouldn't* want to miss it."

"I'd rather have appendicitis," Gethsemane whispered.

"Why don't we get out of here and leave them to their picture-taking," Eamon said. "Or to the devil."

"Gladly," Gethsemane said.

Three

A drink felt in order after her face-off with the happy couple from hell. Gethsemane extracted a half-hearted promise from Eamon not to blast Sunny, Ty, or their entourage with orbs, grabbed her vintage Pashley Parabike, and pedaled to the Mad Rabbit. She spied Frankie Grennan sitting with Verna and her younger sister, Vivian, in a booth at the back. Frankie waved her over.

"I haven't seen much of you this past week," he said.

"I haven't seen much of you this past week." She winked at Verna. Frankie blushed as red as his hair.

"Frankie's been teaching me about roses," Verna said. Frankie, a keen amateur rosarian, had recently won a gold medal in the International Rose Hybridizers' Association's Thirteenth Annual Rose and Garden Show for his hybrid rose, 'Sandra Sechrest.' "You should see what he's done with the old rose garden up at Carnock. You wouldn't recognize it. It looks like a spread from *Irish Garden* magazine."

Gethsemane's hand moved unconsciously to touch the scar on her forehead. Carnock, a desolate hill, better known by the locals as Golgotha, housed the remains of an abandoned insane asylum. Gethsemane's first mystery had nearly been her last when the killer attacked her and set the asylum on fire with Gethsemane in it. The scar was a souvenir of the encounter. She never imagined the tangled brambles that covered the hill could ever be anything but an unredeemable mess of twisted canes and dangerous thorns, but Frankie uncovered the remnants of the rose garden planted when the asylum first opened and had used his award-winning horticultural skills to rehabilitate it. He gave Gethsemane a sneak peek of the work in its early stages, but she hadn't yet seen the finished garden.

"'Fearless Brown' is doing well," Frankie said. "Not that I'd expect anything less from a rambler named for Dunmullach's most intrepid transplant."

"Thank you for naming a rose after me, Frankie," Gethsemane said. "By the way, 'Fearless' is a much better nickname than 'Sissy.'" She made a face at the ridiculous sobriquet her family saddled her with decades ago and her friends in Dunmullach insisted on using to tease her, "so if you want to start calling me 'Fearless' instead..."

"And miss seeing you cringe every time someone calls you 'Sissy'? Not a chance." Frankie winked.

A waitress came over to take their orders. Their drinks arrived and they enjoyed them while chatting about the upcoming school term and about Vivian's, a flutist, doctoral program at University College Cork.

Gethsemane, Bushmills 21 in hand, glanced up from the conversation as the pub door opened. She paused mid-sip as the wedding photographer stepped inside.

Frankie noticed her stare. "You know him?"

"We've met." She turned back to the sisters and tried to resume the conversation.

Too late. Verna had noticed him, too. She paled and her hand shook as she set her drink on the table.

Frankie put an arm around her shoulders. "Vern?"

Vivian swore and jumped up. Her purse spilled to the floor. Its contents rattled and clattered as they rolled under the table.

"He's with them. D'you want me to ask him to go?"

Verna motioned her back into her seat. "Please don't cause a scene, Viv."

"Who is he?" Frankie asked.

"The photographer," Gethsemane said, "for, you know…"

"Ty Lismore," Verna said. "You can say his name."

Vivian mimed spitting. "I'll say he can burn in hell. As can the rest of that bunch."

"You know I'd never pressure you, Vern," Frankie said. "Lord knows there are a few names from my past that won't cross my lips except under duress. But the way you reacted when you saw him here a couple of weeks ago—"

"Who was Ty Lismore to me?" Verna stifled a sob. Vivian reached across the table and laid a hand on hers. "The love of my life, the man I wanted to father my children, the gobshite who ripped out my heart and stomped on it." Tears tracked down her cheeks.

"He left her at the altar," Vivian said. "And now he's come to Dunmullach, of all places, to marry someone else. The bastard."

"Heads up." Gethsemane nodded toward the photographer. "He's coming over."

"Dr. Brown," he greeted Gethsemane when he reached their booth, "allow me to apologize for not calling off Sunny Markham sooner than I did. She's rather much to take. That must have been unpleasant for you." His voice retained hints of the deep South, maybe New Orleans, beneath a general American accent that reminded her of Sunny's. What was the point of flattening out your accent so that no one could tell where you'd come from? To make yourself more marketable? Or to hide from your origins?

Gethsemane shrugged off his apology. "I've dealt with worse." Murderers, vengeful spirits, curses…

"You're gracious. Which is not a word I can use in connection with Sunny. I'm afraid her parents' money bought her a bad attitude."

She craned her neck to get a better look at him than she had at the lighthouse. With his green eyes and boyish face, he appeared younger than he probably was. The resemblance to Eamon struck her again. "Mr...?"

"Malcolm Amott." He shook Gethsemane's hand. His rolled shirt sleeves revealed well-muscled forearms densely inked with finely-detailed tattoos. Vines intertwined with clock faces, eyes, angel wings, and flowers. A vibrant red and orange tattoo depicting a man's hand clasped in a handshake with a monstrous clawed hand disappeared beneath his shirt just above his elbow. He noticed her stare and tugged at the fabric to cover it further. "Youthful mistake. I plan to get a cover-up."

"It's, er, beautiful in a frightening sort of way."

"Are you a fan of body art, Dr. Brown? Maybe you have a violin tattooed in some discrete place?"

Gethsemane laughed. "Not me. My mother would never let me hear the end of it if I got a tattoo, even at my age."

"Vivian's got a thing for tattoos, don't you Viv?" Verna, tears dried, elbowed her sister. The strain in her voice belied the jocular nature of the gesture.

"There's no shame in that, Vern. Everyone's got their kink." Vivian squeezed Verna's elbow and smiled up at Malcolm. "I admire ink on others, Mr. Amott, although I don't actually have any tattoos myself."

Gethsemane gestured to her companions. "Meet Frankie Grennan and Verna and Vivian Cunningham."

"Hello, all." Malcom nodded around the table.

"Haven't I seen you around the village, Mr. Amott—" Gethsemane began.

"Mal, please. They call my father Mr. Amott."

"I think I've seen you around the village, Mal. Before the photo shoot, I mean. You were walking around Our Lady's yard."

"Your lady?" Mal asked.

"Our Lady of Perpetual Sorrows. The large, gothic church in the center of the village."

"Is that what it's called? Our Lady of Perpetual Sorrows? Catholic churches have such creative names. The ones not simply named for saints, that is. I grew up in a non-denominational charismatic church. I worshipped in places with names like Ark of Safety and Holiness Tabernacle."

Frankie leaned closer to Gethsemane and whispered, "Charismatic church?"

Mal overheard. "Sometimes referred to, by non-adherents, as the holy rollers."

Gethsemane nodded at his tattoos. "They didn't have an issue with those?"

"These came much later. My church-going, er, lapsed. I found solutions to my problems outside the church."

"You're an atheist?" Vivian asked.

"Worse," Malcolm said. "I'm a heathen."

"If you've no use for church," Frankie asked, "what were you doing at Our Lady?"

"Scouting locations for Sunny's photo shoots."

Vivian leaned her chin on her hand and her smile broadened. "Did you find a spot? I'd be happy to help you look."

"Thank you for your offer, Miss Cunningham—"

"Viv." Her voice dropped to a sultry octave and her eyes narrowed.

Malcolm bowed his head toward her. "Thank you, Viv. But your Lady, as lovely as she is, won't work. The only area of the garden I could get a good angle on without also getting the cemetery in the shots was the poison garden. A cemetery would be an ill omen for a wedding, and I don't think Sunny would appreciate the humor in me posing her in front of poisonous plants."

"How about inside the church?" Gethsemane asked. "The nave and narthex are lovely. Father Tim wouldn't mind you taking a few photos." The lighthouse decorations came to mind. "Provided you skipped the chiffon."

"I agree with you about the beauty of the church's interior, Dr. Brown—"

"Call her Sissy," Frankie interrupted.

"Call me Gethsemane," Gethsemane corrected.

Malcolm laughed. "I agree, Gethsemane. But Sunny doesn't grasp the concept of a 'few' photos. She insists I take three times as many as I think she needs so she'll have more to choose from as she curates her feed. And the church has a lot of foot traffic. I'd hate for there to be a scene if a parishioner photobombed Sunny while coming to say their prayers."

"Sorry." Gethsemane giggled. "I have an image in my head of a group of church ladies throwing down with Bridezill—with Sunny. The ladies with their leather matron handbags versus Sunny with her designer clutch."

"There's an older part of the church," Verna said. "The subbasement. It's what's left of the original church. Not many people go down there."

Vivian raised an eyebrow. "Wedding snaps in a subbasement? You have a low opinion of weddings?" She winked at Frankie.

Verna countered the wink with an eye roll. "I just thought it would be an out-of-the-way place to take pictures. It would add a gothic flare to the photos."

A flare that symbolized her low opinion of Ty, no doubt. Gethsemane smothered a giggle.

"Thank you for the suggestion, Ms. Verna," Malcolm said. "I

did see the subbasement; I found my way down there through a side entrance someone neglected to lock. I'd have no trouble running some electricity down there for lighting and that old baptismal pool would make a good prop, but Sunny's not big on the gothic look."

"If Sunny Markham is as bad as you say," Vivian asked, "if she's prone to acting the maggot, why put up with her?"

Malcolm frowned. "Acting the maggot?"

"Acting like a jerk," Gethsemane explained. "If you stick around Dunmullach long enough, you pick up a lot of colorful expressions."

"Not that we're suggesting you stick around," Frankie muttered under his breath.

If Malcolm heard, he didn't let on. He addressed Vivian. "Ms. Markham's parents' money buys a great deal of tolerance of Ms. Markham. The pay is phenomenal. And I've convinced myself that running interference between Sunny and the rest of the world is my penance for past sins."

"Mal!"

Everyone turned to see who'd shouted. Ty, flanked by his groomsmen, stood in the center of the pub. They had changed out of the gray linen suits. Ty wore slim-fit navy trousers and a cream linen shirt. A bulge in the trouser pocket betrayed a flask. Waitresses with laden trays shot the group dirty looks as they jockeyed past them.

Verna tensed and buried her face in Frankie's shoulder. Vivian rose from her seat again.

Malcolm looked from the sisters, to Ty, to the sisters. "If you'll excuse me." He made a brief bow. "Apologies."

He joined Ty, Theophilus, and Brian. After a brief, whispered discussion, the four men left the pub.

"They're gone," Vivian said. "Are you all right, Vern?"

Verna closed her eyes for a moment. "I guess I'll have to be all right, won't I? I can't go into hiding until he leaves Dunmullach and I can't have a breakdown every time I see him." She wiped tears with one hand and balled the other into a fist. "I won't let him get into my head again. Not this time. I'd rather..." She closed her eyes again.

Frankie kissed her on the temple. "Dunmullach's not so small that you have to go to ground to avoid him. I'll be your Mal Amott and run interference for you."

"Ty's bridezilla will probably keep him occupied up at Carrick Point posing for 'Insta-perfect' pre-wedding pictures or thinking of musicians to bully into playing the 'Wedding March.' They'll likely be too busy finagling social media sponsorship deals to darken anyone's doorstep." Gethsemane pulled out her phone. "Tell you what. I'll text you when he shows up at the lighthouse and when he leaves so he won't be able to take you by surprise."

Thank you, Frankie mouthed as Gethsemane entered Verna's number into her phone.

Vivian raised her drink and mumbled around her glass. "Text me when he's up there so I can come push him and his horrideous fiancée off the cliff."

Gethsemane's foot hit something. Vivian's wallet. "Your purse."

"Damn." Vivian leaned down to collect her bag and its contents.

"Let me help." Gethsemane motioned to Verna to stay put, wrapped in Frankie's arms, and reached for the items near her feet. She set them on the table as she retrieved them: a comb, a small planner, a silver pen, and a pill bottle, half-full of capsules, their color distorted by the bottle's amber plastic. The prescription label read, "dextroamphetamine." She set the bottle on the table.

Vivian scooped the bottle into her purse. "For ADHD. I also

take nortriptyline. I hate taking the pills but it's the only way I can concentrate on my studies. Sometimes I joke with Vern about giving up on the PhD, chucking the pills, and starting a career as a lifestyle blogger or digital nomad. How much concentration could it require if the future Mrs.—," she glanced at Verna, "if Sunny Markham can manage it?"

"Don't underestimate that one," Frankie said. "I've known women like her. They come across as flighty, fragile hothouse flowers, but really, they notice everything that's going on and they take notes on who said what and when they said it. Then they file the information away as ammunition for future attacks."

"I'll keep that in mind," Gethsemane said.

"Forewarned is forearmed." Frankie raised his glass. "Cheers."

Four

Gethsemane made good on her promise to warn Verna later that afternoon.

Eamon materialized next to her on the sofa in the study where she sat reading a biography of Verdi. His aura shone a mischievous celadon. "Company calls. Lismore." He vanished.

Loud pounding on the cottage's front door prompted a profanity-laced expression of her low opinion of ill-mannered pretty boys who didn't know how to knock. Eamon's disembodied laughter followed her into the entryway. The pounding continued as she sent Verna a text alerting her that Ty was at the cottage.

She opened the door to find Ty lighting a cigarette with a weather-beaten silver lighter. The antique seemed out of place with the modern, pale gray linen suit and Italian loafers that had replaced the navy trousers from the pub. He hadn't included his flask in his wardrobe change. Its tarnished silver top protruded slightly from his jacket pocket. He noticed her looking and slipped the lighter into the same pocket, pushing the flask out of sight as he did so.

"A set," he said. "They photograph well for the social media feed."

"Is that what prompts the frequent costume changes?" She gestured at his suit. "Photo ops?"

"Costume changes?" Ty's eyes widened and his hand flew to his chest in mock offense. "You wound me. My meticulously curated display of sartorial splendor can hardly be dismissed as mere costume changes, as though I were a bit player in some flea bag, itinerant theater troupe."

"Flea bag, itinerant freak show is more what I had in mind."

The offense transformed from mock to real. Ty narrowed his eyes. "Do you have any idea how much these glad rags cost?"

"I do. My grandfather was a high-end tailor. I learned enough about men's fashion by watching him in his shop to realize your fiancée spent a significant chunk of her money to outfit you."

Ty relaxed and shrugged. "The life of an influencer is tougher than you think."

Gooseflesh broke out on Gethsemane's arms in response to his cynical chuckle. "My answer is still no."

Ty looked blank. "Oh, the wedding music." He dragged on his cigarette as realization dawned. "We'll get someone else. Andrea Boccelli, you suggested?" He waved the hand holding the cigarette, sending smoke into Gethsemane's face. "May I use your facilities? Your jacks?" He took a drag on the cigarette. "What is it you Americans call it? Your bathroom? There's none up at the lighthouse."

"What are you doing up at the lighthouse? Not taking more pictures. Don't you have enough?"

Ty dragged on his cigarette again. "As my sweet sunshine says, you can never take too many pictures. Your bathroom?"

"Not with that you can't." Gethsemane nodded at the cigarette. "No smoking."

Ty dropped the cigarette on the porch and crushed it under his heel.

Gethsemane, rooted in the doorway, looked from Ty, to the cigarette, to Ty.

Ty coughed, then picked up the cigarette and put it in his pocket.

"Upstairs." Gethsemane stood aside to let him pass. She waited in the entryway for him to return.

He bounded down the stairs a few moments later. He ignored the open door and sat on the entryway bench. "You're friends with Vern?"

"Is that any of your business?"

"Verna and I used to be close."

"An impressive gift for understatement. You left her at the altar."

"She told you about me."

"No," Gethsemane said, "her sister did. I get the idea Verna would rather talk about boils and toenail fungus than about you."

Ty flashed a smile full of superficial charm. "No need for hostility, is there? I'm just asking about someone who once played an important role in my life."

Gethsemane said nothing.

Ty continued. "The fella she was with at the pub? The ginger. Are they serious?"

"That's even less of your business than whether or not she and I are friends."

"Vern and I go way back. I still care about her and want her to be happy."

"She wants you to be dead. So does her sister."

"Ouch. I'm not going to get much from you, am I?"

"Not this week. So..." She gestured toward the open door.

"You're not easy, are you?" Ty launched into a coughing fit.

She waited until it passed. "Ever think of quitting? Before you cough up a lung?"

Ty waved her question away, a sardonic grin on his lips. "Got it under control. Unlike this situation."

"You cop on fast, Mr. Lismore. Let's hope your darling bride-to-be doesn't cop on to the fact that you're still interested in the well-being of your ex." She opened the door wider. "Better hurry. Your sweet sunshine is probably standing up on Carrick Point, arms crossed, foot tapping, fuming about the Insta-perfect moments you're missing. And you really should do something about that nasty cough. She wouldn't appreciate it if you caught pneumonia and died. You'd cost her a sponsorship."

Ty's smile disappeared. He rose, in no hurry, and ambled toward the door. He paused at the threshold and looked down at Gethsemane, as if he meant to say something. He seemed to reconsider and, instead, smiled again, gave a slight nod of his head, and walked toward the lighthouse.

Gethsemane waited until he reached the end of the drive then called after him. "Why did you abandon her?"

Ty turned.

"Why did you leave Verna at the altar? No one deserves that."

Ty's face remained neutral but his eyes held pure menace. "Blondie-blonde isn't as innocent as she makes out. The poor-me-helpless-female routine's just that, an act. At least with Sunny, I know exactly what I'm getting." He spat the words. "Better warn your red-headed friend to watch his back."

Gethsemane shuddered. Ty reminded her of the husband in one of those twisted domestic suspense novels with "Girl" in the title. He and Sunny were perfect for each other.

As she closed the door, she heard him say, "Give the Cunningham sisters my best. And tell them to be careful who they wish dead."

Five

"I'm telling you, Eamon, it was creepy. Ty Lismore is evil personified." Gethsemane paced the music room.

"You called me by my given name instead of 'Irish.' You must be serious." Eamon's green aura showed that he, on the other hand, was not. He played Debussy's "Golliwog's Cakewalk" on the piano. His fingers disappeared into the keys as he played.

Gethsemane paused her pacing long enough to glare at him. "Not funny."

"You're overreacting," Eamon said. "Lismore and Miss Cunningham had a bad breakup. I'm sure feelings were hurt on both sides."

"Why should Ty care if Verna is serious about Frankie?"

"Some men are that way—possessive wankers whose egos can't handle their exes moving on, even when they were the ones who ended the relationship."

"He threatened her. 'Be careful who you wish dead.' Sounded like a threat to me."

Eamon stopped playing. "Did your warning bells go off?"

"Well, no." Whenever danger loomed, Tchaikovsky's "Pathétique" played in her head, her internal early warning system. She seldom heeded the warning, but it always sounded. "I didn't hear anything."

"Then it was just talk. A gorilla pounding his chest." He

played "Carnival of the Animals."

Gethsemane sat next to him on the piano bench. "I guess. Maybe. What do you think he meant by Verna not being innocent?"

"More ego salvage. Accuse her of being the bad actor, shift the blame to her."

"What if Verna really did something? Cheated on him, maybe."

"Would it matter?"

"No, not really. Unless..." She resumed pacing. "What if she's a habitual cheater? Frankie doesn't deserve that. Yseult put him through enough heartbreak."

"You're letting Lismore get to you."

"I can't help it. It's not only what he said, it's the way he said it. It sounded like more than just talk. Substance lay behind his words."

"Admit it, you smell a mystery and you can't resist it, can you?" Saint-Saens gave way to "Yoda and the Force." "The urge to snoop is strong in this one."

"The urge to protect my friend is strong. Frankie is my friend."

"Yoda and the Force" melted into "When You Wish Upon a Star" from *Pinocchio*.

Gethsemane stuck her tongue out at him. "Okay, okay. I do want to protect Frankie, but I admit I kind of enjoy sleuthing. I seem to have a knack for it. At least this mystery doesn't involve any dead bodies."

"Maybe a skeleton or two." The eerie tones of "La Danse Macabre" replaced the bathetic *Pinocchio* theme.

"Would you stop it with the soundtrack and help me think of a way to find out what really went on between Verna and Ty?"

"Why don't you ask Ty?"

"Even if I trusted him to tell me the truth, which I don't, the thought of having to be civil to him nauseates me. I suppose I could ask Verna. Sometimes you'll tell a gal pal something you wouldn't tell a boyfriend."

"Do you talk about your ex? To anyone?"

"No, but only because there's not much to tell. He wanted an adoring, stay-at-home wife content to live in his shadow. I'd never be that wife, so..." She shrugged.

"Does Grennan talk about Yseult except when he's being questioned as part of a criminal investigation?"

"Point taken."

"How about the sister, Vivian? Orla's sister could never resist gossiping about Orla. She'd have tattled if the devil himself had threatened to nail her tongue to the floor."

"You might be on to something, Irish. No love's lost between Vivian and Ty. Every time she sees him she tries to lay hands on him." Gethsemane walked to the case where she kept her violin, a nineteenth-century antique. "Vivian's a flutist. Think she'd be interested in a close-up look at Vuillaume copy of a Stradivari 'Messiah' violin?"

"Aye, that and a glass or two of Waddell and Dobb Double-Oaked. She'll sing like Kathleen Battle."

Gethsemane rejected the idea of calling Vivian to invite her to Carraigfaire Cottage. She'd have to get her number from Verna, who'd wonder why she wanted it. She'd see Vivian in person.

She rode her bike into the village. Vivian had booked a room at Sweeney's Inn while visiting her sister, claiming she kept odd hours and didn't want to disturb Verna with her coming and going. She also spent time doing research in the Dunmullach library's music collection. Gethsemane had run into her there a few times while doing her own research for the upcoming term's lesson plans. She glanced at her watch. The library closed soon. She'd try the inn.

She parked her bike in front of the Tudor-style structure and entered the lobby. She greeted the clerk at the registration desk.

"I'm here to see Vivian Cunningham, would you call her room to see if she's in, please?"

"She's not in." The clerk nodded toward the lounge. "Ms. Cunningham's in there."

Gethsemane thanked the clerk and headed for the cozy room just off the lobby. Vivian sat with her back to the door, engrossed in conversation with Theophilus Derringer. She didn't notice Gethsemane.

"He's sick. He has to be. No normal person would behave this way. Doesn't he know what he's doing to her?"

"I don't think he sees it that way—"

"What way does he see it? As a couple of old mates reuniting for a walk down memory lane? This is killing my sister."

"I'm sure he didn't mean to cause her pain."

Vivian's harsh laugh turned the heads of other guests in the lounge. "Why did that cow of his choose Dunmullach to get married in? A million bloody lighthouses in the world and she can afford all of 'em. Why here?"

"She didn't—" Theo noticed Gethsemane and broke off. "Hello."

Vivian turned. Her cheeks were damp. "Gethsemane, hello. Sorry, I didn't see you standing there."

"Are you all right?" Gethsemane asked. She glanced at Theophilus.

"I'm fine. I was just, uh—"

"Viv—Ms. Cunningham was hoping I could convince Ty and Sunny to find a different location for their destination wedding. I was explaining that they're both determined people, once they make up their minds, they're not likely to change them."

Gethsemane raised an eyebrow. Vivian must be pretty determined—or desperate—herself to corral a groomsman she hardly knew and try to get him to persuade someone to change their wedding plans.

Theophilus rose, his gaze fixed over Gethsemane's shoulder. "I have to go now."

She and Vivian followed his gaze. Ty, Sunny, Brian, and Sunny's attendants walked into the hotel lobby.

Vivian swore.

Ty smiled, not kindly. "Viv, how are you?"

"Nauseated," she said.

"We haven't had a chance to talk, to catch up on old times."

"I'd rather stick forks in my eyes." She tried to leave the lounge, but Ty blocked her path. "Move."

"Ty," Sunny said in her little-girl voice, with a very adult look of ice-cold threat in her eyes. "Come over here, sweetie. We have an appointment with the director of catering. We *mustn't* keep them waiting. That would be *so* rude."

Ty stepped aside and Vivian rushed past. Gethsemane followed her. She caught up to her in the inn's courtyard.

Vivian sank onto a bench. "I'm sorry. You must think I'm not the full shilling."

"I think something terrible happened between Ty and your sister, something worse than leaving her at the altar.

Vivian buried her face in her hands.

Gethsemane sat next to her. "What happened?"

Vivian didn't answer. Her shoulders shook with near-silent sobs.

Gethsemane placed a hand on her shoulder and waited for the crying to stop. "Vivian, what happened?"

Vivian shook her head.

"If it's something Frankie needs to know about, something

that could hurt him—"

"No, no," Vivian lowered her hands, "it's nothing like that. Vern would never do anything to hurt Frankie, I swear. He's the first man since—" Vivian took a deep breath. "Ty Lismore murdered our brother."

Didn't see that coming. "Murdered your brother?"

Vivian nodded. "Patrick. They were mates, he and Ty. They both worked at Berridge Lodge up in Connemara, Ty as estate manager and Patrick as gamekeeper. They went out shooting one day, hunting for hare. Only Ty came back."

"I'm so sorry. I..." What more could she say? No wonder the Cunningham sisters reacted so violently when Ty walked into a room. How would she react if someone murdered one of her brothers and she ran into the murderer in town? "Why isn't Ty in prison?"

"Because the state concluded 'accidental shooting.'" Vivian filled the words with acid. "No motive for intentional homicide they said. Never even went to trial. An accident. Hah! It was daddy's connections and an expensive solicitor is what it was. That bastard got away with murder as sure as I'm sitting here."

"All things considered, you've modeled restraint. What keeps you from jumping over a table and ripping his throat out?"

"Don't think I haven't considered it. Vern's the only one who keeps me from doing to him what he did to Patrick. She blames herself. She brought Ty into our lives. She introduced him to Patrick."

"She couldn't have predicted her fiancé would shoot her brother."

"She stuck by him after it happened, at least for a while. She chose to believe him, right up to the day she found herself standing alone at the altar. She believed him when he told her it was an accident. Most of the family never forgave her. Ma and

Da disowned her. They haven't spoken to her since Patrick's funeral."

Worse and worse. "I can't fathom why Ty would want to get married in the village where the sisters of the man he killed lived, even if he honestly believed the shooting was accidental."

"I'm sure he's enjoying it. He's cruel. Evil. I'm sure he gets off on the thought that he's torturing us."

"I wish I could say something to make you feel better."

"You can. You can tell me you found his lifeless corpse at the foot of a cliff," Vivian said. She gasped and swore as the object of her hatred appeared in the courtyard entrance.

"Speak of the devil," Gethsemane muttered.

"I have nothin' to say to ya, Ty." Vivian spat the words. "At least nothin' I'd say in front of a witness. Why don't you go back to hell and leave us in peace?"

"Relax, Vivian." Ty stepped into the courtyard and looked around, his gaze at ground level instead of on the two women. "Unlike so many of the men in your orbit, I'm not after you." He bent to peer under a bench.

"Lose something?" Gethsemane asked.

"My flask. You haven't seen it around anywhere, have you?" He peered behind a flowerpot. "I don't know where it's got to."

"If I find it, I'll be sure to return it filled with poison," Vivian said.

"In that case," Ty straightened up, "I'd better find it before you do. No worries, I'm sure it'll turn up." He smiled but made no move to leave the courtyard.

Gethsemane pointed toward the entrance. "You can get out the same way you came in. Or was there something else you needed help with?"

Ty's smile tightened, giving him the appearance of a venomous reptile. "Why do you dislike me? Viv and I have history, sure, but you and I have only just met."

"Why do I dislike you?" Gethsemane shrugged. "General principle? Because to know you is to loathe you? Maybe it's because even a few minutes spent in your company is long enough to know that you don't fall into the category of 'decent guy.' You are not a good person."

"But I'm a gas at parties." Ty winked.

"If I gave you the eye roll that remark deserved, I might sprain an eye muscle. Shouldn't you scurry along to find your keeper? She probably has another photoshoot planned. Gotta keep the sponsors happy."

"Anything for the sponsors. You have to give it to my sunshine. She's a marketing genius. The wedding of her dreams on someone else's dime." He bowed his head to Gethsemane and Vivian. "Ladies."

They watched as he disappeared back into the inn.

Vivian closed her eyes and spoke through clenched teeth. "I hate him so much. Lord forgive me, I wish Ty Lismore nothing more than a slow lonely death." She grabbed Gethsemane's arm so hard, Gethsemane almost didn't notice "Pathetique" playing in her head.

She pried Vivian's fingers from her arm. "You wouldn't act on your feelings for Ty, would you? He's not worth going to prison for."

Tears pooled in Vivian's eyes. "I don't know. Heaven help me, I really don't know." She choked back a sob and ran for the inn.

Six

Gethsemane left Vivian in the inn's bar with a bottle of Bushmills and a promise from staff to see that she got back to her room. She toyed with her phone as she exited the inn. Should she call Frankie and tell him that his girlfriend's ex-fiancé killed her brother? Was that the kind of thing you tell a friend? Should she call Verna and tell her she knew what happened and encourage her to tell Frankie? Did Frankie wonder why his girlfriend lost it every time her ex walked into the same room? Or did he just assume her ex was as twisted as his and satisfy himself, leaving it at that? Yseult hadn't killed anyone. Probably.

She wandered, preoccupied. She looked up when she tripped over the step leading up to the iron gate surrounding the parish church, Our Lady of Perpetual Sorrows. A sign. She'd talk to Father Tim. Father Tim Keating gave good advice, wise counsel, and the occasional paranormal insight gleaned from the library of occult books he inherited from his late brother, also Father Keating, an official exorcist for the Catholic church.

She found Father Tim at home in the rectory.

"Gethsemane, welcome." He greeted her with a hearty handshake, both of his hands clasped around hers. "Come in, come in. A cuppa tea? Or—" He studied her face.

"Some advice," Gethsemane said.

Father Time ushered her into his study. "Tell me what's troubling you. No angry spirits or curses, I hope."

"A mundane problem this time." She retold Vivian's story. "What should I do? Part of me feels telling Frankie would be little more than gossiping but another part of me feels like not telling him would be disloyal, holding out on a friend."

"Why don't you reach out to Verna? Offer her your support and understanding. If she realizes people who care about her won't judge her, she'll tell Frankie herself."

"You're right, of course. I knew you'd give me solid advice. I'll talk to her tomorrow."

"How about that cuppa tea, then?" Father Tim headed toward the kitchen. He soon returned to the study with a loaded tea tray. He served them both and they settled in to enjoy their Bewley's.

A knock at the door interrupted them. Father Tim excused himself to answer it and returned with one of Sunny's attendants. A carnation pink cardigan over a calico sundress had replaced the salmon pink silk gown she'd worn at the lighthouse.

Father Tim introduced her to Gethsemane. "This is Miss Baraquin."

"Rosalie." She shook Gethsemane's hand. Away from Sunny, the slim, American, brunette seemed bright and cordial, if a bit nervous, not like the vapid clotheshorse Gethsemane had initially taken her to be. "I know your name, of course. Nice to officially meet you."

"Join us for a cup?" Father Tim asked.

"Not for me, thank you. And if I've come at a bad time..." She bit her lip.

"Something's troubling you." Father Tim made it a statement rather than a question.

"No trouble..." She hesitated and glanced from Father Tim

to Gethsemane. She pushed the sleeves of her cardigan up.

Gethsemane spied an ornate "27" superimposed on a heart shot through with an arrow and surrounded by circles tattooed on Rosalie's inner forearm. So, Mal wasn't the only one sporting artist-quality ink. Rosalie must have used makeup to hide hers earlier, up at the lighthouse. The salmon-colored slip dress certainly hadn't covered it. The skimpy dress hadn't covered much of anything.

Rosalie noticed her stare and pushed her sleeves back into place. "I'll come back later, Father."

"Please stay." Gethsemane drained her teacup and stood. "I'd better run. It's getting late and I want to ride back to the cottage before it gets dark."

"Please don't let me run you off Dr. Brown," Rosalie said. "I can come back—" She toyed with the cuff of her sweater.

Gethsemane waved off the suggestion. If she'd been one of Sunny Markham's bridesmaids, she'd need spiritual guidance, too. "No. You stay. If something's troubling you, Father Tim's the man to see. He'll get you sorted. And call me Gethsemane."

"Will I see you Sunday?" Father Tim asked her.

"At the late service. You know me and early mornings." Although an Episcopalian, Gethsemane attended Catholic services at Our Lady. Father Tim delivered the best sermons she'd ever heard and the hospitality committee's coffee rivaled that of any Episcopalian church.

Father Tim escorted her to the door.

Rosalie called after her. An apprehensive expression flickered across the bridesmaid's face. "Please, be careful," she said.

"Going home? Don't worry, it's an easy ride. And this is a pretty safe village." Despite the string of murders that had occurred since her arrival.

Rosalie didn't answer right away. Apprehension battled

with uncertainty for control of her features. The moment passed and the non-committal, social media-appropriate expression she'd worn at the lighthouse took over. "Yes, going home. That's what I meant. Be careful going home. Like you said, it's getting dark. Time for the haints and boo hags to come out. Kidding," she added when Gethsemane didn't laugh.

"They call them *taibhse* and *Cailleach* around here. Kidding," she added when Rosalie didn't smile.

Gethsemane bid priest and bridesmaid goodnight then stood on the porch for a moment after Father Tim closed the door behind her. If Rosalie had only meant be careful going home, why had Tchaikovsky's "Pathétique" gone off in her head like a clarion?

When she arrived back at the inn, she found Ty holding her bike with one hand, a cigarette in the other.

She snatched the bike. "Why are you here?"

He indicated the cigarette. "No smoking in the inn." His shoulders shook with a coughing spasm.

"Sounds like you shouldn't be smoking outside the inn, either. What I meant was, why are you here in Dunmullach? Really? And don't tell me you're only here to marry Sunny. You can afford to get married anywhere in the world. You could court sponsors in Paris, London, or Timbuktu as easily as you could in Dunmullach. I doubt your wife-to-be is thrilled by the thought of planning her future with you while your ex hangs about in the background."

He dragged on his cigarette and narrowed his eyes at her.

"What's that look?"

"I'm studying you. I can't suss you out. Not something I say often. I pride myself on knowing everyone's game."

"I'm easy to figure out, Ty. I just want to know. Why. Are.

You. Here?"

He dodged the question. "I'm surprised Vern hooked up with your friend. Redheads were never her type."

"Oh, don't even." Gethsemane drew herself up to her full five-foot-three and stepped toward Ty. "Don't go there. You will not interfere in their relationship."

"Who'd stop me?" Smoke streamed from his nostrils. Coughs followed.

She stepped back, fear of contagion outweighing her anger. "I'd stop you. If that foulness in your chest doesn't stop you first."

"Foulness? You mean my cold, shriveled heart?"

"That, too, but I was talking about your cough."

"I'll pretend your concern for my health is genuine. I've got things under control." He pulled two pill bottles from his pocket and shook them. "Or soon will."

"Drugs? Is that how you deal with Sunny? By staying constantly under the influence?" She glanced at his other pocket. Flat. Empty. "Find your flask yet?"

"You're a wee snarky one, aren't you?"

"I do my best."

Ty grinned and shook the bottles again. "It's medication legitimately prescribed by a licensed health care professional." He tossed one of the bottles her way. "See for yourself. I've nothing to hide."

Gethsemane caught the bottle mid-air with an overhand catch, pleased to see Ty's surprised expression. "High school softball champ," she explained. "And, as for you having nothing to hide, you're as rotten a liar as you are a human being."

"Ouch." Ty crushed his cigarette butt under his heel and lit another. "I protest. I'm a much better liar."

Gethsemane turned the bottle over in her hand. Through the amber plastic, the capsules looked like Vivian's ADHD medication. "What are these?"

Ty held out a hand and Gethsemane tossed the bottle back. "An antibiotic. Evoxil. That and some Benylin," Ty tapped the other bottle, "and I'll be right as rain, as they say."

"I hope you keep better track of your meds than you do of your flask."

"Your concern for my well-being touches me."

"Sorry, it was a reflex, basic humanity-level concern for a fellow being. I forgot for a minute you're inhuman."

"Such flattery. I'm surprised you don't have all the men chasing after you with sweet talk like that."

"I'm surprised no one's pushed you in front of a bus. Tell me how you avoid succumbing to justifiable homicide."

"I manage. Tell me, how do you plan to stop me from reminding Verna what she's losing out on? Let me guess, you're going to run to your ginger mate and tattle on me. Tell him I'm after his mot."

"Since I don't have time to wait for the cocktail of meds and nicotine and whatever you keep in that mercurial silver flask to do you in, how about I run to *your* ginger fiancée and tell her that I caught you with your hand up Verna's skirt?"

"You mean you'd lie about me."

Did she imagine the fleeting look of admiration in Ty's eyes? "I thought you'd appreciate that."

Ty grinned, the closest she'd seen to a genuine smile. "You fight dirty. I admire that in a woman. But you'd better be careful who you take on."

"As should you. Push me or my friends too far and—"

"And?"

She'd almost said she'd summon the hounds of hell to kill him in his sleep. But, given her recent dealings with ghosts, curses, and vengeful spirits, best not to joke.

One of the inn's bellmen approached. "Sorry, to interrupt."

He nodded at Gethsemane and then at Ty. "Someone turned this in at the front desk for you, sir. You left it behind at the bar." He held out Ty's flask.

"The prodigal flask returns. Thank you." Ty held the silver vessel near his ear and shook it. "Did you top it off for me?"

"No, sir," the bellman deadpanned.

"Anyone slip you a few Euros to drop some poison in it?"

"No, sir." The bellman nodded again. "Please excuse me."

After the bellman had gone, Gethsemane asked Ty, "You know Vivian was kidding when she—"

"When she threatened to kill me for the umpteenth time?" Ty yawned. "Vivi does tend to perseverate. She becomes tedious. She was not, however, kidding. Both Cunningham sisters would happily stab me in the heart, given the chance. Luckily, like the man in the movie, my heart is my least vulnerable spot."

"Don't ruin *Casablanca* for me." She loathed the thought of sharing anything with Ty, even love of a classic film. "If you really believe Vivian or Verna would kill you, I repeat my previous question. Why are you here?"

"What's life when lived without danger?" He added, in response to Gethsemane's frown, "You don't believe I'm afraid of either of those two? They're as much of a threat to me as a mouse is to a ravenous lion."

"Don't underestimate the mouse."

A coughing spell cut off his response. Gethsemane turned her back on him and knelt to examine her bike.

Ty choked down a couple of pills from one of the bottles. "Problem?" Cough subsided, he dragged on his cigarette. A stream of smoke escaped from a corner of his mouth.

"Checking to make sure you didn't sabotage anything."

"Don't you trust me?"

She climbed onto the Pashley. "Any other stupid questions you want to ask before I go?"

Ty flicked his cigarette onto the pavement. "Not today. Ride safe."

"Evening, Gethsemane, Ty."

Gethsemane turned to see Malcolm exiting the inn, headed for the parking lot.

"Sunny's looking for you Ty," the photographer said.

"That's my sunshine. Consistently persistent," Ty said. "Where are you off to?" he asked Mal.

"No place in particular." Malcolm addressed Gethsemane. "I thought I'd further explore your charming village. Any suggestions?"

"Have you walked along the cliffs? The view out over the bay is spectacular," Gethsemane said. "And St. Brennan's Boys' School has some gorgeous gardens. You won't be able to get into the buildings, but the campus is open. Head down to the boathouse; the dock gives you a great view of the lake."

"Lake?" Malcolm's eyes brightened. "And a boathouse. Can I take a boat out? Nothing better than an evening sail, is there, Ty?"

Ty shrugged. "I wouldn't know."

"Or are they shells instead of sailboats? My rowing's a bit rusty but I think I could manage not to fall in."

Ty snorted.

"Sailboats and shells," Gethsemane said, "but for students and faculty, only. Sorry."

"My luck." Mal laughed, not seeming upset. "I love being out on the water. Sailing, fishing, rowing...How about you, Ty?"

"I prefer dry land."

"If you're looking for something more challenging than a stroll along the cliffs or through a garden," Gethsemane said, "you can hike around the lake and from the lake back to the village by following the stream. It runs under Our Lady and the market square before feeding into the river that goes out to the bay. You can follow the stream as far as the park across from the Garda station."

"Any place else in the village where it surfaces?"

Gethsemane shook her head. "I don't think so, not now, anyway. It used to come up by the original Our Lady—they used it to fill the old baptismal pool—but it's been built over."

"Mal!" Vivian bounded toward him, arm raised in greeting. She stopped mid-wave when she saw Gethsemane and Ty. Her smile morphed into a scowl. "Oh. Sorry to interrupt."

"You're not," Malcolm said. "I asked Gethsemane to recommend some local attractions. I've opted for the hike around the lake."

Vivian glared at Ty, her hands clenched into fists, an engorged vein tracing an angry path from her temple to her neck. Ty smirked and lit another cigarette.

"You ever consider giving those up, Ty?" Malcolm asked.

"Nope," he answered around a stream of smoke. "Something else will kill me before these do, right, Viv?" He winked at her.

Gethsemane and Malcolm stepped between Ty and Vivian as Vivian lunged forward. Malcolm put a hand on her arm. "Why don't you join me? I'd enjoy the company."

Vivian stepped back and unclenched her hands. She kept her eyes on Ty as she spoke. "Thank you, Mal. I'd love to join you. I need some fresh air."

"Have fun," Ty said.

"Crawl in a hole and die," Vivian responded.

Malcolm gestured toward the parking lot. "Shall we? Best we get started before it gets too late."

After a final expletive directed at Ty, Vivian strode away. Malcolm turned to follow her but paused to ask over his shoulder. "By the way, Ty? Did you get your flask back? I found it on the bar and asked the front desk to hold it for you. If I'd known I'd run into you, I'd have given it to you myself."

Ty displayed the flask.

"That's all right, then," Malcolm said. "Gethsemane, good evening."

"Same to you," she said.

He hurried to catch up with Vivian.

Gethsemane watched Ty for several seconds. He puffed his cigarette and stared back. "You really are the devil incarnate, aren't you?"

"Nah," he said. "The devil's got nothing on me."

"T-y-y-y?" Sunny's lilt carried from some unseen location. Gethsemane cringed at its irritating, sing-song quality.

"Where are you, sweetie?" Sunny sounded closer. "I need you. Don't make me look for you. You know how I hate to have to look for you." The girlish tone carried an undercurrent of malice.

"I bet she pulls wings off flies during her downtime," Gethsemane said.

Ty chuckled and swigged from his returned flask before answering. "Over here, dearest sunshine, heart of my heart."

"Bane of my existence," Gethsemane muttered.

Ty chuckled again. Sunny appeared around the corner of the inn. A frown creased her brow when she spotted Gethsemane, replaced by an expression of charmed surprise so quickly, Gethsemane wondered if the frown had ever been there.

"Doc-tor Brown," Sunny said as she threaded her arm through Ty's. She pulled him close to her, away from Gethsemane. "Thank you for babysitting my man. I hope he didn't trouble you too much."

Ty smiled down at Sunny. His flask disappeared into a pocket. "I'm not a bit of trouble." He paused, then added with a sidelong glance at Gethsemane, "Am I, Doctor Brown?"

Was he daring her to say something about Verna? Or

threatening her not to? Either way, he had it coming. "No trouble to *me*—" she began.

Sunny cut her off. "Of course, he wasn't. My Ty's a peach. A yummy, perfect peach." She kissed him.

"An Insta-perfect peach," Gethsemane said under her breath.

"Speaking of perfect," Sunny said, "we'll be up at the lighthouse later this evening. Just Ty and me, to take some night shots. You won't mind." It wasn't a question.

"Just you and Ty? You're taking selfies?"

"Of course not." Sunny made a disdainful noise. "We'll bring Mal. I'm paying him a fortune; I'm going to use him."

"Speaking of Mal, where'd you find him? He doesn't fit my image of a wedding photographer."

"Oh, I don't know." Sunny gestured as if nothing Mal did before working for her mattered. "Some gallery. In New York? New Orleans? Where was it, Ty?"

"Your mother introduced him. She attended his show at that artists' co-op. What was it called?" Ty snapped his fingers. "You know the one."

"Whatever," Sunny said. "Mal's a smart man. He knows that photographing the wedding event of the era is far more lucrative than taking artsy photos of rocks or buildings or whatever it was he was doing."

"He says he plans to use the money to further his art," Ty said.

Sunny snorted. "Once my photos hit social media and the sponsors line up like starving seals at a fish market, Mal will forget about 'art.' He'll be far too busy juggling offers from influencers. They'll go after him like—"

"Starving seals?" Gethsemane asked.

Sunny looked daggers at Gethsemane. "Not that any other influencers can match me, of course." She kissed Ty again.

"Come on, sweetness. We've got a couple of hours before we need to be anywhere. Remind me how much you want me."

Ty scooped Sunny up and spun her around. His flask slipped from his pocket and clattered to the ground.

"Honestly, Ty," Sunny said, "if you can't keep up with it, why carry it around?"

"It's my trademark." Ty put his fiancée down and retrieved his flask. "Part of my brand."

"It's time to discuss re-branding." Sunny grabbed him by the arm. "Come on."

Gethsemane shivered despite the still summer air as she watched the couple go into the inn. Ty and Sunny's match had been made far from heaven. She didn't put much stock in happily ever after, being more a pragmatist than a romantic, but she wouldn't give even odds on those two achieving contented enough for the time being. "Pathétique" swelled in her head, accompanied by images of Ty and Sunny as the subject of a Women's Network show about murderous spouses. No surprise if one of them ended up as a skeleton in a footlocker before their third anniversary. But which one of them was Tchaikovsky warning her about?

A breeze sprang up, carrying with it the faint aroma of leather and soap. The breeze grew into a gentle wind that swirled the scents, echoes of Eamon's cologne and soap that often heralded his arrival, around her.

"Come out from wherever you're hiding, Irish."

Eamon materialized next to her. "I wasn't hiding."

"From wherever you were lurking, then."

"Someone's in a foul mood this evening. No need to eat my head off."

"I'm not—" She took a deep breath and started again. "I didn't mean to sound cross."

"You're worried."

"I can't shake the feeling that one-half of the unhappy couple isn't going to make it to the honeymoon."

"Shouldn't you tell O'Reilly? Or Sutton?"

"Seriously? Tell the Dunmullach Garda's chief cold case or chief homicide inspector that I have a hunch—not evidence, only a hunch—heralded by music that only I can hear, that some unknown unpleasant thing will happen to some unknown person at some unknown time? You want them to arrest me for wasting police time?"

"Don't look at me like that." Eamon's aura glowed a scolding platinum. "No offense, darlin', but your track record of hunches leading to dead bodies is enough to send the guards scrambling for an arrest warrant."

No denying Dumullach's murder rate had jumped since she'd arrived, a statistic that made her a frequent, if unpopular, visitor to the Garda station. She'd spent more time in interrogation rooms in her months in the village than she had in the rest of her thirty-eight years combined. "I can't tell Sutton. If I mention murder within earshot of him, he's liable to arrest me on principle. I'll talk to Niall." She counted the head of the Garda's cold case unit as a friend. "In the morning. I'm going to have to sell him on the idea and I need to sleep on it before I craft my pitch. Not that I have any idea what he could do about the possibility of a crime occurring in the future."

"Tell him it's a courtesy heads-up."

"Speaking of heads-up," Gethsemane lowered her voice as a movement beyond Eamon caught her eye, "here comes Rosalie Baraquin. You better vanish."

"She can't see me. Nor hear me."

"But I can see you and hear you. And I'm liable to answer you. Which I'd have a hard time explaining."

"I'll be quiet. You'll manage." Instead of vanishing, Eamon appeared more solid.

Gethsemane bit back her opinion of his ability to remain silent as Rosalie neared. She greeted the bridesmaid. "Are you—all right?"

"All right?" Blankness gave way to remembrance. "Oh, you mean since my visit to Father Keating. I'm sorry if I ran you off."

"You didn't run me off. You seemed upset. Or worried."

Rosalie didn't respond.

"Anyway, you obviously needed him more than I did at that moment. I hope he helped."

"Yes, he did." Rosalie's shoulders relaxed as if the priest's counsel had come back to her as a palliative. She raised her arm to massage her neck, exposing her tattoo again.

"It's beautiful," Gethsemane said before Rosalie could hide it. "Such intricate detail. It reminds me of Mal's. Do you two have the same tattoo artist?"

"No." Rosalie tugged her sleeve down. "I mean I don't know. I have no idea where Mal had his ink done. I'm sure any similarity is just coincidence."

"What's your tattoo symbolize? The twenty-seven and the heart?"

"Nothing. I mean—" Rosalie paused. When she spoke again, her tone sounded more convincing. "The tattoo was a youthful mistake. I made a deal with someone a long time ago."

"A matching tattoo pact? Or a lost bet?"

Rosalie shuddered and rubbed her arms, a faraway expression on her face.

"I'm kidding."

"What?" Rosalie snapped back to attention.

"Are you sure you're all right? You seemed to be..." Gethsemane waved her hand in the air, suggesting Rosalie had been anywhere but here.

"I just..." Rosalie shuddered again. "Cold chill. Someone must be walking over my grave." Her mirthless laugh died abruptly and she stared at the space next to Gethsemane.

Gethsemane forced herself not to look at Eamon.

"No." Eamon seemed to guess her thought. "She can't see me." He hesitated. "I'm almost positive." He screwed up his face and made a rude gesture. Rosalie didn't react. "Nope. She can't see me."

Rosalie turned her stare on Gethsemane. "Why are you here?"

"I, um, came to get my bike. I ran into Ty and—"

"No, I mean why are you here in this village, so far from home? Your family's not here, you've no roots here. Why are you in this place?"

Why had she stayed? Directing a boys' school music program hadn't been part of her grand plan. Nor moving into a haunted cottage. She hadn't even believed in ghosts. And yet, she loved her job, she'd made friends, she liked her ghost. And, if she was honest, she got a thrill from her new-found sleuthing abilities, a sense of purpose from keeping innocent people out of jail, and a sense of satisfaction from bringing killers to justice. She shrugged. "I don't know. I guess Dunmullach feels like home now."

"This place feels like..." Her words trailed off and Rosalie shook her head as if to clear it. "Sorry. Guess I'm not much for small towns. There's something...creepy about them. Give me the big city, any day. Excuse me." She went inside the inn.

Gethsemane waited until she'd gone, then asked Eamon, "You're certain she couldn't see you? Or hear you?"

"If you saw me make that gesture at you—"

"I'd have reacted. She didn't see you."

"Doesn't mean she couldn't sense me. I run across people from time to time who know something's quare, even if they can't say what."

Gethsemane took a deep breath. With Eamon this close, she

detected notes of cedar and pepper intermingled with the leather and soap. "Maybe she smelled you."

"Maybe you should be wide around that one. She's more than vapid smiles and overpriced clothes."

"This whole bloody wedding party is more than I can deal with right now. I'm tired, I'm hungry, and," she shifted with growing discomfort, "I have to pee."

"Use the jacks in the inn."

"I'll wait 'til I get back to the cottage. Don't worry," she said in response to his doubtful hickory-brown aura, "I've held it all the way through Mahler's 'Third.'"

"Which isn't the same as bumping along on a bike over rural Irish roads. You won't make it past the post office."

"How do you know?"

"Have you forgotten I was married to a woman? Have you any idea of how many toilets I've waited outside of? I've got some idea of how it works. Go on." Eamon pointed to her bike and sent it rolling to rest against a wall. "I'll wait here."

No point arguing. Gethsemane went inside in search of the ladies' room. She turned down a hallway off the inn's lobby. Rosalie and the other bridesmaid stood at the far end, heads close together in intense conversation. The other bridesmaid punctuated her words with jabs at Rosalie's arm. Gethsemane hung back and tried to overhear what they said but they kept their voices too low. Rosalie looked up and saw Gethsemane. She nudged the other bridesmaid into silence.

"Um, ladies' room?" Gethsemane pointed to a door behind them. They moved to let her pass.

A short while later, Gethsemane stepped back into the hall. Rosalie and the other bridesmaid were gone. Gethsemane continued through the lobby on her way out of the inn. She spied Rosalie in one of the armchairs near the fireplace. She clutched a piece of paper in one hand. The other, balled into a fist, pressed against her lips. Gethsemane moved close enough to peer over Rosalie's shoulder. She glimpsed an intricate line drawing before Rosalie noticed being watched. Startled, she crumpled the paper and shoved it between the seat cushion and the arm of the chair.

"Bad news?" Gethsemane asked.

"No, uh…" Rosalie retrieved the wadded paper, smoothed it, and folded it neatly, careful to keep whatever was on it hidden from view. "Just, um, a message from…someone."

Gethsemane waited for Rosalie to say more but the other woman remained silent. After a few seconds, Gethsemane spoke. "I hope everything's okay. If you need anything—"

"Father Keating issued an open invitation. Thanks for asking." She rose and headed for the stairs.

Gethsemane watched her disappear onto the second floor then headed outside to find Eamon.

"Feel better?" he asked.

The story tumbled out. "Someone sent Rosalie a note, some kind of drawing. It upset her, but she made a point of not telling me why it upset her nor who sent the note. She also made sure I didn't get a second look at the drawing. She actually crumpled the note rather than let me see it. And, yes, I feel better."

Eamon's aura glimmered an amused green.

"What's funny?" she asked.

"You've got that I-know-something's-going-on-and-I'm-going-to-find-out-what look on your face."

"Rosalie took time off from bridezilla watch to see Father Tim about something, something troubling. A little while ago, I saw her in the hall in a heated discussion with the other bridesmaid—"

"You left that part out."

Gethsemane told Eamon what she saw outside the ladies' room. "They may not have been arguing. But they looked serious about whatever they were talking about. And a few minutes after that, Rosalie got a note that disturbed her, a note whose message she hid. Doesn't that add up to...something?"

"The note could have been a letter from an ex or bad news from home."

"It was a drawing."

"Maybe it was a new tattoo design."

"Why would she be upset about that?"

"I thought you were concerned with the future Mr. and Mrs. Lismore."

"I was. I am. I'm concerned about Rosalie, too." She pressed the heels of her hands hard against her temples. "None of this is making sense."

"What do you want me to do, he asked like a proper sidekick," Eamon said.

"Pop into Rosalie's room and get that note."

"I don't pop. I—"

"Translocate. Can you translocate into her room and get the note? Or at least get a good look at it?"

"To be clear, you want me to enter a woman's room uninvited—"

"Don't pretend you have any qualms about that. You translocate into my room whenever you feel like it."

"Correction. I translocate into my room. You just happen to be occupying it."

"Stop nitpicking."

"As I was saying, you want me to enter a woman's room," Eamon raised an eyebrow as if daring her to contradict him, "uninvited, and steal a private message?"

Gethsemane met his gaze. "Yes."

"Fine. Just wanted to make sure I understood the plan."

She closed her eyes and counted to three. "You enjoy this, don't you?"

Eamon's aura glowed bright green with his laughter. "More than you know. A ghost has to have some fun."

"You're worse than my brothers. By the way, you can get inside, can't you? Sweeney's has been here since 1902." Eamon could only enter places as a ghost that he'd visited during his lifetime—except the church. Buried in error in unhallowed ground as a supposed suicide, he couldn't go past the church's gate. "I assume you've been inside at least once."

"Sweeney's is the grandest place in the village. Every wedding reception, graduation, First Communion, and mother's birthday has been celebrated there since they opened their doors. I've been inside countless times."

"Good. Then you'll have no trouble getting into Rosalie's room. What are you waiting for?" She motioned for him to hurry.

"And here I thought Orla was the only woman I couldn't say no to." He vanished with a wink.

A moment later, he reappeared. His green aura had transformed to a disappointed puce tinged with an apologetic magenta.

"What happened?" Gethsemane asked. "You couldn't find the note?"

"I couldn't get in."

"But you said—"

"I know what I said." Mauve annoyance flared between the puce and magenta. "I'd no trouble getting inside Sweeney's. But Rosalie Baraquin has barred her door."

"You lost me. You can pop—translocate—through doors, windows, walls—"

"Not against charms, I can't. The Baraquin woman's worked some sort of spell or used a talisman or something to prevent supernatural entities from crossing her threshold."

"Since she doesn't know you exist, she can't be trying to

keep you, specifically, out. You're sure she can't see or hear you?"

"For the last time, I'm sure. I'm as sure she can't see nor hear me as I am of my own name. Besides," his aura flared with all the colors of indignation, "if she could see or hear me, she wouldn't want to keep me out."

"Eamon McCarthy, proof that ego persists after death," Gethsemane said. "If not you, then who? Is some other ghost hanging around?"

"Darlin', have you forgotten where you are? This is Ireland. The place is lousy with ghosts. But none other than yours truly in the immediate vicinity. Unless you've conjured another sea captain or vengeful princess..."

"I have not. I learned my lesson." She had, in the past, called an eighteenth-century sea captain back from the other side by accident when she recited a summoning spell then played the tones—a sea chanty—that vibrated as his harmonic likeness. "Don't recite summoning spells unless you know exactly who you're calling. Kind of like not hitting 'reply all' on your emails. But the vengeful princess—" who'd almost succeeded in destroying Dunmullach's first-born male population "—was not my fault. Whose Rosalie trying to keep out?"

"Not trying. Succeeding. She knows what's she's doing. Like I said, be wide with that one, be dog wide. And I'm afraid you'll have to find a mundane way of getting a look at that note."

"How'm I going to do that?" She'd broken into more than one room—gained unauthorized access, she preferred to call it— in the course of an investigation but Frankie, her usual accomplice, had Verna to worry about. He wouldn't be up for skulking about the inn or running interference for her. She certainly couldn't ask Niall, a garda, to help her. And asking Tim, a priest, didn't seem right, either.

"You'll think of something," Eamon said.

"Not standing out here, I won't." She climbed on her bike. "I'm heading back to the cottage. Maybe I'll think of a plan on the way."

Seven

The sun gravitated toward the horizon as Gethsemane pedaled toward Carraigfaire. Our Lady of Perpetual Sorrows' wrought iron fence came into view as she crested a hill. A detour was in order. The virulent animosity between Ty and the Cunningham sisters, concern for Frankie, anxiety over Sunny and Ty, and a sense of dread about Rosalie conspired to make her head throb. The persistent strains of Tchaikovsky didn't help. Father Tim had a gift for wrestling calm from the center of a maelstrom armed with nothing more than wit, common sense, and a pot of Bewley's tea. He'd help her make sense of things.

She found him in the rectory's kitchen, an array of batter-caked bowls, spatulas, and measuring cups spread before him on the counter. He stood with his elbows propped amidst eggshells and vegetable peels, chin in hands, studying a book whose worn covers and yellowed pages gave it an ancient appearance.

"Brushing up on your Betty Crocker?" she asked. "I hope you don't mind me letting myself in. The door was open."

"Course I don't mind." Tim brushed a hand across the book's pages, raising a small, white cloud that could have been dust or flour. "I left the door open to keep from setting off the smoke detectors. The fire brigade convinced the bishop we needed them, but the kitchen's so small, you can hardly boil a kettle without the steam setting the bloody things off."

"What are you, um, baking?" She picked up a pan filled with thick, lumpy batter the color of beets.

"A medieval veal and vegetable pie."

"Rephrase. Why are you baking?" One whiff of the pan convinced her to set it down and push it aside. No amount of nose wrinkling could get rid of the smell. "This reminds me why I don't cook."

"Saoirse's studying the culinary history of the British Isles and Europe. We've reached the medieval period. Have you ever tried to convert a sixteenth-century recipe to the metric system?"

Gethsemane pictured mischievous, blonde, twelve-year-old Saoirse Nolan in the kitchen with Father Tim. The prescient, precocious young genius, privately tutored by the priest since her parents discovered the local schools had run out of subjects to keep her brilliant mind occupied by the time she turned seven, displayed talent, skills, and abilities in broad areas. Cooking, however, was not an area in which she'd shown any interest.

"Wouldn't Saoirse rather study medieval weapons?" Gethsemane asked.

"That's next month." Tim closed the cookbook. "'Tis hopeless. I've made a right bags of the kitchen."

"I'm sorry I stopped by at a bad time. I should have called."

"Nonsense. You saved me from," he waved his hand over the counter, "all this. Care for a cuppa tea?"

Gethsemane surveyed the culinary detritus. "Let's skip the Bewley's this time."

She followed Tim into the study. "I apologize for coming by this late, but I'm stuck. I can't shake this feeling that something bad's about to happen. I've got no evidence, only a feeling—" And Tchaikovsky, she almost added.

Tim settled in a chair across from her. He leaned forward, elbows on knees, hands clasped, with no indication he took her anything other than seriously. "What do you think's going to happen?"

"These days, my bad feelings usually mean dead bodies. I don't know what or how. Who? Ty? Sunny?" She hesitated. "Or Rosalie? What did she talk to you about earlier?"

Tim leaned back in his chair, concern drawing his brow into a frown. "You know I can't discuss that. Miss Baraquin came to me in confidence. What's happened to make you think she may be in danger?" A raised eyebrow displaced the frown. "Sadly, I don't need to ask what concerns you about Mr. Lismore and Miss Markham. Even if they weren't the hottest topic on the local gossip circuit, their behavior makes it obvious theirs is a union created somewhere south of heaven. But you're suggesting Miss Baraquin is in danger. You're afraid some harm might befall her?"

"Yes. Rosalie received a note from someone that...upset her. Her reaction seemed..." What? Out of proportion? By whose standards? What had Rosalie really done, aside from telegraph the message that her business was none of Gethsemane's? And consult a priest. And deploy a charm to keep supernatural entities out of her hotel room? "She wasn't happy about the note, which was a line drawing. I only glimpsed it for a few seconds, but I didn't see any words. It seemed an odd reaction to a picture. Ea—someone suggested I talk to Niall. But when I hear myself tell the story and lay out the details—well, I don't have any details. At least not the kind I'd take to law enforcement. So I came to you." She studied Tim's face. Not dismissive, not judgmental, not shocked. Did he wear this same inscrutable expression during confession when penitents confided their sins? "Should I go to Niall?"

"The inspector's a man who operates on evidence. He

knows you well enough not to discount you, but he'd need something tangible to act on." Tim cocked his head. "You don't have anything tangible, do you? Like the note?"

Niall wasn't the only one who knew her well. "No. I, er, couldn't figure out a way into Rosalie's room."

Tim drummed his fingers on the chair arm. "I'll visit Miss Baraquin in the morning to see how she's doing after our chat. If you don't mind me mentioning your name, I'll tell her you noticed she appeared perturbed and offer my assistance. Perhaps she'll open up to me."

"Thank you. You always come up with the most reasonable course of action. You're impressively level-headed."

"Wish my dear aul wan, God rest her soul, could hear you say that. Growing up, my brother was the straight man and I was the one given to acting the maggot."

"Your brother, the exorcist, was the strait-laced one, and you, the parish priest, were the wild child?"

"Sums it up," Tim said.

"There's a concept for me to wrap my head around—the Keating brothers, a study in contrasts." Gethsemane stood. "Thanks, again, for listening and, in advance, for your help. And for giving me something to ponder besides wedding disasters, social media, and cryptic messages."

"Always glad to help." He escorted her to the door. "I'll call you after I see Miss Baraquin. I hope I'll be able to tell you there's nothing to worry about."

Gethsemane pedaled home in semi-darkness, somewhat reassured by Tim's promise to speak with Rosalie. He stood a good chance of finding out what upset—or frightened—her. Few people could resist opening up to the priest. She'd hold off on telling Niall her suspicions until after she heard from Tim. She wanted to offer the inspector something concrete, something that couldn't be dismissed as a hunch, feminine intuition, or jiggery-pokery.

She almost missed it. Sudden movement flashed in her peripheral vision. She turned her head just in time to see Vivian dart around a bend in the winding road leading to Carrick Point and barrel into her path.

"Oh!" Gethsemane jerked the wheel of her bicycle to one side to avoid plowing into Vivian. She lost balance as her tire skidded on a rock. Curse words died on her lips as the road loomed toward her. She let go of the bike and twisted sideways, landing on her shoulder. "Oof!"

"Shite!" Vivian squatted beside her. "Are you all right? Anything broken?"

Gethsemane, stunned and winded by the impact, didn't answer. She struggled to sort out what had happened. Her bike lay on its side, wheels spinning, a few feet from where she lay. She stared up at a worried Vivian. Vivian? What was Verna's sister doing up on Carrick Point road?

"Gethsemane? Are you all right?" Vivian held up her cellphone. "Shall I call an ambulance?"

The thought of a night in the hospital snapped her out of her confusion. "No. No ambulance. I'm fine. Sore, but fine. I think." She wiggled her fingers and flexed and extended her elbows. At least those worked. She could hold a baton or a violin. She flexed her toes, knees, and hips. They worked, too. "I'm fine. Help me up?" She extended a hand.

Vivian helped her stand then retrieved her bike. The Pashley had earned a few new scrapes and dings but, overall, remained intact. Vivian held onto it while Gethsemane brushed gravel from her elbows. "You've ruined your dress." She pointed at Gethsemane's skirt.

Gethsemane examined her dress. A grease stain marred the

blue linen and the hem hung loose where the fabric had gotten entangled in the bike. "Nothing a good dry cleaner can't fix. Or," she took a closer look at the grease stain. The skirt would probably have to be shortened to remove the damaged area, "a good tailor." Too bad she couldn't take it to her grandfather.

Vivian apologized. "Can you forgive me? I know I should have been watching were I was going, but—" She giggled and clutched her purse to her chest.

"What are you doing up here?" Gethsemane leaned on her bike and massaged a sore spot in her hip. "I thought you'd gone for a walk with Mal."

"I did. Then he had to meet Ty and Sunny up at the lighthouse for another damned photoshoot. I helped him carry his gear."

She'd forgotten Sunny wanted night photos. But why would Vivian help Mal schlep his equipment, knowing that going up to the lighthouse would put her in Ty's vicinity? "Why would you want to be anywhere near Ty?" Unless...Gethsemane's throat tightened. "You didn't push him off the cliff, did you?"

"No. Tempted, but..." Vivian giggled again and reached into her purse. "I wanted to get close enough to Ty to grab this." She pulled out his silver flask. "Actually, I didn't get that close to him. He dropped it again. Sunny made him pick her up and spin her around like a scene from a third-rate telly advert for fabric softener or teeth whitener or something. It slipped from his pocket mid-spin and landed in the grass."

"You stole his flask?"

"Borrowed it. Mal and I finished setting up before they got there so I'd been hiding behind some rocks, waiting for the chance to sneak away, when the flask fell. I nicked it and ran." Vivian pouted the way Gethsemane's niece did when caught doing something naughty. "Don't worry, the wanker can have it back. Eventually. I'd like to put poison in it."

"But you're not going to."

"No. Not poison." Vivian shook the flask. "Nearly empty. Figures. I'd drink, too, if I was marrying Sunny Markham." She unscrewed the flask's top, horked saliva, and spat into the container. She screwed the top back on and shook the flask. "Mix well."

Gross. Gethsemane curled a lip. "How do you plan to return that to Ty?"

"I'll give it to Mal to give to him. Mal's his mate—well, his fiancée's employee—so he won't be wide if Mal hands it back." She frowned at Gethsemane. "You think this is a childish, petty stunt, unworthy of even the youngest of your schoolboys. You're right. But what else can I do? The thought of that cute hoor prancing about in his fancy duds with his fancy mot, acting as if they're the king and queen of all they survey, not giving a damn about the pain he's causing Verna, getting off on it, even. I just—" She bit off her words and squeezed her eyes shut. She shook with an almost palpable rage, the flask clenched so tightly, Gethsemane feared she'd break her hand if the metal didn't collapse.

Bruised muscles and damaged skirt forgotten, she extended a hand toward the distraught woman. "Vivian?"

Vivian took a deep breath and held it. The shaking ceased and she opened her eyes. A wan smile flickered across her lips. "God forgive me, I want Ty dead. But I'm too much of a coward to spend the rest of my life in prison for murder. So, I settle for petty sabotage, like spitting in his whiskey. Pathetic, right?"

"Frustrated. Desperate. Understandable."

"Thank you." Vivian slipped the flask back into her purse. "Thank you for not making me feel like a hysterical idiot. Neither Vern nor I have been feeling good about ourselves since Ty showed up."

"How's Verna doing?"

"Not well. At least she's got Frankie. I don't think she'd be able to get through this without him. He's a good man."

"He knows a thing or two about sociopathic exes. Speaking of which—" She recalled Ty's un-subtle threat to drive a wedge between Verna and Frankie. "Ty's planning to cause trouble for them. He didn't come right out and say so, but he dropped more hints than there are clues in an Agatha Christie novel."

"I'll kill him, the lousy gobshite. I swear, I'll kill him. If he ruins this for Verna, I'll kill him, prison be damned."

"I promised him I'd lie to Sunny about him making a pass at Verna if he didn't leave her and Frankie alone. Of course, there's the chance that Sunny would blame Verna for enticing Ty, but any threat to her social media happiness would set Sunny off. The allegations, unfounded or not, should create enough drama to keep Ty's focus on saving his meal ticket instead of on pouring salt into old wounds."

Vivian grabbed Gethsemane in a bear hug. "You're brilliant, d'ya know that? I'm glad you're on our side."

"Frankie's my friend. He's been through a lot and he deserves some happiness. Verna's given him that."

"Pathétique" flared in her head. She willed the music to shut up. Frankie did deserve happiness and she wouldn't stand by and watch it denied him. Tchaikovsky be damned.

Eight

"What happened to you?" Eamon, surrounded by a worried saffron aura, materialized in Carraigfaire's entryway as Gethsemane let herself into the cottage.

"Vivian Cunningham happened. She showed up unannounced on Carrick Point Road for a rousing game of dodge the pedestrian."

"You're all right?"

"The bike and I are both fine. My dress is the only casualty." She filled him in on what had happened between Sweeney's and home as she led the way into the study.

Eamon's elbow disappeared into the wood of the rolltop desk as he leaned against it. "Lismore's such a gobshite, I'll forgive Vivian for adulterating whiskey."

Gethsemane winced as she lowered herself onto the sofa.

"Are you sure you're all right?"

"Fine," she said in defiance of her shoulder's and hip's protest. "Nothing a few dozen naproxen won't fix. What were you up to while I was convincing a priest to snoop and crashing my bike?"

"I went up to Carrick Point to watch Sunny and Lismore put on their holy show. You should be proud of me. I resisted the urge to blast them off the cliff, despite their turning my lighthouse into a backdrop for their theater of the grotesque."

"Then you saw Vivian?"

Eamon shook his head. "She must've gone before I arrived. Sunny, Lismore, and Amott were the only three I saw. Sunny'd decked herself out in some diaphanous, grass-green fairy get-up, complete with wings. She looked like Titania if Titania had been styled by the costume designer from the Dunmullach Amateur Dramatical Society. No doubt the Bard's rolling in his grave. Honestly, Sunny was so over-the-top, I probably wouldn't have noticed the Duchess of Cambridge riding through on a horse. I assume Vivian left before I got there."

"Did you see anything to clue you in to impending danger?"

"You mean like Lismore pacing off in the distance to the cliff's edge or Sunny testing the weight of largish rocks? No, nothing like that."

"Maybe it's Rosalie." Sore muscles transformed a deep sigh into a short, sharp intake of breath.

The saffron in Eamon's aura intensified.

"I promise I'm okay. I just need to give up sleuthing for the night and go to bed."

"Then I'll bid you good night. May Queen Mab guard you against troublous dreams that make you sad."

"You're butchering your Shakespeare."

Eamon bowed like an actor taking a curtain call. He began to dematerialize, feet first. "If this shadow has offended..."

Gethsemane chuckled.

Translucency ascended his legs. "...think but this and all is mended..."

"G'night, Irish."

Stars, framed by the window behind him, came into view through his nearly transparent torso. "...that you have but slumbered here, while these visions did appear..." He vanished.

Gethsemane finished the quotation. "And this weak and idle theme, no more yielding than a dream. Lord, Irish, I hope so."

Shakespearean good wishes failed to bring peaceful sleep. Tossing and turning in bed mirrored thoughts of Ty, Sunny, and Rosalie tossing and turning in her mind. Rosalie and her mysterious note rose to the top of the list of worries. No obvious human force threatened her. But a supernatural one? What if whatever she kept out of her hotel room went after the rest of the village? What charm would protect everyone else?

She conceded defeat to insomnia and sat up. Frustrated, she threw a pillow, which sailed through the chest of a saffron-hued Eamon. He hovered near the foot of her bed.

"Look out the window," he said.

She went to the window and looked out. The full moon cast enough light for her to recognize Verna walking alone along the road from the lighthouse.

"What's she doing?"

Gethsemane shrugged. "Walking."

"At this hour?"

"It's the twenty-first century. Women are allowed out after dark. Even without a chaperone."

"You don't go out walking this late."

"That's me. It's a hang-up." She tucked hair back into her head scarf. "My mother's convinced there's no legit reason to be outside after midnight. Whenever I think about going out that late, I get a mental image of my mother staring at me in disapproving silence. Other women go out this late."

"You're a grown woman and your ma's three thousand miles away."

"Doesn't matter. She will always be my mother and she will

always be in my head. One day, possibly one day soon, I will turn into her."

Eamon jerked his thumb toward the window. "Your ma would want to know what Verna's doing out this late."

"She would. But she wouldn't go out and ask. She'd wait until after sun-up and ask her then." Gethsemane opened the window and leaned out. Verna's back remained visible in the distance as she passed the cottage around the bend in the path that led down to the main road.

"What are you doing?" Eamon asked.

"I am not yet my mother so I'm watching to see if Verna is being followed." She leaned farther out. "She isn't. She isn't running, she isn't crying, and she isn't casting worried glances over her shoulder." Vivian's dash into the path of her bike and Rosalie's paranoid behavior bubbled up in her memory. "Nor did she run in front of a moving vehicle or toss salt over her left shoulder. No boo hags are lurking—are they?"

Eamon's saffron hue intensified. "No, no *cailleach feasa* are out tonight. Would you come back in before you fall?"

Gethsemane's pajama top tented toward the room's interior in response to Eamon's pointed finger. "And Tchaikovsky, mercifully, keeps silent." She pulled her head back in. "Verna, like me, is a grown woman. Unlike me, she chose to go for a late-night walk, probably because she needed some solitude to process the turmoil happening in her life. I am not going to disturb her. I'll take a page from Mother's playbook and say something to her later, at a decent hour." She yawned. "Now, I'm going back to bed."

She fell asleep just before dawn. Pounding on the cottage door awoke her almost as soon as she'd drifted off. Cursing, she dragged herself out of bed, retrieved her head scarf from under the pillow where her tossing and turning had dislodged it, fumbled on a robe, and went downstairs.

Inspector Sutton, head of the Dunmullach Garda homicide squad, greeted her with a scowl.

She re-tied the scarf. "It can't possibly be a good morning if you're standing on my porch at a quarter after oh-dark-thirty, Inspector."

"D'ya mind telling me why a dead man is hanging from your lighthouse?"

Nine

Inspector Sutton waited for her to throw on some clothes before marching her up Carrick Point Road. She followed him to the edge of the cliff and looked up at the side of the lighthouse that overlooked the bay. No mistake, a human figure hung from the end of a rope attached to the lantern room's catwalk. Even from a distance she could see the head tilted at an unnatural angle. The clothes looked like the suit Ty wore the last time she saw him. She couldn't see the face. From what her brother, Zeb, a physician, had told her about hangings, that was a mercy. Uniformed gardaí milled around the base of the lighthouse. Two more up on the catwalk took photos.

"Not exactly Insta-perfect," Gethsemane mumbled.

"His name's Ty Lismore," Sutton said.

"I know him. Knew him. He and his fiancée rented the lighthouse for their wedding in October."

"Hope she can get her deposit back." Sutton strode toward the uniformed guards on the ground. Gethsemane hurried to keep up with him. "Who wanted him dead?"

Besides damned-near everyone? "How should I know?"

"Because," Sutton's scowl deepened, transforming his brow's ever-present furrows into crevasses, "any time there's a dead body in this village, you know something about it." He ran a hand over his thinning hair. "Feck, I hate mornings."

One thing, the only thing, she and Sutton had in common. "What are you doing here, Inspector? I mean, how did you know about—" She gestured toward Ty's body.

"Got a call at the station, anonymous, of course. They're always anonymous. Voice disguised. Couldn't tell if it was a man or a woman. Any idea who might have called?"

"No. I don't know anything about this. I was asleep. You woke me up. I..." She looked up at Ty again. The gardaí on the catwalk had gotten ropes around him and were pulling him up. He seemed small and harmless, so different from the malignant bully who'd threatened to ruin so many lives. She shook her head.

"Did you hear or see anything last night or early—earlier—this morning?"

Her heart skipped a beat. She saw Vivian running away with Ty's property. And she saw Verna walking from the lighthouse late last night. Verna, who had even less reason to be at Carrick Point than her sister. "No, nothing." She swallowed hard.

Sutton cocked his head. "This isn't your first body. You've seen almost as many as me."

For the first time in her life, she was glad to be misunderstood. "Does it ever get easy?"

Sutton looked up at the catwalk. "When it does, it's time to bunk off and take up fly fishing. Are you sure there's nothing you can tell me that would shed light on how a man in Dunmullach to plan his wedding ends up swinging from the top of the venue?"

"I saw him yesterday. Spoke to him."

"About?"

She shrugged, nonchalantly, she hoped. Uncaffeinated, semi-wakefulness worked in her favor. "Photography. He, and the rest of the wedding party, are—were—in the village for a pre-wedding photoshoot. His fiancée, Sunny Markham, is a social media influencer. Pre-wedding photos attract sponsors for the wedding. Get enough sponsors, get the wedding paid for." She added, under her voice, "Not that she can't afford to pay for the wedding herself."

Sutton grumbled. "Social media influencer. What's the world come to when that's a fecking job description?" He frowned at Gethsemane "Photos? That's it?"

"That's it."

Sutton frowned and lowered his voice. "If I find out you're holding out on me…"

"It's too early in the morning for me to be disingenuous."

"All right, you can go. I know where to find you." A garda called to Sutton. The inspector went over to him and left Gethsemane standing at the cliff's edge.

Gethsemane forced herself to maintain a normal pace as she walked back to the cottage. As soon as she'd gone far enough down Carrick Point Road to be out of sight of Sutton and the rest of the gardaí, she ran.

Back at the cottage, she ignored Eamon hovering near the door and raced upstairs to grab her phone from her purse.

Frankie answered on the third ring.

"Where's Verna?" she asked. "Is she there? Tell me she's with you."

"She's not here." Frankie sounded as sleepy as she'd felt before she saw Ty's body. "She left around ten to go back to her place. Said she had to meet Vivian." He paused. When he spoke again, the sleep had vanished from his voice. "Why are you asking for Verna?"

No way to sugar coat it. Best to rip the bandage off. "Ty Lismore's dead. The gardaí found him hanging from Carrick Point Lighthouse earlier this morning."

Silence.

"Frankie?"

"Yeah, I'm here. Look, I can't talk now. I've got to find Verna."

"I understand. And, Frankie, I didn't tell Sutton about Verna's and Ty's past."

"Thank you, Gethsemane." He ended the call.

Eamon materialized at the foot of the bed. "You lied to Inspector Sutton."

"Don't start in on me, Irish. I only half-slept, my least-favorite garda woke me up early to see a dead body dangling from my lighthouse, and I haven't had coffee yet. This is not a good morning."

"My lighthouse. And I wasn't going to start in on you, I was going to say fair play. I'm no fan of the guards." Incompetent police work and a cover-up resulted in Eamon being falsely accused of murdering his wife, Orla, and killing himself—which resulted in his haunting Carraigfaire Cottage. "And, anyway, neither of us liked Lismore."

"Not liking is not the same as wanting dead." She remembered her unspoken threat about the hounds of hell. "Not really. You say things when you're angry that you don't really mean."

"Vivian and Verna meant it. The Misses Cunningham really wanted him dead."

The same thought nagged her. "Oh, don't say that."

"You know it's true."

"I can't think my friend's girlfriend or his girlfriend's sister killed a man. I can't."

"What about Grennan?"

"Frankie didn't kill anyone," she said.

"We know that but what's Sutton going to think? Grennan has motives—defense of his lady love, jealousy. And wouldn't Sutton love to have another go at him?"

Poor Frankie. Inspector Sutton had him all but convicted of murdering the man who'd wrecked his marriage. It had taken all of Gethsemane's sleuthing ability, plus a hefty dose of help from Eamon and Inspector Niall O'Reilly of the garda cold case unit, to prove him innocent. Now this. Please let Frankie have an alibi after ten.

Eamon's aura softened to a sympathetic coral. He sat next to Gethsemane, sinking part way into the mattress. "It's been a rough month. I'm sorry."

"Rougher for others than for me. Although we'll all be in Sutton's line of fire when he finds out the woman who used to be engaged to his murder victim is now dating my friend and I lied about it."

The edge of the bed dipped as Eamon sat on it. A thought intruded into Gethsemane's anxiety: Why do ghosts have enough mass to weigh down a bed and leave impressions in bedcovers but not enough to sit on a bench or lean against a wall without passing into the object? She forced the question from her head. Ty was dead and her friends were suspects. This was not the time to analyze the physics of a haunting.

Eamon spoke. "Lismore was a wanker. Folks will line up from here to Dublin to dance on his grave. The gardaí will have plenty of suspects to focus on besides Grennan and the Cunningham sisters."

"Like who? Sunny? She might've killed Ty after the honeymoon, but before the wedding? She wouldn't do anything to jeopardize her sponsorship opportunities."

"Unless she thought playing the grieving, heartbroken fiancée would sell more of whatever it is she's selling. She's as mercenary as they come. I wouldn't put anything past her."

"If she found out Ty wasn't done with Verna, jealous fury might have won out over mere greed."

"And what about the rest of that miserable crew? The grim

groomsmen and those scared rabbit bridesmaids. You'd find more gleeful folks at a funeral."

"Having to spend time attending Sunny Markham's whims is enough to make even Pollyanna gloomy. That's not cause to murder Ty."

"Maybe there's more behind their bad moods than Miss Markham's sparkling personality. Do you really think the Cunninghams are the only ones Lismore ever hurt?"

She shook her head. "Guys like that leave trails of broken spirits like Hansel and Gretel left a trail of breadcrumbs."

"Maybe one of them decided that murder is the best revenge."

"Maybe. How wrong of me is it to say I hope so? Not that I want any member of the wedding party to be a murderer. But if there has to be a murderer, I'd rather it be one of them than Vivian or Verna."

"What are you going to do?" Eamon pointed. The bedcovers turned back and the remaining pillow plumped itself. "Crawl back under your covers and hope this all goes away?"

"You know me better than that." She jabbed her elbow through Eamon's ribs. An energizing shock zipped up her arm. "I'm going to find out who killed Ty Lismore. I just have to figure out how I'm going to do that without triggering the wrath, and the arrest powers, of Inspector Sutton and how I'm going to do it without hurting my friends."

"Here's where we start: I'll make coffee while you get a shower. Then you track down Frankie and the misses and get your stories straight."

"We?"

"Did you think I wouldn't help?"

"What will you be doing while I'm comparing notes with Frankie and the Cunninghams?"

"I'll haunt up at the lighthouse and the Garda station and

see if I can suss out some details about the demise of the unlamented Mr. Lismore."

"Keep this up and you might make a good amateur detective someday." She paused, unsure, for once, what to say next.

Eamon studied her face. "What's that look?"

"Ty being dead means Rosalie and Sunny are off the hook. Safe, I mean. In terms of my premonition of danger. Right?"

"One of them could be a murderer."

"True." She paused again.

"What?"

"I'm bombarded with the feeling something terrible is going to happen and something terrible happens. A man—a despicable man, but a man, nonetheless—died. Times like this, I hate being right."

Ten

Refreshed by a hot shower and a hotter cup of coffee, Gethsemane rode her bike to St. Brennan's. Frankie lived in Erasmus Hall, the on-campus bachelor faculty quarters. He hadn't answered her calls or texts, but she guessed he might be holed up in his apartment with Verna, trying to avoid Sutton.

She turned onto the path leading from the main campus to faculty housing when, without warning, a young girl stepped out of the bushes that lined the path and stopped in front of her.

"Saoirse!" Gethsemane yelled. She swerved, bringing herself and the Pashley down into a patch of wildflowers. "What the—" She swallowed the swear words that filled her mouth and took a deep breath. "What on earth are you doing? I almost ran over you." Two near-miss pedestrian accidents in two days had to be a record. Why did people keep jumping out in front of her?

"I'm sorry, Miss." The girl, Saoirse Nolan, helped her stand. "I didn't mean to startle you."

Gethsemane brushed off her knees and elbows and righted her bike. She studied Saoirse. Her blonde ponytail, shorts, and t-shirt portrayed a picture of a preteen enjoying a carefree summer day. Her worried green eyes and ill-at-ease stance suggested something more serious. "What's happened?"

"He's not here, Miss."

"Who's not here?"

"Mr. Grennan. He's with Miss Cunningham and her sister up at Carnock."

Of all the places to hide. "How do you know? Did you see them go up there? Did Mr. Grennan ask you to tell me?"

Saoirse, a prescient, shrugged. "I just know." The preteen often knew of events before they happened and knew information without being told.

"Thanks," Gethsemane said. "Now, do me a favor, and go home."

"No one's home but Colm and Aengus and Feargus. They're playing video games and won't let me play." Colm Nolan loved his younger sister but, at sixteen, often preferred time with his schoolmates than her. "Can't I come with you?"

"No, you can't. You're twelve."

"Almost thirteen."

"Which is still too young to be involved in a murd—unexplained death."

"I'm mature for my age. Everyone says so."

"You are as precocious as you are brilliant, but the answer is still no." Gethsemane smiled at the girl. She'd displayed similar perseverance at that age. "You've already been a tremendous help, Saoirse. I appreciate it, but—"

"I know, Miss." Saoirse scuffed the toe of her shoe on the gravel path and sighed the way only a twelve-going-on-forty-year-old can. "How would you explain it to my parents?"

"Hey, why don't you stop by Our Lady? I think Father Tim just got a copy of Pliny's *Naturalis Historia*." In addition to tutoring the young, homeschooled genius, the priest gave her unlimited access to his collection of Greek and Latin texts and pretended not to notice when the occasional occult book made it into her TBR pile. "I bet he'd let you borrow it."

"He'll make me sample his veal pie. Have you ever tasted a medieval meat pie?"

"No, eating medieval meat pie does not number among the unusual things I've done in my life." But never say never. Not so long ago, investigating a murder had been on her never-tried-it list.

"If anyone offers it to you, Miss, tell them you're a vegetarian."

Saoirse gave a sad wave and headed toward the village. Gethsemane watched her go then mounted her bike. Carnock rose on the horizon like a bad omen. Gethsemane took a deep breath, said a silent prayer, and headed for it.

The road to Carnock wound through desolate ranks of gnarled trees that conspired to blot out all sunlight. Gethsemane pedaled fast, her eyes fixed on the road. *Rudolph Ash, one-sixty, Jim Brown, two-sixteen, Bingo DeMoss, three-oh-nine, George Dixon, three-forty-two.* She recited Negro League batting averages to ease her anxiety and keep memories of killers at bay.

"Honestly, Frankie," she said aloud, "couldn't you have found a better hiding place? You know how much I hate it up here."

She pulled up in front of the burned remains of the old asylum and scanned the desolate area. Where would Frankie be?

"Duh." Where else? "The rose garden."

She left her bike against a tree and walked to the remnants of the asylum's main entrance. The front door hung weirdly on two hinges. Her hand shook as she reached to push it aside.

"Nope." She shook her head. "Not enough Negro League stats in the world." So much for the shortcut through the building. Her scar throbbed at the thought of creeping through its dark, fire-damaged halls. "I'll take the long way 'round."

She returned to the main drive and picked her way around the side of the building, through overgrown grass and assorted rubbish, to the rear. She stopped short and gasped at what greeted her. What she remembered as inhospitable brambles had been transformed into an oasis of beauty. The tops of tree roses peered over low stone walls, a bower of pink and white rose blossoms arched over the entry way. And along one wall, the rambler Frankie had named 'Fearless' in her honor, trailed over the stones and carpeted the wall with a blanket of fully double, deep red blooms.

"Sissy."

She jumped at the sound of Frankie's voice. He sat on a bench in a corner near the rear wall, his arms around Verna. Vivian sat on the end of the bench next to her sister.

"My god, Frankie," Gethsemane said, "what kind of horticultural wizardry did you work up here?"

Vivian jumped up. "What's happened? Do you know? What's going on?"

Verna pulled her sister back onto the bench. "Give her a chance to talk, Viv."

Gethsemane forced herself to push aside images of Ty dangling from the catwalk. "Around dawn, Inspector Sutton from the Garda homicide unit woke me up. I followed him up to Carrick Point. When we got to the lighthouse, he showed me a body hanging from the tower. He'd already confirmed the victim's identity—Ty Lismore."

Verna sobbed and buried her face in Frankie's neck.

"Good riddance," Vivian muttered.

"I know Sutton didn't let you off that easy." Frankie had endured one of Sutton's interrogations during a recent murder investigation. "We're the usual suspects. Which of us is he pointing the finger at? You or me?"

"Neither, yet. He said he got an anonymous call alerting him to the body. Then he assured me he knew where to find me later."

"That's it?" Vivian asked.

Gethsemane nodded. "For now. Not that Sutton would tell me any more than he had to."

"He must suspect someone," Vivian said.

"He didn't say who." She eyed the Cunningham sisters. "He did ask me if I knew anything about it."

"Why would you know anything about it?" Frankie asked.

"Other than the fact that it's your lighthouse." Vivian's stare challenged Gethsemane.

"I didn't mention running into you on Carrick Point Road," she said. "Must've forgotten."

Vivian dropped her gaze.

"Sissy," Frankie asked, "do you know something?"

Verna turned her head enough to look at Gethsemane with one eye.

"I also saw you, Verna," she said. "I saw you walking on Carrick Point Road late last night."

Vivian sucked in her breath.

"What are you accusing her of?" Frankie tightened his hold on Verna.

"I'm not accusing her of anything. I'm just letting her know I saw her walking on Carrick Point Road last night, heading back toward the village. From the direction of the lighthouse."

"And you told Inspector Sutton you saw her," Vivian said.

"No, I didn't. I didn't tell Inspector Sutton anything about seeing Verna last night nor about her past relationship with Ty. Guess that slipped my mind, too. My memory isn't what it used to be."

"Vern?" Frankie asked.

Verna raised her head. "All right. It's true." She kept her gaze on Gethsemane. "I did go up to Carrick Point last night. I met Ty at the lighthouse."

Frankie withdrew his arms. "Saw him? About what?"

Verna grasped his hand. "I saw him to tell him to leave me—leave us—alone. I worked up my nerve and confronted him. I told him he was making me miserable, begged him to stop torturing me." She laid her forehead against Frankie's and held his face in her hands. "That's all, I swear. I told him I'd moved on and asked him to go away and let me be happy." She turned to Gethsemane. "I swear I left him alive. Alive and laughing at me."

"I believe you," Gethsemane said. "You're half Ty's size, if that. You couldn't have hanged him. Even if you'd gotten a rope around his neck, you couldn't have thrown him over the catwalk's railing."

"I've known you long enough to know there's a 'but,'" Frankie said.

"Let's be honest, Frankie. If—when—Sutton finds out Ty planned to come between you and Verna and finds out Verna confronted him about it and that he humiliated her..."

"He'll be delighted to blame me for killing the bastard."

Verna threw her arms around Frankie. "I'm so sorry."

"Who says Sutton has to find out?" Vivian asked. "None of us are going to tell him. Are we?"

"We don't have to," Gethsemane said. "He can get the story from Sunny Markham, her attendants, the groomsmen...What if he bragged to one of those guys about his plan to lure Verna back?"

"He'd do something like that, the gobshite," Vivian said. "What are we going to do?"

"First," Gethsemane said, "we need to find out exactly what Sutton knows. He won't tell me anything, but I've got a, er, someone sniffing around."

On cue, Eamon materialized next to her. "You rang?"

A startled expletive escaped before she could cover her surprise at the ghost's unexpected appearance.

"What is it?" Frankie asked.

She covered. "Uh, nothing. I just remembered something."

"Who's sniffing around for you?" Vivian asked.

"I do not sniff," Eamon said, "I observe. And I observed—"

"I'd rather not say," Gethsemane answered Vivian. "I mean, he'd prefer to remain anonymous."

"I observed the coroner's preliminary report. Suicide."

Gethsemane forgot the others couldn't see or hear Eamon. "What?"

Frankie raised an eyebrow. "Sissy, are you sure you're all right?"

"I'm fine, I just—" Beethoven's "Fifth" jangled in her purse. She pulled out her phone. "Saved by the ring tone," she mumbled as she answered the call.

Inspector Niall O'Reilly's voice came over the line. "Sissy, can you talk?"

"Niall, hi. I'm with Frankie." Best not to tell him about the Cunningham sisters. Friend or not, he was still a garda. If Sutton was out for Verna and Vivian, Niall wouldn't cover for them.

"I thought you'd like to know what the coroner thinks about Ty Lismore's death."

"Yes," she repeated for the benefit of the others, "I would like to know what the coroner thinks about Ty Lismore's death. Can I put you on speaker?" She switched the phone to speaker mode and held it so the others could hear.

"Nothing's official yet, you understand," Niall said, "and you didn't hear this from me, but Lismore's death looks like suicide."

Vivian and Verna gasped. Gethsemane held a finger to her lips.

"Who else is there with you, Sissy?" Niall asked.

"Just Frankie," she said. "Your news caught him by

surprise."

"It's not my news—"

Eamon interrupted. "No, it's mine."

"Remember, I didn't tell you this. It looks like Lismore tied a rope around his neck, probably one he found in the lighthouse, climbed over the railing, and jumped. Snapped his neck, lucky for him."

"Could someone have pushed him?"

"No signs of struggle," Niall said. "No scuff marks, no bits of anything under his nails, no torn clothes, no bruises. Lismore seemed like a fit fella. Doubt he would have gone over the side without a fight unless he went on his own."

"Thanks for telling me, Niall. And I don't mean to sound unappreciative but, why did you tell me?"

"Simple," Niall said. "To keep you from poking your nose into garda business. No need for you to snoop because there's no murder. No killer for you to uncover, no reason to risk your neck."

"Thanks for looking out for me."

"That's what I'm doing, yeah." He raised his voice. "That goes for you, too, Frankie." He hung up.

"That's that, then," Vivian said. "Suicide, case closed. No need for Sutton to pick at scabs and open old wounds."

"I'd like to go now, Frankie," Verna said, "if you don't mind."

Frankie, Verna, and Vivian rose. Frankie started to speak. "Gethsemane, I—"

She waved it away. "No worries." She watched him lead Verna and her sister to his new car, which she hadn't noticed parked on a side path.

"So, Vivian's right? That's it, then?"

"Sure. Suicide. Case closed."

"You don't buy that."

She faced Eamon. "Sure I do. Why wouldn't I?"

"Because you're still hearing Tchaikovsky playing in your head. I recognize the look by now. And because nothing in your life is ever that simple."

Eleven

As if Eamon's assessment about the complexity of her life needed proving, Sunny Markham appeared to complicate matters that same afternoon.

"Gethsemane Brown!" Pounding on the cottage door punctuated Sunny's shouts. "I know you're home!"

Gethsemane threw open the window in the upstairs parlor and shouted down. "Doesn't anyone in this damned village know the proper way to knock?"

"She's not from here." Eamon materialized beside her. "Better see what she wants before she breaks the door."

Gethsemane stomped down the stairs and yanked the door open to an infuriated Sunny, her heaving chest and flared nostrils giving the impression of an enraged harpy rather than a put-together social media influencer. Inspector Sutton appeared in the doorway behind the bereaved bride, an aggrieved expression on his face. This couldn't be good.

"Apologies, Dr. Brown. Miss Markham insisted—"

"Don't apologize to her," Sunny interrupted, all traces of little-girl sweetness and curated coolness gone from her voice. She spoke with pure wrath. "Someone murdered Ty and she—" She jabbed a finger in Gethsemane's direction. "—knows who did it."

A muscle twitched in Sutton's jaw. "Miss Markham insisted

I speak with you."

"Damned right I insisted!" Sunny yelled. "I'm not going to let you brush Ty's death under the rug, write it off as a suicide so you don't have to do any work. She knows who killed Ty. Maybe she was in on it. I bet she was in on it. Arrest her, make her talk."

The muscle twitches spread from Sutton's jaw to his neck. His eyes narrowed. Since she wasn't already in the back of a police car on the way to the Garda station, Gethsemane assumed the anger was aimed at Sunny.

"Miss Markham," Sutton said, "if you don't stop shouting, I will arrest you for disturbing the peace."

Eamon appeared in the entryway next to Gethsemane. "And waking the dead."

Sunny huffed and plopped onto the entryway bench.

"May I offer you a drink, Inspector?" Gethsemane asked as she shut the door.

Sutton's eyes brightened, then he shook his head. "Thank you, no. I'm on duty." He glanced at Sunny. "I need my wits about me."

"It's probably poisoned." Sunny spat the words at Gethsemane. "Murderer."

Gethsemane bit back a caustic remark. "I'm confused, Inspector. Murder? I'd, er, heard a rumor that Ty Lismore committed suicide."

"Hah!" Sunny snorted. "Suicide. Ty wasn't depressed. He didn't have enough emotional depth to suffer from depression. Do you really think that arrogant nitwit would off himself? Do you think anyone loved Ty Lismore more than Ty Lismore?"

"Odd way of talking about your late fiancé, Miss Markham," Sutton said.

"Not to mention you shouldn't speak ill of the dead," Eamon said.

"Oh, grow up, Inspector," Sunny said. "Are all you country cops so naïve? I didn't love Ty and he didn't love me. He was marrying my money and I was marrying his social appeal."

Gethsemane stifled a laugh. "You mean you were marrying Ty because he was Insta-perfect?"

Sunny scowled. "What of it? Our engagement photo gained me an additional 10k followers. Do you have any idea what that's worth in brand endorsement deals? Four different couture houses begged me—*begged* me—to let them do the gowns for me and my bridesmaids. A high-end luggage company offered to pick up the transportation tab, half a dozen hotels were competing to have us stay with them on our honeymoon."

"You're coddin' me, right?" Sutton asked. "You were going to spend the rest of your life with a man just to gets some likes?"

"Of course not. Two years, four at the most, maybe a kid or two, then divorce." Sunny rolled her eyes. "Rest of my life. Hah."

Sutton pressed the heels of his palms into his eyes. "I'm getting too old for this."

Sunny jerked her thumb at Gethsemane. "Aren't you going to take her in for questioning?"

"No, Miss Markham, I'm going to ask Dr. Brown a few questions right here. She's going to answer them fully and truthfully. And then we're going to leave."

"Never thought I'd see it," Eamon said to Gethsemane, "someone who aggravates Sutton more than you do."

"Dr. Brown," Sutton said to Gethsemane, "is there any reason you can think of why Miss Markham would believe you knew more than you told me about Ty Lismore's suicide?"

"Murder," Sunny interjected.

"Death," Sutton continued.

Better to have him for her than against her. "I'm friends with Frankie Grennan and Frankie dates Verna Cunningham—and Verna used to be engaged to Ty."

"You didn't tell me this before because...?"

"Because I assumed you knew, Inspector. It's not a secret."

"You see," Sunny jumped up, "there's motive. Verna Cunningham wanted Ty back. She was jealous because he wanted me, not her, so she killed him."

"Verna Cunningham is smaller than you are," Gethsemane said.

Eamon laughed. "Fair play."

"How could she possibly have hanged Ty from the catwalk?" Gethsemane asked.

"She's not that small," Sunny said. "And maybe her new boyfriend helped her. Or maybe he did it by himself. Maybe he was the jealous one."

Damn. Gethsemane kicked herself. She'd forgotten to ask Frankie if he had an alibi.

"Francis Grennan didn't kill anyone last night, Miss Markham," Sutton said. "I can vouch for him."

Gethsemane, Sunny, and Eamon stared.

Sutton continued. "I ran into Grennan last night at the Rabbit. He and O'Reilly were there from half past ten until Murphy kicked us out at three this morning. Grennan didn't look like he was in condition to drive, so I drove him to St. Brennan's then dropped O'Reilly off at the station to retrieve his car. Ten minutes later, Mr. or Ms. Anonymous called to tell me about a body dangling from Carrick Point."

"Before ten thirty—"

Gethsemane cut Sunny off. "Frankie was with Verna until ten." Sutton shot her a look. "He mentioned it when I called to tell him about Ty."

"You reported, Miss Markham, that you, Lismore, and Malcolm Amott were at Carrick Point lighthouse taking photographs until half-past nine. At that time, one of your bridal attendants," Sutton consulted a notebook he'd pulled from his pocket, "Ms. Agnes Haygood, excuse me, Hay*wood*, arrived in a taxi to escort you back to Sweeney's Inn. Lismore opted to remain behind and help Amott collect his gear."

"I know what I said, Detective."

"Inspector." Sutton checked his notes again. "Lismore's mates, Theophilus Derringer and Brian Nishi, reported seeing both Lismore and Amott in the lobby of Sweeney's Inn around ten o'clock. Lismore and Amott parted ways and Lismore joined his mates in the hotel bar. They saw Amott again at about half-past eleven when he returned a silver flask that Lismore had lost someplace. Lismore, Nishi, and Derringer remained in the bar until shortly after midnight. Lismore went out for a smoke about a quarter after twelve. His lighter malfunctioned so he asked the doorman for a book of matches, which the doorman provided." Sutton snapped his notebook shut. "Several witnesses at the inn, including Amott, the bartender, and the doorman, confirm the timeline. Your fiancé was seen alive almost two hours after Frankie Grennan sat down for a pint with a couple of gardaí."

Gethsemane calculated the math. If Sutton dropped Frankie at home at three a.m., or a little after if you figured in the time to drive to Erasmus Hall, and the anonymous call alerting Sutton to Ty's body came in at three twenty or three thirty—no way Frankie could have made it to Carrick Point, murdered Ty, and made it back home. Verna, on the other hand...She had admitted to being with Ty at the lighthouse. She dismissed the thought. Suicide. Ty died by his own hand, not someone else's.

"I don't care about your witnesses or your stupid timelines." Sunny stomped her foot and brought Gethsemane back to the present. "Ty did not kill himself. Someone murdered him. Murdered." She stomped her foot again, hard enough to rattle the door hinges. "That one—" She pointed at Gethsemane. "—knows who killed him. One or all of her friends was responsible and she's covering up for them. It's your job to prove it, Inspector. Start by taking her in for questioning."

"Speaking of questioning," Gethsemane attempted to channel her inner ingénue and asked in her most innocent, artless voice, "if Ty really was murdered, how do we know you didn't do it Sunny? Isn't the significant other usually the murderer, Inspector Sutton?"

Sutton struggled to keep his lips from curling into a smile. "Either the significant other or the butler."

Sunny's face flushed as red as her hair. "You are not. Seriously. Suggesting. That I, Sunny Princess Randolph Markham—"

"Of the Newport Markhams," Gethsemane interjected.

Sunny balled her hands into fists. "How could I possibly have hanged Ty? As you pointed out, Doctor Brown, he wasn't a small man."

"Maybe someone from your past then," Gethsemane said. "A heart broken and trampled on your way to social media stardom. Dreams and desires bloodied as you clawed your way to verified badges on your accounts. Any skeletons in your closet with murderous intentions?"

"What are you talking about?" Sunny asked. "My closet's full of Emilia Wickstead, Markarian, and Pippa Holt. There's no room for skeletons, literal or figurative."

"I bet you discarded boyfriends like you discarded last year's fashions. How do you know one of your exes didn't follow you here and kill Ty in hopes of reclaiming his spot in your social media feed?"

"That's, that's," Sunny stammered, "that's ridiculous."

"Is it, Miss Markham?" Sutton asked. "Perhaps you'd come down to the station with me and provide me a list of names to check?"

"No, I won't." She narrowed her eyes and brought her

clenched fists up to her chest. "How dare you suggest—" She stopped and looked back and forth between Gethsemane and Sutton. Her face relaxed into a thousand-watt smile and the little girl voice returned. "Inspector Sutton, surely, you *don't* suspect me of having *anything* to do with Ty's death. I'd *never* be involved with anything so *horrible*. No one from my past would be cruel enough to kill anyone. I would *never* associate with anyone capable of murder. Just look at me—"

"Yes," Gethsemane said, "let's take another look at you. I'm still sold on the idea of the significant other as the most likely suspect."

"What?" The little girl voice vanished.

"Did you kill your fiancé, Sunny? Assuming for the sake of argument that he was murdered. You found out Ty wanted to rekindle things with Verna. You became jealous, afraid an affair would ruin the image of the happy couple you were shopping to sponsors. You're smart, you wouldn't let size stop you from eliminating a threat to everything you'd worked for. You could have lured him up to the top of the lighthouse, coaxed him into putting a rope around his neck, talked him into climbing onto the railing for some kind of extreme selfie—"

"You!" Sunny flew at Gethsemane who ducked out of reach. Inspector Sutton intercepted her. He grabbed her around her waist with both arms and pulled her back. Sunny struggled against him, but he held her tight with her feet several inches above the floor.

"That's enough of that, Miss Markham." Sutton dodged a kick aimed at his shin.

Gethsemane averted her eyes to keep from laughing.

Sunny squirmed and struggled. "Did you hear what she said? What she accused me of?"

"No more than what you accused her of. I think it's best if we go now." Sutton backed toward the door, socialite in arms.

The door swung open, aided by Eamon. Sutton half-carried, half-dragged his uncooperative cargo through it. Gethsemane hoped he didn't remember that she'd closed the door when she'd invited him in. She shut it again after Sutton loaded Sunny into his car.

Eamon densified until he appeared solid. "I'd hate to get on the wrong side of that one. She's more terrifying than a lioness who hasn't eaten for a week."

"Where were your blue orbs when she attacked me?"

"She'd have caught one and thrown it back at you."

Gethsemane went to the study and poured herself a shot of Waddell and Dobb. "Do you think she was right? Could Ty have been murdered?"

"By who?" Eamon asked. "Grennan has Sutton as his alibi. The Cunningham sisters are both too small to hoist a grown man over a rail. And I don't see Ty posing for any extreme selfies with them."

"One or both of the groomsmen?"

"No signs of a struggle, remember? How would they have gotten him over? Dared him?"

"I wish I'd looked at the clock when I saw Verna. She says she left Ty alive. Sutton got his call not long after three a.m. Ty must have been dead by three. Verna could have been there at the same time as the killer, could have seen or heard—"

"What killer?" Eamon asked. "Don't let that she-devil get to you and turn a straightforward suicide into a murder that didn't happen."

"But what if it wasn't really a suicide? What if it was actually murder, staged to look like suicide? You know what that's like. You waited twenty-five years after your death to prove you didn't kill yourself."

"Damn." Eamon followed this up with a string of more profanities. His aura glowed a blue-saffron mixture of anger and worry. "I just thought of something."

"What?"

"If—and this is only conjecture—but if Ty's suicide wasn't a suicide, if he was murdered but he's buried as a suicide—"

"Like you were."

"He'll never be able to rest in peace."

"Meaning?"

"Meaning he'll roam as a ghost like me, condemned to haunt the place where he died until someone sets things right and clears his name." Blue sparks popped and sizzled. A tiny blue orb whizzed past Gethsemane's ear.

She felt the heat as the ball of energy flew by. "Hey, take it easy. You'll burn the house down."

"I'll burn the whole bloody village down. Dunmullach be damned if I'll be stuck co-haunting Carraigfaire with that bollocks for all eternity."

Twelve

"Thank you, Father Tim," Gethsemane said to the priest on the other end of the phone. "In the meantime, I'll try my luck at Arcana Arcanora. An occult bookstore ought to have at least one book on how to keep ghosts away. Which reminds me, have you spoken to Rosalie?"

"Ay," Tim said. "Not that I got any answers about the note. I went to Sweeney's this morning to see her. Of course, Ty, God rest his soul, was foremost in mind. Lots of angst and confusion among guests and staff alike. I prayed with more than one. Gardaí were everywhere, asking questions. I think they interviewed everyone in the inn. I only had time to ask Miss Baraquin how she was holding up before a garda whisked her off for an interview. I didn't see her again."

"Thanks for trying. Not that it matters much now. Ty was the one in danger, not Rosalie. Although, I'd still like to know why she blocked her doorway."

"Religious practice, superstition, habit. Plenty of people take precautions against things they can't see and may or may not believe in but want to be on the safe side of, just in case."

"You're right. I won't put a hat on a bed, just because Grandma said not to. Even my skeptical, rational, citified mother won't do it. Grandma never told us why we couldn't put hats on beds, she just told us not to. Probably nothing. But why chance it?"

"I am sorry I couldn't be of more help," Tim said. "I can try again later, if you like."

"That's okay. Don't trouble yourself any further. Like I said, it doesn't matter now and you're likely to be busy. As much as I detested Ty Lismore, I realize his sudden, violent death must have hit his friends hard. At least some of them will be seeking spiritual guidance and solace."

"Hopefully, I'll have better luck finding a spell to ensure the peaceful repose of that poor soul. Of course, I've prayed that eternal rest be granted to him, but a back-up spell wouldn't hurt."

They rang off and Gethsemane turned to Eamon. The ghost stood next to the kitchen counter, arms crossed, aura a sullen teal blue.

"Stop sulking," Gethsemane said. "Father Tim's going to search his collection for a spell to prevent someone from coming back as a ghost—he's already prayed—and I'm going to the occult bookstore to search for the same. We don't want Ty's ghost to come back to haunt any more than you do." The coffee pot, visible through Eamon's semi-transparent chest, simmered full of rich, dark liquid and the earthy, caramel aroma that gave her almost as much pleasure as hearing the Biber Mystery Sonatas played on a Stradivarius violin filled the room. "Coffee's ready."

Eamon nodded at a cabinet. It swung open and a mug levitated across the kitchen to the counter. The coffee pot floated up, tilted, and filled the mug before settling itself back on the counter. The mug drifted across the kitchen and set itself down on the table in front of Gethsemane.

"You shouldn't drink that stuff so late in the day," Eamon said. "Have a cup of tea instead."

"Tea contains caffeine, too." Gethsemane sipped coffee.

"And 'this stuff,' as you so dismissively call it, gives me the energy to do things like find ways to prevent dead louts from becoming ghosts and to figure out whether said louts killed themselves or if someone did it for them." She drained her cup. "Have to go. Bookstore closes soon."

She arrived at Arcana Arcanora, Dunmullach's occult bookshop, in time to find a young man with purple hair and pierced face wheeling a cart full of books from the sidewalk into the bookstore. Faint strains of Nina Simone's cover of "I Put a Spell on You" spilled through the open doorway.

"We close soon," the man said as she approached.

She slipped past him into the shop's crowded interior. "Ten minutes. I know what I want."

"Why don't you tell me what that is and we'll make it five minutes?"

"A grimoire." She pointed at a sign, labeled "Spell Books," that hung from the ceiling at the far side of the store.

"Any particular incantation you're looking for? Romance, money?" He looked her up and down. "Youth?"

A spell to turn smart-mouthed store clerks into toadstools? She reminded herself she'd have to be nice if she wanted the clerk's help. "I need an incantation to prevent someone who died from coming back as a ghost."

"Takes more than just the incantation, you know. You have to perform rituals, as well."

"Yeah, I know. Trust me, I have some experience with ghosts." She tapped her watch. "The book?"

The young man led her through narrow aisles filled with tarot cards, incense, scrying mirrors, and numerous other occult items. Gethsemane couldn't guess what half of them were for.

"What happened to the other clerk?" she asked. "The young

woman with the chiffon and tattoos?"

"Got married and moved to Dublin." He stopped under the "Spell Book" sign and scanned the jumble of titles on the floor-to-ceiling bookshelf. "Hmm, I don't see anything. We have several books with rituals for preventing someone from coming back as a vampire but nothing to prevent revenants, strigori, or duppies. I thought we had one but..." His finger hovered over a book spine as he shook his head. "No, sorry. Have you tried Father Tim at Our Lady of Perpetual Sorrows? He owns a comprehensive occult library. Maybe you'd have better luck there."

Father Tim's occult collection was one of the worst kept secrets in Dunmullach. "I called him already. He's checking for me."

"Sorry. Say, you're not worried about that fella who hanged himself from Carrick Point lighthouse coming back as a haunt, are you?" The clerk pulled a small, red book from the shelf and handed it to her. *Profilaxie Vampyras.* "Maybe you should try this instead. People who commit suicide are at high risk for becoming vampires."

"Thanks, but," Gethsemane handed to book back, "ghosts are my concern. By the way, how did you know about—"

"Ty's suicide?" a familiar voice interjected.

Gethsemane and the clerk turned toward the speaker.

Rosalie approached them. "Everyone in this village knows what happened up at Carrick Point in the wee small hours of the morning. Dunmullach's just like small towns at home. Bad news spreads like a virus." She held up a deck of tarot cards. "I'd like to get this, please."

The clerk grumbled about customers waiting until almost closing time to come in as he took the cards and led the way to the cash register.

"Have you ever had a reading, Dr. Brown?" Rosalie asked.

"A tarot reading, I mean."

"It's Gethsemane. And, no, I haven't. I'm not really a believer." Ghosts, she believed in, and Russian symphonies playing in her head as harbingers of doom. But fortune telling? She wasn't quite there yet.

"You don't have to believe in something for it to be true. You should have a reading. Try it. You'd be amazed at the insights tarot can provide."

"How are you doing?" Gethsemane asked. "Ty was a friend—"

Rosalie interrupted. "To no one. Ty Lismore was a deeply unpleasant individual who left things worse off than when he found them. He never did anything to make the world a better place and no one misses him. Least of all his fiancée."

Harsh words. No hesitation to speak ill of the dead. Not exactly the image of the bridesmaid's post-tragedy demeanor she'd gotten from Father Tim. "I, er, saw Sunny earlier. She seemed quite upset about Ty's death. Nearly hysterical." Not exactly with grief, but hysterical, nonetheless.

"Sunny Markham thrives on drama, chaos, and manipulation. Or hadn't you noticed?"

"Aren't you her friend? You're serving as one of her bridesmaids, so I assumed..."

"Emphasis on 'serving' and 'maid.'" Rosalie bit her lip, then sighed and continued. "It's complicated. There are to be ten bridesmaids, total. Agnes, that's Agnes Haywood, the other woman you saw at the lighthouse, and I are maids of honor. That means we've the 'honor,'" Rosalie made air quotes, "of being Sunny's primary whipping posts and scut monkeys."

"You mean you're not clamoring to be in the wedding party for the social media exposure opportunities?"

Rosalie snorted. "Hardly. Ten million followers wouldn't be adequate compensation for putting up with Sunny Markham.

Her money and family connections ensure she gets whatever, and whoever, she wants. If you refuse her, she finds a way to make you pay. The job you were after suddenly disappears, your name drops to the bottom of the waiting list for the apartment you coveted, you're a social pariah. And if the threat of becoming a social outcast fails to keep you in line, Sunny resorts to full-on conniptions. She throws tantrums that put two-year-olds to shame. People cave to avoid a scene. Mal's the only one able to talk her down. I don't know why, they haven't known each other that long. But Mal's got some sort of gift for dealing with her lunacy. He's the only one she responds to. He's a drama queen whisperer. We call him The Lord of Chaos." She glanced toward the door. "But not when Sunny's in earshot."

"Ty, the man she planned to marry, had no influence over her behavior? He couldn't calm her down?"

"Not Ty. Sunny's outrageous behavior suits—" she corrected herself, "suited Ty. His particular gift was for directing her wrath at others. He'd manipulate her into a tirade then step out of the line of fire and enjoy the spoils of war. As long as Sunny focused her terror on others, Ty could spend her money—usually on cigarettes, booze, and other women—without fear of detection. It's not like you could tell her, after the fact, what Ty had gotten up to. Sunny's ego won't allow the possibility that anyone would prefer any company over hers. And Ty seemed to have a knack for shifting blame for his sins to other people."

"Why do you think he—"

"Hanged himself? You mean other than to get out of marrying Sunny?" Rosalie flushed. "Sorry, that was flip. No, it wasn't. Death would be preferable to a life of hell with Sunny Markham. But Ty had a plan to help himself to a large part of her fortune as compensation." Rosalie shrugged. "Maybe the devil made him do it."

Gethsemane shuddered. The opening measures of

"Pathétique" blared in her head, catching her off guard. Damn. Now what? Ty was dead. So why the warning? "Ty didn't tell you—"

"About his plans to relieve Sunny of the burden of wealth? No, he told Brian and Theo. And Brian is a gossip."

"Excuse me," the clerk called to Rosalie, "that'll be eighteen ninety-five."

Gethsemane waited while Rosalie paid for her tarot cards. She followed her out as the clerk locked the door behind them.

The Tchaikovsky persisted. Had she been wrong about the warning being for Ty? Was Rosalie the one in danger and Ty's death a tragic coincidence? Was there a connection between them? Rosalie was no bigger than Verna. She couldn't have thrown Ty over the railing. Maybe her cryptic note mattered after all.

She caught up to Rosalie, several paces ahead of her. "I get that you're not going to weep for Ty but are you sure you're all right? About that other thing, I mean."

Rosalie kept walking. "What other thing?"

"The note you received at Sweeney's. The one you didn't want me to see. The one with the line drawing."

"I didn't want you to see it because it was no business of yours."

"If you read my tarot cards, you'd find out that I have a penchant for sticking my nose into business that's not mine."

"That's not how tarot works."

"Sorry. Bad joke. But I'm serious about that note."

Rosalie spun without warning and collided with Gethsemane. "You don't quit, do you?"

"No." Gethsemane rubbed her nose where it had impacted Rosalie's collarbone. "Quitting is not one of my character traits."

Rosalie's shoulders slumped in resignation. "The note was a...message, like a calling card. From an old business associate, warn—letting me know he'd be 'round to see me soon."

"Granted, I only glimpsed the note for a few seconds, but I didn't see any words, only a drawing. You got all that information from a drawing?"

"It was a pictograph. The drawing contained all the information I needed. And that's all I'm going to say about that." She walked on.

Undeterred, Gethsemane followed. "When is this friend, sorry, associate coming to visit?"

Rosalie stopped again and held up the shop bag containing the tarot cards. "Are you sure you don't want me to do a reading?"

Neither woman spoke. Gethsemane waited. Was Rosalie going to answer her question about her pictograph-writing visitor? Several seconds passed in silence. Apparently, Rosalie had meant it when she'd declared she had no more to say about her note. Gethsemane debated bringing up the charm Rosalie had used to protect her door but explaining how she knew about the charm would be tricky. She conceded the round. Time to change the subject.

She spoke first. "I'll pass on the cards, thanks."

"Are you sure?" Rosalie asked. "You might learn something."

The truth about whether or not Ty killed himself? She imagined Rosalie's offended response that tarot didn't work that way. "I might not like what I'd learn," she said.

Rosalie warmed to the topic. "Insight always benefits, even if it's hard to accept. Wouldn't you like to gain a deeper understanding of the teachings of your grandparents? The wisdom of your elders?"

"My grandparents?" A tailor and teacher on her father's side and farmers on her mother's. Alarms from her claptrap meter replaced warning notes from Tchaikovsky. Rosalie's wisdom-of-the-elders spiel sounded like a carnival barker's con job. "What do my grandparents have to do with anything?"

"They must have passed some rural Virginia folk wisdom on to you with the family lore. People connected to the land possess a great deal of knowledge. When they share it with family it may not be in a form the recipients understand or appreciate. The tarot can help make sense of what you already know."

Gethsemane's maternal grandmother had shared African American folk tales and legends, in addition to family stories, with her—at least until her no-nonsense, psychiatrist mother had put a stop to it. But how could Rosalie know that? Or was she just guessing?

Rosalie smiled. "I read in a magazine somewhere that your mother's people came from rural Virginia. An interview you gave." She held Gethsemane's gaze for a moment, then tossed her hair, as if the motion changed a channel or turned a page. "Are you, by any chance, performing while we're here in Dunmullach?"

"What?" Something Rosalie said nagged at her and the sudden topic change caught Gethsemane off guard. "Um, no, I don't have any scheduled performances." How much did she hate Ty that she was trying to score concert tickets the day he died? "Maybe open mic night at the pub, but nothing formal."

"That's too bad. I'd love to hear you play your violin. A Vuillaume from the eighteen hundreds, isn't it?"

"Yes, a copy of a Stradivarius 'Messiah.' You know violins? You're a musician?"

"No. I read that somewhere, too. I have an excellent memory for things I read." She laughed. "Of course, I had to look Vuillaume violins up on the internet. An impressive pedigree."

Gethsemane agreed with her about the violin.

"Hopefully, someday I'll get the chance to hear you play it. One of the instrumental passages from 'The Damnation of Faust.' If you take requests." She winked.

"You're a Berlioz fan?"

"I find the story of Faust fascinating. What's worth selling your soul to the devil? Money, power, love, fame? What's worth the cost of eternal damnation? What would you give up in order to gain everything you thought you wanted? Do you ever wonder, Gethsemane," she fixed her with an intense stare and lowered her voice, "how far you'd be willing to go?"

"Not recently, no." Had she underestimated Rosalie Baraquin? Though she be but little...What was she capable of? The idea of a connection between Ty's death and Rosalie didn't seem so fantastical all of a sudden.

"I'm sorry." Rosalie's face relaxed into a smile and her voice returned to normal. "I'm weirding you out. I can tell. I have that effect on people sometimes. I don't mean to, I just..." She circled her hand in the air then shrugged. "Sunny complains all the time. Calls me Rosal-eerie. Speaking of whom," she checked her watch, "I'd better go. Sunny's been in uber-high-maintenance mode since Ty's death. You know she thinks he was murdered?"

Boy, did she know. "I heard something along those lines."

"Murder may be a sin, but on occasion, it's understandable. And sins can be forgiven, right?" She jiggled the bag with the tarot cards. "If you ever change your mind."

You'll be the last one I call. Gethsemane watched her go. Something nagged her. It hit her as Rosalie disappeared around a corner. She'd given dozens, if not hundreds, of interviews in her career. She hadn't mentioned her grandparents in any of them.

Thirteen

Gethsemane, on the chance Father Tim had tracked down a spell to keep spirits on the other side of the veil, aimed her bike toward Our Lady. She halted in front of the Mad Rabbit when she spied Theophilus Derringer and Brian Nishi walking in. Were they distraught over Ty's death? Or were they, like Rosalie, shedding no tears? One way to find out. She parked her bike and followed them into the pub.

"May I join you?" she asked as she neared their table.

Theophilus rose from his seat and pulled over an extra chair. "Please, sit."

Brian nodded, then turned his attention back to his drink.

"I'm sorry about Ty," she said. "This must be a tough time for you both."

"No picnic for you, either." Theophilus's mellifluous accent reminded her of a BBC adaptation of a Jane Austen novel. "Considering the circumstances of how, you know..."

Brian looked up from his drink. "Did you see anyone? Or hear anything? The road to the lighthouse runs right past your cottage."

"No," Gethsemane said, "nothing." No reason to tell him about Verna's late-night trek up to Carrick Point, nor her run-in with Vivian. "How long did you know Ty?"

"Since university," Theophilus answered. "The three of us,

Bri, Ty, and me, were suite mates."

"We knew him a damn sight longer than that header he got mixed up with," Brian said.

"Sunny, he means." Theophilus called to a barmaid, "Same again," then asked Gethsemane, "Did you want anything?"

"Nothing for me, thanks." She came to snoop, not to drink. "You didn't approve of Ty's relationship with Sunny?"

"I approved of it the way I'd approve of going before a firing squad," Brian said.

Theophilus toyed with his glass. "I'm afraid Sunny was the only one looking forward to the upcoming nuptials. And she was mostly looking forward to the photo ops. I guess Mal may have been looking forward to them. Sunny was paying him a bloody fortune."

"He'd have earned it," Brian said. "Probably would've developed a repetitive motion injury of his trigger finger. No amount of money's worth being saddled with that horrideous cow, not even for as long as it'd take for the ink on annulment documents to dry. Ty should've stuck with Verna. Probably be alive now if he had."

Gethsemane leaned closer. "Verna? You know Verna?" Because Verna had claimed she didn't know either of them.

"Sure, we know her," Brian said. "Sweet girl. Theo's sister introduced her to Ty."

"My sister apologized to Verna for that." Theophilus drank a good portion of his drink before continuing. "Ty was my mate and all, and I hate to speak ill of the dead, but Ty didn't treat Verna as well as she deserved. She was good for Ty, but Ty wasn't so good for her."

Brian slammed a fist on the table. Glasses rattled. A few heads turned. "None of this matters now, Theo, does it? Ty's dead and what's past is past."

Theophilus didn't answer right away. "No, none of that

matters now." He emptied his glass. "Where's that barmaid got to?"

"Don't you think you ought to slow down, mate?" Brian arranged Theophilus's empty glasses, one, two, three, in a row on the table.

"Are you my nanny now, Bri?" Theophilus ordered a fourth.

Gethsemane waited until both men finished their drinks and the silence grew uncomfortable. "Do you think Ty killed himself? Sunny doesn't."

Brian swore. "Let me guess. She can't imagine that anyone would rather be dead than with her. What's her explanation? Autoerotic asphyxiation gone horribly wrong?"

Theophilus shot Brian a look. "I don't see how it could be anything but suicide, given where he was found."

"Was Ty suicidal?" Gethsemane thought back to the red flags her mother, a psychiatrist, had spoken about. "Did he put his affairs in order? Make a will? Seem emotionally distant? Distracted?"

"No more so than any other bloke about to take the plunge." Brian cringed. "Sorry. Get married."

"He lived in what I guess you'd call a bachelor pad," Theophilus said. "He had to sell his apartment and furniture—"

Brian interrupted. "Sunny made it clear none of *his* furniture would be welcome in the family home."

"Give notice at work—he and Sunny planned to live in the States, you see," Theophilus continued. "Don't know if he made a will."

"Signed a prenup," Brian said. "Sunny's idea."

"What about visiting old friends?" Or ex-fiancées? Had he tracked down Verna to say a final goodbye? "Making amends with family? Ruminating on past events, losses?"

A glance that Gethsemane couldn't decipher passed between Theophilus and Brian before Theophilus answered. "Ty wasn't one for dwelling on the past. No profit in it, he said."

"Ty focused on future plans, not past accomplishments," Brian said. "Always had an eye out for his next big opportunity. As far as he was concerned, anything that happened more than six months ago was ancient history and best forgotten."

"Doesn't sound as if he was at high risk for suicide."

"But who would've killed him?" Theophilus asked. "Who could have? Verna's not got killer instinct. Plus she's half Ty's size. No way she could've gotten him over a railing."

"Sunny wouldn't have done it," Brian said. "I don't doubt she's capable of murder. If Ty had turned up dead *after* the wedding, she'd be number one on the suspect list. She'd probably even post the kill shots on her social media feed. But she'd never have ruined her wedding plans and lost out on all those influencer endorsement deals."

"Not even if she discovered Ty loved her money more than he loved her?" Gethsemane asked.

Brian shook his head. "She knew Ty was marrying her money. She didn't care, as long as he played his part in front of whatever smartphone camera happened to be pointed in their direction. She turns that little girl voice on and off like a tap and makes cow eyes at any male over the age of twelve she thinks may be of use to her, but the helpless female routine is just that, a routine. She's as cold-blooded and pragmatic as they come and suffers no illusions about what she's—she was—getting into with Ty."

"Besides," Theophilus said, "Sunny's also too small to have hoisted Ty over a railing."

"You're both convinced Ty took his own life?"

Theophilus shrugged. "What other explanation is there?"

"Doubt we'll ever know why," Brian said. "In the end, does it matter? Dissecting Ty's past searching for an answer won't bring Ty back, will it? I say leave it alone."

She couldn't leave it alone. Not after Sunny barged into her house, insistent a murder had occurred. And not after she caught her friend's girlfriend in a lie about not knowing the dead guy's best friends.

She flagged down a barmaid. "On second thought, I'll have that drink."

Not even her favorite whiskey, Bushmills, kept her from ruminating on Sunny's and Verna's behavior. Was Sunny vicious enough to kill the man she planned to marry if she found out he'd made a play for a woman he'd dumped? Had Verna really told him to go away? With two big lies to her credit, she ranked low on the credibility scale right now. And what about Vivian? Had she gone back up to the lighthouse later that evening? She seemed protective of her older sister. Could she and Verna have teamed up to toss Ty off the catwalk? But how would they get the rope around his neck?

She continued to brood as she pedaled home. Was Brian's joke about autoerotic asphyxiation really a joke? Or did Ty have a kink that a killer might have exploited to trick him into participating in his own murder? If he'd put the rope around his own neck and climbed up onto the railing, a push would have sent him over. Even a small woman could shove an unsuspecting narcissist off a railing he'd perched on. Sunny, Verna, Vivian. Of the three, Verna was the one who'd lied. Why? Sure, she wouldn't want anyone to know she'd been one of the last people to see Ty alive, but why lie about knowing the groomsmen? Even if you forgot you knew Brian, you certainly wouldn't forget you knew a guy named Theophilus.

Suddenly, a chill shot down Gethsemane's spine. The hair on her neck and arms stood up as she stopped her bike in the middle of the road. She rubbed at the gooseflesh on her arms and looked around. Nothing but trees. She listened. No Tchaikovsky.

"Eamon?" she whispered. "Is that you?"

Silence. She squinted to peer into the woods that surrounded her. The "insufferable gloom" Edgar Allan Poe described in "The Fall of the House of Usher" crept over her. She shook her head to clear it. She'd ridden this way hundreds of times without incident. What creeped her out now?

"Eamon," she said, her voice a little louder, "if that's you, knock it off. You're scaring me."

Sunset loomed on the horizon. The gathering gold and orange and pink filled her with angst instead of awe.

"Eamon?" she whispered again. "Please let that be you."

An ear-splitting wail rent the twilight. Gethsemane froze, a breath caught between lung and throat.

"It's a banshee."

She yelped and spun, clenched fists raised. The Pashley crashed to the road.

Eamon appeared before her. His frightened mauve aura failed to reassure her.

"Jaysus, Mary, and..." Gethsemane exhaled her relief and dropped her hands. "What the—"

"Did you hear what I said?" Eamon asked. "It's a banshee."

"A banshee." She ran through her mental bestiary. "A folkloric female believed to be a harbinger of—"

"Of nothing good." Eamon pointed at the Pashley. The bike righted itself and rolled to Gethsemane. "Get on and let's go. I'll walk you home."

She climbed onto the bike. "A banshee is a harbinger of death. Hearing a banshee's cry means—"

"There'll be another violent death in Dunmullach soon."

Fourteen

She didn't sleep that night. Images of Ty hanging from the lighthouse plagued her when she closed her eyes and thoughts of Verna's lies, Sunny's machinations, and Vivian's possible involvement plagued her when she opened them. Every creak and groan of settling walls and floorboards reminded her of the banshee. Paranormal experiences, both pleasant and deadly, over the past several months meant she couldn't dismiss the wail as harmless superstition. She sighed and threw the covers back. Some nights, she missed being a skeptic.

She went down to the kitchen. Nothing in the fridge looked sleep-inducing. Coffee was out of the question. She picked up the phone.

Niall did not sound happy to hear from her. "Do you have any fecking idea what time it is?" He yawned.

"It's late." Too late to play coy. "Could Ty have been murdered? How sure is the coroner about suicide?"

Niall's voice faded, as if he held the phone away from his mouth. Not so far away that she couldn't hear the torrent of swear words he unleashed. "Why are you doing this to me?"

"I'm not doing anything to you. Except disrupting your sleep. I'm concerned a murder may be misclassified as a suicide and a murderer may escape justice."

Niall sighed. She imagined him massaging the bridge of his

nose, his tell when she got on his nerves. "Not every case is the Eamon McCarthy case."

"And Eamon McCarthy's death isn't the only one to have been mislabeled."

"What dosser's doin' a number on ya to get you all worked up about this?" She thought she heard him mumble, "So I can throttle them."

"Ty's fiancée is convinced he was murdered."

"I heard she paid you a visit." He chuckled. "Boy, did I hear about it. She put on a holy show at the station. Sutton threatened to arrest her for interfering with garda business. That wedding photographer showed up and managed to corral her and coax her out of the building. Poor Sutton went home early with a headache. You didn't take her rants seriously?"

"Not at first. And not only because of what she said. I talked to Theophilus Derringer and Brian Nishi."

"The groomsmen?"

"Yes. And neither of them remembered Ty as suicidal. They've known him for ages, and they described a man looking forward to the next phase of his life." A phase filled with crazy amounts of money. "They couldn't understand why he'd take his own life."

"But they agree he did?"

"Only because they couldn't think of anyone who might have wanted him dead who, physically, could have killed him. The main suspects are half Ty's size."

"Suspects? Plural?"

Damn, he caught that. Note to self, watch your grammar when speaking to a cop. "Sunny…" She couldn't bring herself to say it.

"And?"

Gethsemane took a deep breath and silently apologized to Frankie. "And the Cunningham sisters."

Another sigh. "What do you know?"

She told him about her collision with Vivian and Verna's late-night meeting with Ty at the lighthouse and her failure to acknowledge her acquaintance with his groomsmen.

"Maybe Verna didn't know Nishi and Derringer well," Niall said. "Maybe she forgot them."

"Forgot a big, blond guy with a scar on his face and a name like Theophilus?"

"Point taken. And even if she had legit forgotten Nishi and Derringer, she wouldn't have forgotten meeting her ex a few hours before he died. So she lied." A pause. "Have you spoken to Frankie?"

"No. I don't particularly want to. He already knows about her meeting Ty. She told him she begged Ty to leave her alone. He seemed to believe her."

"You doubt her?"

"No. Not exactly. Well, maybe." She searched for words. "I mean, her story sounds reasonable. A jerk from her past threatens her current relationship so she tells him to get lost. And I understand why she wouldn't tell Frankie about the meeting. But..."

"But catching her in a second lie, a lie that doesn't serve much purpose, makes you wonder."

"And there's Vivian. She's quick to rush to her sister's defense. Is her loyalty limited to verbal attacks or would she amp it up a level?"

"Hanging a man is amping it up more than a level. And Vivian's no bigger that Sunny and Verna, so how—" He swore. "Now you've got me doing it."

"You'll take another peek at the coroner's report?"

"Yes, I'll look, if you promise to hang up and not call me again before sunrise."

"I promise. I—"

The call ended.

Eamon materialized. "Thank you. And you don't have to figure out who killed Ty to keep him from haunting Carrick Point. Just keep him from being wrongly buried in unhallowed ground as a suicide."

"You've known me for the better part of a year. Do you really think I can leave the job half-done? Especially if Frankie's girlfriend played a role in his death?"

"No. But you can't blame a ghost for trying."

She wasted no time getting to the Garda station as soon as the sun rose. She arrived before Niall and waited under a tree next to his usual parking space.

Several minutes later, Niall pulled into the parking space. He exited his car but stopped when he spied Gethsemane. The brim of his hat, a small-brimmed fedora he'd inherited from his father, didn't hide his frown. He approached her. Gethsemane left her bike by the tree and met him halfway.

"Before you ask," he said, "no, I haven't spoken to the coroner. Nor have I taken a closer look at her report. Because the office opened," he looked at his watch, "about three-and-a-half minutes ago. D'you know what time it is?"

"You keep asking me that." She tapped her own watch. "I have a watch and I know what time it is. But I—"

"Am convinced something sinister is happening and am overly eager to prove it. I know. I should be used to it by now."

"I am not overly anything. I—" She held her hands up in the shape of a "T." "Truce. I'm going over to the coffee shop. I will wait there patiently—"

Niall rolled his eyes.

"Okay, I will wait impatiently. But I will wait until you call me."

"And I'll speak to the coroner first thing, I promise." He readjusted his hat and walked toward the station.

Gethsemane crossed the street to Roasted, the village coffee house, and joined the short line at the counter.

"Your usual large caramel latte?" the barista asked.

"I think I'll change it up today. How about a hazelnut cappuccino? Large."

She scanned the room while the barista rang up her order. The crowd, somewhat thin at this hour—summer being the time when many villagers, students and educators among them, chose sleep over caffeine—filled about half the tables. A familiar figure sat at one near a window—Agnes Haywood, Sunny's other maid of honor.

"That's five twenty-four."

"What?" Gethsemane turned back to the barista.

"Five twenty-four. The cappuccino."

Gethsemane paid for her coffee and headed toward Agnes. She hadn't taken much notice of her when she first saw her with Sunny at the lighthouse, so she looked at her more closely now. Thick braids crowned smooth, dark skin, darker than Gethsemane's. She rested her head on a slim hand, elbow propped on the table. She turned pages in a book with the other hand. A coffee mug sat nearby.

"Hello," Gethsemane said, "May I join you?"

The woman didn't answer right away. She finished reading the page she was on, pulled a bookmark from beneath the book cover, marked her place, then pushed the book aside a few inches before she acknowledged Gethsemane. She gestured toward the empty seat opposite her.

"I'm Gethsem—"

"Gethsemane Brown." The woman sipped her coffee and watched Gethsemane over the mug's rim. "I remember you from the lighthouse." Her accent put her origin somewhere in New

York.

Gethsemane took a long sip of her own drink. "I don't remember Sunny introducing you."

"She didn't. She wouldn't. I'm Agnes Haywood."

"Rosalie mentioned your name. How are you doing?"

Agnes raised an eyebrow.

"Holding up, I mean. Ty Lismore's death. It must've hit you pretty hard. It was—unexpected?" She made it a question.

"Yeah." Agnes set her mug down. "I still can't wrap my head around it. Ty seemed like—Ty. Like his usual self. I've known him for years. Knew him for years. I didn't see any signs to make me think he planned to kill himself. His death doesn't seem real to me. It'll probably hit me when I get back home." She gave a brief, sardonic laugh. "I'll save my emotional meltdown until I'm safe on my home turf. Won't do to show vulnerability around Sunny. Jackals go for the weakest gazelles, don't they?"

"You were close to Ty? Good friends?"

"That's hard to believe?"

"I assumed," Gethsemane said, "you were more Sunny's friend. Since you're one of her maids of honor. At least that's what Rosalie said."

"Rosalie talks too much. I knew Ty first. Long before he met Sunny. I wanted to be one of his groomsmen, but I didn't look good in a morning coat." A smile flickered across her lips. "That was a joke. Not a good one. I'm terrible at jokes. Ty always said so."

"You're from New York?"

"Manhattan born and bred."

"How did you meet Ty? He spent time in New York? Or you spent time in the UK?"

"Why do you care? You've only just met us, and you don't like us." She cut off Gethsemane's protests. "Most people dislike us, especially at first acquaintance. We're clique-y and vain and high-maintenance and suffer no illusions about ourselves. I think that's why we were drawn to each other, Ty, Brian, Theo, and me. Rare breeds flock together. Well," she toyed with her coffee mug, seemingly lost in a memory, "less so, Theo. He's the 'nice one' of the bunch. He mediates between us and ordinary people." She snapped back from wherever she'd been and frowned at Gethsemane. "So, why do you care?"

Why did she care? Because she suspected one of these rare birds might be a murderer? Or because she feared her friend's girlfriend might, however justifiably so, be one? Gethsemane sipped her cappuccino. It was cold. "Ty was found hanging from my lighthouse. Every time I look out my windows, I see the place where a man died. I feel compelled to find out more about him. Especially since, from what little I've heard about him, his suicide surprised everyone, his fiancée the most."

"Sunny notices Sunny. Brian, Theo, and I were the ones who—you're right, suicide was something we never saw coming. To answer your question, I met Ty in New Orleans. He, Theo, Brian, and his girlfriend at the time, Verna, were there for Mardi Gras. You know Verna, don't you?"

"Yes, I know her." Another past acquaintance Verna had failed to mention. "We both teach at the same school."

"And she dates your red-headed friend. The rumors about small towns being gossip hotbeds are true. I've picked up more dirt on people in my two weeks here than I get in a year back home. If I had this intelligence network in New York, I'd be invincible."

Gethsemane swigged coffee, disguising her distaste for Agnes as a reaction to the undrinkable liquid. "You traveled solo to Mardi Gras? I'm a fan of solo travel. You're not beholden to anyone else's sightseeing plans."

"I was there with—" Agnes stopped.

"With?"

"Just some guy I'd met. Anyway, we ran into Ty and his crew at a bar and ended up hanging out for the rest of the week."

Just some guy. She couldn't remember her date's name but she remembered Ty, Theo, Brian, and Verna. Either the date had been a loser or the others had been the life of the party. "Must've been a great week, you remained friends this long."

"It was a," Agnes looked down at the table, "memorable week."

"As memorable as time spent with Sunny? How'd you become friends with her, anyway?"

"Since Rosalie talked to you, I'm sure she explained that Sunny Markham doesn't have friends. Hangers-on, lackeys, and obstacles to be overcome, but not friends. I tolerate her for Ty's sake."

"'Tolerate' is a far cry from 'maid of honor.'"

Agnes shrugged. "I'm a good actress. I pretend Sunny's particular brand of toxic doesn't bother me. Anything for Ty."

"So he introduced you?"

"No, Rosalie's to blame for that. She introduced Sunny to Ty and the rest of us. She once joked—half-joked—she needed to throw Sunny some fresh meat to stop her from gnawing on her bones."

"I don't understand. No one seems to like Sunny—not her maids of honor, not her fiancé's groomsmen, not even her fiancé. Granted, it's not hard to see why. Five minutes in her company is four minutes of your life you'll never get back. She's dreadful, personified. But why put up with her? No one has *that* much money. Do they?"

"Her family has that much money. And influence. And power. They used to have more but their 'fortunes turned for the worse,' as her mother puts it to anyone within earshot, during the Depression. They've resented it ever since. They feel entitled to be in the top one percent of the one percent and have been clawing and manipulating and maneuvering their way back to the top for the past eighty years. Sunny's like that woman who founded that sham medical device company, Theta. What was her name, Becky Harris? Based on the strength of some dead relatives' names on buildings and an absolute conviction that she's entitled to whatever she desires, she gets people to go along with her—or give in to her. She keeps secrets, she lies when it serves her, she plays sides against each other. She surrounds herself with chaos, which keeps everyone in her orbit off guard and on their toes. And, on the rare occasion someone works up enough courage to challenge her openly, she turns to Mommy and Daddy for the kill."

"Rosalie did mention something about losing jobs and apartments if you crossed her."

"You're blacklisted. A social outcast, untouchable. People have literally changed their names and moved out of the city to start over. And she can count at least one person's suicide to her—credit, if you can call it that." Agnes dropped her gaze. "Maybe two, if you count Ty."

"Sounds like you'd get a better deal selling your soul to the devil."

Agnes looked up and crossed herself, then blushed. "You must think I'm superstitious, crossing myself when someone mentions the devil."

Once upon a time she might have but now... "No."

"Well, I am superstitious. Ty used to tease me about it. Sunny mocks me for it. Rosalie keeps me supplied with talismans."

"She offered to read the tarot cards for me."

"You should let her. She's good. She has some sort of gift. I can't explain it, but I can't deny it, either. Did she tell you she studied hoodoo? Her grandmother taught her."

"African-American folk magic? But Rosalie's—"

"White? Yeah, but her great-great-great grandmother was as Black as you and I. Folks whose ancestors hail from the River Road area are likely to be at least a little bit of everything. Rosalie descends from a long line of conjure women. I wondered why she never put a hex on Sunny."

"Did you ever ask her?"

"Yeah. She said, what did I think Ty was?" Agnes leaned back in her chair. "I know some people, maybe most, find Ty—found Ty—difficult to deal with. He was arrogant, he had a mean streak, he'd do anything for money, even marry Sunny. But he was also funny and charming, full of energy. You were guaranteed a good time in his company. He treated me all right."

"You said he teased you."

"Don't your friends tease you?"

All. The. Time. "Yeah, a bit."

"He was dangerous, but in an exciting, daring way. Not an anxiety-provoking way, like Sunny. I liked him." Agnes shrugged. "Who knows why some friendships form? But Ty was my friend, a true friend, and, like I said, I'd have done anything for him."

"Even serve as one of his fiancée's maids of honor."

"Could've been worse. He could've asked me to put my eyes out with hot pokers. And being one of the special, chosen ones, comes with a few perks. That's why Rosalie and I got to come along on this all-expense paid pre-wedding promotional trip. I know we're mostly here as backdrop for Sunny's photos, but a free trip to Ireland is still a free trip to Ireland. Ty made a good call on this one."

"Ty?"

"Dunmullach was his idea. Sunny wanted to have her wedding in Paris but Ty convinced her it was overdone. He talked her into a wedding in Ireland because it 'went with her looks,' and in a small, picturesque village because it would complement her instead of compete with her the way a big city would. You must admit, this place looks good on film."

So, Ty had chosen Dunmullach, not Sunny. Maybe not so much of a coincidence that his ex-fiancée lived here after all. "You mentioned Ty was with Verna when you met him."

"Verna was two engagements and three 'serious' relationships before Sunny. As serious as any relationship could be for Ty. He craved women more than he craved nicotine. Verna didn't tolerate Ty's proclivities the way Sunny does. Their relationship didn't work out."

Understatement of the century. And no mention of abandoning Verna at the altar. Undoubtedly, Ty's spin on events. She started to ask about Verna's brother but Agnes spoke first.

"Ty cheated chronically. And enthusiastically. Full disclosure, a few times with me. More than a few times."

"Friends with benefits? Sunny put up with it? Or didn't she know?"

"Preferred it, I think, as long as we were discreet. At least with me, she knew Ty was with someone who had no long-term designs on him. A harmless diversion, not a serious threat."

"Sunny doesn't strike me as the sharing type."

"Unfaithful husbands are a Markham family tradition. They make the Kennedy men seem like altar boys. In fact, family legend has it her great-grandfather and Joe Kennedy, Sr. shared mistresses as well as a bootlegging business. And an uncle was rumored to have had an affair with Marilyn Monroe at the same time as JFK."

"Was it only Ty's infidelity that ended his relationship with Verna or did her brother's death factor into it? Ty's involvement must've put a strain on—"

"It was an accident. A tragic accident, yes, but still an

accident. Accidents happen, you know. People die sometimes but it's no one's fault. That's the definition of accident." Agnes stood. "I have to go." She stared out the window past Gethsemane's shoulder.

Gethsemane turned to see where she looked. Rosalie Baraquin stood across the street.

"Sunny's put together a memorial for Ty at Our Lady of Perpetual Sorrows. For show, mostly. I'm walking over with Rosalie. Later, Theo, Brian, and I will get together for a real memorial. At the pub or up at the lighthouse with a bottle." She added an afterthought. "You wouldn't mind, would you? If we went up to Carrick Point to say goodbye?"

"No, I wouldn't mind." Eamon might, but she wouldn't.

Agnes pulled out her phone and sent a quick text. Gethsemane watched as Rosalie across the street reached into her bag and pulled out her phone. She read the screen then looked up and waved at the coffee house.

Agnes dropped her phone back into her purse. "No one ever accused Ty of being a saint. No one's ever accused me of that, either. But Ty was my friend and I miss him, and I think he deserved better than what he got."

Gethsemane watched as Agnes left Roasted and crossed the street to Rosalie. The two bridesmaids walked together in the direction of the village center. Gethsemane pulled out her phone and checked for messages. No missed calls or texts from Niall. She debated calling Frankie. He'd probably be with Verna. She needed time to digest Verna's selective memory—her lies, to be blunt—before she talked to him. How much did he know? Maybe Verna had been more honest with him. She doubted it. Damn. Frankie had already had his heart broken by one deceitful woman. Ty wasn't the only one who deserved better.

Fifteen

"Wait patiently." Her two least favorite words. Her phone rang just as she decided to go back to the Garda station instead of continue to wait for Niall's call.

She answered on the first notes of Beethoven's "Fifth Symphony," her ringtone. "Niall?"

"Tim," the priest answered. "Can you come to the rectory?"

"I'll be right there," she said, glad to have something to occupy her.

Father Tim met her at the rectory door.

"Must be serious," she said as he ushered her inside. "You aren't conducting Ty's memorial service?"

"Miss Markham asked to use the nave, however, my services weren't needed. I got the impression the event is to be non-denominational. I will, of course, continue to offer prayers for the repose of Mr. Lismore's soul. And, yes, it is serious."

She followed Father Tim into his study. Saoirse sat on the sofa, surrounded by stacks of ancient, leather-bound books. "Hello, Miss." She lifted a tome the size of a prayer book from the pile nearest her and flipped it open.

"Hello, Saoirse. You found something?"

"My brother's books contained any number of banishing spells." Father Tim held up a few books from one of the piles. "But we did locate an ancient prayer that will prevent Mr.

Lismore from becoming a ghost in the first place." He held up a small, battered, leather-bound book the size of an index card. "Then there'll be no need to banish him."

"You didn't call me over here because of Ty, did you?"

Tim glanced at Saoirse. "Step into the kitchen with me," he said to Gethsemane.

"Saoirse knows everything, anyway. Don't you, Saoirse?"

The girl didn't look up from her book. "Yes, Miss."

"Humor me," Tim said. "Prescient or not, she's still a child and I'm old fashioned that way." He led the way to the rear of the rectory.

"Tea?" he asked when they reached the kitchen. He turned the kettle on without waiting for an answer.

Gethsemane took a tea pot, teacups, and Bewley's from cabinets. "What *did* you find? Considering Saoirse's in there," she jerked her head toward the study, "happily reading incantations to banish ghosts, find one's fortune, clear up acne, and who knows what else, I'm nervous about something you don't want to discuss in front of her."

"I received this message this morning, not long before Saoirse arrived. Someone slipped the envelope under the door." He pulled a plain white envelope from his pocket and handed it to Gethsemane.

She opened it and removed a slip of writing paper with a solitary black-and-white drawing in the center. "A Jerusalem cross surrounded by an arrow, seven circles, a heart, and some squiggles, in a ring labeled with letters. What is it, some kind of cipher?" What did it remind her of?

"It's a sigil, or seal. A sort of pictograph used in medieval ceremonial magic."

A pictograph, like Rosalie's message. "From the expression on your face, I gather medieval ceremonial magic isn't a good thing."

"It's not inherently any better nor any worse than any other form of magic. But that," he pointed at the drawing, "was never used for anything good."

"What are sigils used for?"

"Summoning angels, demons, and spirits."

"Let me guess. This particular sigil was not used for summoning angels and spirits." If Rosalie had received a similar message...

Tim shook his head.

...No wonder Rosalie was upset. Gethsemane pinched the paper between two fingers and dangled it by its corner. "This is for summoning demons?" Rosalie had described it as a calling card. Was she expecting a demon to drop in for a visit? Who described a demon as a business associate?

"Not demons, plural."

The kettle whistled. Gethsemane started and dropped the paper.

"Let's have tea first." Tim poured hot water into the pot.

She retrieved the picture and laid it on the kitchen table. She studied it while the tea steeped. "I can't make any sense of it."

"On its own, it doesn't make much sense. It's meant to be esoteric. Only someone in on the secrets would understand what it meant. An uninitiated person who found it would think it no more than a strange doodle. But combined with the proper incantations and rituals—"

"And harmonic likeness. Each ghost resonates to a particular tone so you'd have to combine the right harmony with the sigil and the proper summoning spell in order to bring a spirit back from the other side."

"Not needed for demons, I'm afraid. Unfortunate, because requiring that extra step might discourage people from dabbling. During a ritual, that sigil would stand in for the name of whatever entity, angelic or demonic, the magician wanted to summon. Especially with demons, as the entity's true name, the sigil would give the conjurer some control over the entity." Tim filled their teacups and sat across from her.

Gethsemane ignored the rich, brown, malty liquid and pointed at the drawing. "These squiggles and symbols translate to a name? Whose name? Can you translate it?"

"No, I can't translate it," Tim said. "But I don't have to. I recognize it. My brother showed it to me once, as a warning."

"A warning about what?" Gooseflesh peppered her arms. Did she want to know the answer?

"The only spell that particular sigil is used with is a spell to conjure the devil. It's a spell for revenge. A magician who wanted revenge on his or her enemies, but who didn't expect to live long enough to wreak it, would summon the devil and make a deal. In exchange for their soul, the devil would keep them alive long enough to exact retribution."

Gethsemane shuddered. Be careful what you ask. "Someone delivered that to you? As a warning? Is someone out to get you?"

"I can't think of anyone angry enough with me to sell their soul to the devil for a chance to get at me. Can't recall doing anything worse than putting people to sleep with my sermons."

"Tim, this is serious. A person willing to suffer eternal damnation just to get back at someone, must really, really, really want to get back at someone."

"I agree it's serious, but I don't think it's meant as a warning for me. You wouldn't put your target on notice. That would give them the chance to conduct some magic of their own to protect themselves. What's the saying about revenge? That it's a dish best served cold?"

"I see your point." She slid the drawing close to herself and traced the outline of the central cross. "Why send it to anyone at all? Selling your soul to the devil doesn't seem like the type of thing you'd advertise." She pushed the drawing away and said a silent prayer of protection.

"Don't know," Tim said. "As a heads up? A professional courtesy? Or maybe to brag, to thumb your nose at the Church, announcing that there's nothing the Church can do to stop you? Whatever the motivation for sending it, we need to find out who sent it and why. If the devil's on the loose in Dunmullach, we need to do something about it. We have to stop him."

"I can see why you don't want Saoirse involved in this." She'd refused to let the girl become involved in violent death by human agency. Satan-powered vengeance was definitely not in the realm of appropriate concerns for pre-teens. It wasn't in the realm of appropriate concerns for adult musicians and parish priests, for that matter. "Should we be involved in it? Maybe we should call one of your brother's colleagues?"

"An exorcist? It's not that simple, I'm afraid. You need hard evidence of demonic activity for the Church to sanction an exorcist's involvement. We have a piece of paper."

Gethsemane snapped her fingers. "We have Rosalie Baraquin."

"Miss Baraquin? How can she help?"

"She's a conjure woman." She described her chat with the other maid of honor. "According to Agnes, Rosalie's experience with folk magic dates back generations. And that note she wouldn't discuss with me? The drawing on it looked a lot like this sigil. Not exactly like it," she reassured Tim as he paled, "but close enough to remind me of it. Maybe she knows something about this one."

"Knows something about it as in, knows who sent it? Or are you thinking maybe she sent it herself?"

"I'm not sure what to think about Rosalie. One minute she seems like an average bridesmaid, the next I feel like I should check over my shoulder to make sure she's not following me."

She pulled the sketch back around and scrutinized it. What else, besides Rosalie's note, did it remind her of? Something...Her tattoo. It resembled one of Rosalie's tattoos even more than it did her note. Gethsemane snapped a picture with her phone. "It'll be interesting to see how she reacts to this."

A loud commotion outside carried into the kitchen. Gethsemane, Father Tim, and Saoirse rushed into the church yard to find Sunny and her wedding party gathered in the cloister.

"You stupid, stupid, stupid cow!" Sunny, her complexion as scarlet as her hair, stood inches from Agnes and yelled in her face. "How dare you?"

Agnes, eyes narrowed and fists clenched, yelled back. "Shut up! You inbred, histrionic, malicious brat! The EPA's cleaned up chemical spills less toxic than you!"

"*You* shut up, you insignificant wanna be. You should be on your knees thanking me for the chance to be in my wedding."

"You should be on your knees thanking me for not punching you in your head."

Rosalie, Theophilus, Brian, and Malcolm stared, open-mouthed, at the screaming women.

Father Tim hurried over and stood between Agnes and Sunny. "May I be of assistance?"

"Yeah," Agnes said, "You can pray I don't knock her pearly white implants right down her throat."

Tim held up his hands. "There's no need for violence."

"What happened?" Saoirse asked.

"What happened," Sunny said, "is this middle-class nobody dared to call me, *me*, common. The Markhams are not common. We trace our lineage back to—"

Agnes broke in. "The Mayflower and Columbus and the Emperor Charlemagne. Yadda, yadda, yadda, all the way back to Cain and Abel and nobody cares. And I didn't say you were common, I said you were trash. I've met cleaning women and hot dog peddlers with more class than you."

Saoirse asked Gethsemane, "Aren't they friends?"

Rosalie snorted and covered a laugh with her hand.

"Sunny doesn't have friends, kid," Agnes said. "You have to be human to have friends. This sociopathic, narcissistic, borderline snake has victims, people she manipulates and abuses."

"You're jealous," Sunny said, "because Ty chose me over you. He was going to marry me. You wanted him but I got him."

"I had no interest in marrying Ty, you self-absorbed twit. I didn't need to because I 'got' him every other week and twice on holiday weekends. You might want to check your credit card statements a little closer, sweetie. Those restaurant and hotel charges were for two."

"Why you—" Sunny flew at Agnes.

Agnes stepped back while Father Tim stepped forward. Malcolm jumped in front of the priest and intercepted Sunny. He wrapped his arms around her, pinning her arms at her side, as she struggled to reach her bridesmaid. "Sunny, please," he said. "This is a house of God. Well, His front yard, anyway."

She kicked at him. "Let go of me."

Malcolm's grip tightened. "Not until you calm down. What good will attacking Agnes do?"

"Snatching those braids out of her hair will make me feel good."

"You try it." Agnes raised a fist. "There aren't enough Instagram filters in the world to disguise what I'd do to you."

"Miss Haywood," Father Tim slipped an arm around Agnes's shoulder. "Perhaps you'd like to come into the rectory for a cup of tea."

Agnes shook him off. "What is it with the Irish and tea? Any trouble that happens, you make tea. Shouting match—tea.

Fistfight—tea. Natural disaster—tea. Second coming—tea."

"Nothing a hot cup of Bewley's Irish Breakfast can't solve," Brian said.

Theophilus put his arm around Agnes. "Come on, Aggie, let's you, Brian, and me head back to the inn. We can swing by the off license on the way, pick up a bottle of something stronger than tea, and get drunk in my room. Like we did with Ty and Verna in New Orleans. Remember?"

Sunny sneered. "I'd think you'd all want to forget New Orleans."

Brian's eyes narrowed. "I'd think you'd want to shut your gob, Sunny."

Malcolm shifted, blocking Sunny's view of anyone but him. He smiled down at her. "C'mon, they're not worth it. Let's go for a walk around the village square, calm down. Or maybe a walk around the church gardens. See how beautiful they are." He kept his eyes on Sunny as he spoke to Tim. "That would be all right, wouldn't it, Father? A stroll through the grounds?"

"Certainly," Tim said. "Our Lady's gardens are open to all. I find a walk 'round the church yard to be quite therapeutic."

"That's a lovely poison garden you have, Father." Agnes nodded at a small garden several yards away, isolated from the main garden by a high wrought iron fence and gate. "That's where Mal and Sunny should stroll. And he should feed her a few samples." Agnes's baleful expression made the hair on Gethsemane's neck stand up. She'd gotten a taste of the poison garden's bounty, not so long ago, not an experience she'd wish on anyone.

Sunny went for Agnes again and, again, Malcolm stopped her.

"Let's go, Aggie," Theophilus said. "This isn't how we want to remember Ty."

Theophilus and Brian steered Agnes toward the exit gate

while Malcolm led Sunny in the opposite direction. Gethsemane, Rosalie, Tim, and Saoirse stared after them.

"Wow," Gethsemane said. "What was that?"

"Sunny being Sunny," Rosalie said, "and Agnes's last nerve snapping. Sunny started in about how Agnes and the guys meant nothing to Ty. Agnes lost it."

"Nice job Mal running interference."

"The Lord of Chaos."

The four fell silent as they watched Malcolm escort Sunny past the poison garden to the church cemetery.

"Strange place to walk, isn't it, Miss?" Saoirse said.

"You walk through the cemetery, Saoirse," Gethsemane replied. "You like to read the old tombstones."

"That lady doesn't look like she's fond of tombstones, Miss. Far too posh."

"Don't believe everything you see, kid," Rosalie said.

Speaking of things seen...Gethsemane pulled out her phone and showed Rosalie the photo of the sigil. "Do you have any idea what this is?"

Rosalie paled and recoiled. "No. Why would I?"

Gethsemane's gaze drifted to Rosalie's arms, covered by long, gauzy sleeves. "It reminds me of your tattoo. The one with the twenty-seven and the heart."

Rosalie crossed her arms. "I'm sure it doesn't. It's nothing like any of my tattoos."

"Okay, your note, then. The one from the business associate announcing a visit. It resembles the pictograph."

"No." Rosalie looked ill. "It's nothing like that note. You barely even got a look at it; how would you know what it resembles? The design in that photo is nothing like the note, it's nothing like my tattoos. It's nothing to do with me."

"You're an occult expert. Agnes said—" Something stopped her from telling Rosalie what Agnes said about Rosalie's hoodoo background.

"Agnes said what?"

"Just that you read tarot. You offered to do a reading for me."

"Which hardly makes me an occult expert. And, even if I was, I wouldn't have anything to do with that."

"How do you know you wouldn't have anything to do with it," Saoirse asked, "if you don't know what it is?"

Rosalie scowled. "Didn't anyone ever tell you children should be seen and not heard?" She hurried across the yard, toward the exit gate, without waiting for a reply.

"Saoirse's right," Father Tim said. "If Miss Baraquin didn't know what that thing was, she wouldn't have been afraid of it. And it terrified her. She recognized the sigil. Could she have slipped it under my door?"

"I don't think so," Gethsemane said. "You saw the way she reacted. If a photo of the sigil has that effect on her, I doubt she'd touch the actual drawing, let alone seal it in an envelope and hand deliver it."

"Which brings us back to, who did?" Father Tim said. "And why? Is it a boast, a warning, or a threat?"

"I vote for a warning about Rosalie. I don't care what she says, the sigil does resemble her tattoo with the twenty-seven and it resembles the pictograph in the note she received. Maybe someone's warning us to watch out for her."

Tim frowned. "Or maybe they're directing a threat toward her. Maybe she recognized the threat or who it came from and that's why she's so jumpy. Maybe we should watch over her instead of out for her."

"If it was meant as a threat toward Rosalie, why send it to you?"

"The sender might have been afraid to leave it at the inn. Too many potential witnesses, a chance the maid might sweep it up. Maybe whoever sent it believed a priest would recognize its significance and connect it to Rosalie."

Gethsemane shook her head. "I don't know, Tim. I'm still inclined toward warning about her. Rosalie Baraquin may not be physically large enough to have tossed Ty over a railing, but she knows more than she's—" Beethoven's "Fifth" sounded from her phone. A text from Niall filled the screen:

You were right.

"I have to go," she said.

"Something serious?" Father Tim asked.

"As serious as murder," she said.

Sixteen

Niall met her in the Garda station's parking lot. "Let's go up to my office."

"Your office? No." She responded to Niall's puzzled look. "Every time I step into that building, I end up in an interrogation room. Sutton's gone weeks without hauling me in, I don't want to run into him."

"My office isn't on the same floor as homicide."

"Doesn't matter. I'm not chancing him finding me."

"You know he likes you."

Gethsemane laughed. "No, he doesn't."

"Yeah, he does. He admires intelligent women. His wife's a nuclear chemist."

"He's got a funny way of showing his admiration. How'd he act if he hated me?"

"Don't ask. Can we at least find a bench to sit on? Don't make me eat my hat standing in a car park."

Gethsemane led the way across the parking lot to a small park opposite the station. Niall unfolded a piece of paper as they sat on a bench near the park's entrance.

"What's that?" she asked.

Niall handed it to her. "Read it."

Niall's full name and title, "Iollan Niall O'Reilly, Inspector," marched across the To: line of an official-looking email. The CC:

line included Sutton's name. The sender's title read "Coroner." Gethsemane jumped to the end of the message. "Homicide," she read aloud.

"I bet you skip to the end of novels, too."

She rolled her eyes then went back to the top of the page. "Amphetamines and phencyclidine found on preliminary tox screen." She stopped reading. "Phencyclidine, that's PCP."

Niall nodded. "A hallucinogen."

"Ty was doing drugs?" She resumed reading. "Given the hallucinogenic properties of both amphetamines and phencyclidine, it's possible the deceased may have been hallucinating when he jumped or fell from the catwalk of Carrick Point lighthouse. Further investigation is needed to determine whether he ingested the substances on his own or if they were administered to him. Although suicide remains a possibility, I am inclined to officially classify the death as either 'death by misadventure' or 'homicide.'" She handed the email back to Niall. "Does Sutton know?"

"Not yet. Figured I'd let him enjoy a cuppa before I ruin his day."

"I find it hard to believe Ty was on drugs. Granted, I only saw him a few times, but he always appeared sober. A gobshite, but never high, never even drunk, despite carrying a flask in his pocket. Chain smoking seemed to be his main vice, aside from ruining people's lives."

"He may have been selective about where and when he indulged. The coroner found a fair bit of alcohol in him. And none in his flask. Maybe Lismore reserved his drinking and drugging for times when no one was around."

"Like late at night? Atop an isolated lighthouse?" Verna hadn't mentioned Ty being under the influence when she confronted him at Carrick Point. Surely, she'd have noticed. And, surely, she'd have said something. Wouldn't she? Or would she, if she had slipped him something? If she'd agreed to a conciliatory drink and he'd handed her the flask and she'd—

Niall snapped his fingers. "Hey, where are you?"

Gethsemane shook her head. "Sorry. I was just trying to picture Ty on PCP. I can buy amphetamines," she said, "but PCP? In this day and age? It seems so—1980s."

"Old fashioned or not, it's still used."

"Is illness a side effect of amphetamines and PCP? I mean illness like you've got a sinus infection or pneumonia."

"Dunno. Why?"

"Ty had a nasty cough. I assumed he was ill from smoking. He was taking prescription meds, Evoxil and Benylin."

"Those sound familiar. I think one of my sisters took those for a bad dose she had a while back. I'll check with the coroner. Thanks for the tip." Niall rose. "I have to run. I've got a meeting with the Superintendent."

"You know I'm going to tell Frankie about this."

"Yeah, I know. You notice I didn't bother warning you not to. While you're at it, you might warn Verna and Vivian not to leave the village."

"Because?"

"Don't play coy. I don't need to tell you to cop on. If it turns out Lismore had some help getting those drugs into his system, the Cunningham sisters, Verna in particular, jump to the head of the suspect list. Sutton knows about her past relationship with Ty."

"Nothing stays secret for long in Dunmullach, does it?"

Niall tipped his hat and headed back to the station.

Eamon materialized next to her on the bench. "You can handle it."

"Handle what?" Gethsemane asked without looking at him.

"Handle delivering Grennan the bad news about his bure."

"I need to tell him before Sutton gets to him, don't I?"

"Remember how Sutton treated him the last time?"

"I need to tell him before Sutton gets to him. Damn."

"He's a grown man."

"Who was betrayed by the woman he loved with the man he was later accused of killing. And he's fallen hard for Verna. I can tell, even if it doesn't show through that curmudgeonly façade. Why'd she have to turn out to be a liar?"

"No one's perfect."

"She may be a murderer."

"You don't know that."

"She had motive. She hated Ty. She had opportunity. She was at the lighthouse alone with him the night he died, while he was under the influence of hallucinogens. Maybe she convinced him the rope was a necklace and that he could fly."

"You're jumping to conclusions."

Gethsemane sighed and hid her face in her hands. "Yeah. But you have to admit, things don't look good for our lovely blonde Latin teacher. That's the conclusion Sutton will jump to as soon as he checks his email."

"What about the other one, Vivian?" Eamon asked. "She hated Ty as much as Verna. And she's the bolder of the two sisters. Maybe Vivian went back to the lighthouse later that night. Maybe she followed her sister up to the catwalk and did what Verna couldn't. Just because you didn't see her walking back to the village with Verna doesn't mean she was tucked up in bed. Maybe Verna is covering for her."

"Meaning maybe Verna's an accessory to murder instead of a murderer. Small consolation for Frankie."

"Less prison time for Verna."

"Not funny."

"I know. I'm sorry." Eamon floated closer to her, sending an electric buzz down her arm where her shoulder passed through his. "But you can't help who you fall for and sometimes that person turns out to be someone other than who you thought they were. If Grennan's got to hear the news, I'm sure he'd rather hear it from a friend than from a guard."

Gethsemane grasped at a thread. "Ty's death could be no one's fault but his own. Death by misadventure."

"Here's another ray of hope. One of Ty's crew could have done him in. Agnes or one of those fellas."

"Theophilus or Brian? They're Ty's friends."

"So they say. But have you noticed how cagey they get whenever someone brings up New Orleans?"

"How do you know about that?"

"Being a ghost makes earwigging easy, darlin'. Just because you don't see me, doesn't mean I'm not around."

"Are you spying on me?"

"No, I'm assisting in your investigation. And keeping an eye on you."

"How could you eavesdrop on me and Agnes? Roasted wasn't here when you were alive. I thought you could only go places you'd been before...you know."

"Before I was murdered. You can say it. True, there was no posh coffee house while I lived. But the building was there. A pool hall. I got thrown out regularly from the ages of ten through sixteen. By the way, whose idea was it to charge five euros for a cuppa coffee? That's criminal." Eamon's aura shown an energetic tiger orange. Gethsemane jumped as he poked a finger through her knee. "Now quit stalling and get over to Erasmus Hall before Sutton reads his email." He vanished.

Seventeen

Gethsemane stared up at the façade of Erasmus Hall, the bachelor faculty quarters on the east end of St. Brennan's campus. Her heart pounded. Repeated swallowing failed to relieve her dry mouth. But Eamon was right. Better from her than from the police. She turned to her trick of reciting Negro League baseball stats to steady her nerves. She recited the batting averages of the starting lineup of the 1933 Homestead Grays then climbed the stairs. A quick run through of Josh Gibson's averages from 1936 to 1938 and she knocked on the door of Frankie's apartment, 1B.

Frankie opened the door after the third knock. Miles Davis's "Enigma" drifted into the hall. "Sissy."

"Hi. May I come in?"

"Is it that bad, then?"

"Excuse me?"

"You didn't eat my head off for calling you Sissy. Whatever it is must be brutal. It's not another body, is it?"

If only. "No, not another body. News about Ty."

Frankie started to speak, then swallowed hard and opened the door wide. "You better come in."

Verna rose from the couch as Gethsemane entered the living room. She frowned. "Gethsemane, how are you? You look—"

"Like you could use a drink." Frankie switched off the record player. "I know I could."

"May I get you something?" Verna asked. "Wine? Tea?"

"Whiskey?" Frankie pulled a bottle from his liquor cabinet and poured liquid two fingers deep into a double old-fashioned glass. "Tullamore D.E.W."

She held up a hand. "Nothing for me thanks."

"I guess we should sit." Frankie crossed back to the couch and sank next to Verna. "Just tell us. It can't be much worse than what we already know."

Gethsemane sat, then stood, then sat again. "Ty may not have killed himself. The coroner found evidence he had hallucinogens, amphetamines, and phencyclidine—PCP—in his system. He may have died by misadventure. Or by—" She took a deep breath. "Homicide. Niall told me."

"Shite." Frankie drained his glass. More expletives followed.

"Excuse me." Verna choked back a sob and raced from the room. The reflection from the bathroom light bounced off the ceiling. Retching noises traveled down the hall.

"I'd better..." Frankie went after her.

Gethsemane pushed herself up from the armchair and wandered over to a window. She rested her forehead against the glass and closed her eyes. Thoughts of places she'd rather be filled her head—conducting the Reykjavik Philharmonia with the Northern Lights dancing over the concert hall, performing Stravinsky with the Dallas Symphony Orchestra, composing a piano-vocal score for a community chorus, scrubbing a toilet—anywhere other than in her friend's living room, blowing up his world.

"She's lying down."

Gethsemane opened her eyes to Frankie coming back into the room. He sank onto the couch. "Let me have the rest."

"As soon as Inspector Sutton reads the coroner's email, he's going to come looking for Verna and Vivian. He knows about Verna's past with Ty."

"Because this is Dunmullach, where not even the dead's secrets are safe." Frankie pressed the palm of his hand into an eye socket. "Damn, damn, damn."

"Niall suggested no one leave town."

"Vern's not a murderer."

"She hated Ty."

"I hated Ty. So did you. So did anyone who spent more than ten minutes in his cursed company."

"Verna admits to being alone with Ty the night he died."

"Whose side are you on?"

"Yours."

Frankie sprang from the couch so quickly, Gethsemane stepped back. He paced. "She didn't do it. How could she have? You said yourself she's too small—"

"The drugs. If she slipped Ty hallucinogenic drugs, he might have jumped off the catwalk thinking he was diving into a swimming pool or that he was being chased by, by, by—"

Frankie cut her off. "Verna doesn't have any drugs to slip to anyone. She's a Latin teacher fer chrissake, not a drug pusher. Where would she get amphetamines and PCP? PCP! Who has that nowadays? Verna did not drug Ty Lismore then stand back and watch as he wrapped a rope around his neck and swan-dive off a fecking lighthouse. She didn't!"

"But that's what the guards think happened, isn't it?" Verna, eyes puffy, nose red, stood in the living room doorway. "That I doped Ty and made him kill himself."

"Vern, hon." Frankie wrapped his arms around her.

"Isn't that what they think?" she asked Gethsemane.

"Yes," she said. "It's what Sutton will think, anyway. He's prone to thinking the worst."

"Do you think that's what happened?" Verna asked.

Gethsemane said nothing.

"Sissy," Frankie said, "she asked you a question."

Gethsemane shoved her hands in her pockets.

Frankie pressed her. "I'm asking you that question."

She addressed Verna. "What happened in New Orleans?"

"N-New Orleans?" Verna stuttered.

Frankie frowned. "New Orleans? What's New Orleans got to do with anything?"

"New Orleans," Gethsemane said to Verna. "When you and Ty met Agnes and Brian and Theophilus. What happened?"

"Vern?" Frankie pulled back from his girlfriend but kept his arms around her. "What's she on about? Ty's the only one of that lot you knew before they turned up here."

Verna looked back and forth between Frankie and Gethsemane, then stared at the floor.

Frankie let his arms fall to his sides. "Verna? What's Sissy on about?"

Pounding on the door precluded her answer. No one moved. The pounding repeated. Frankie swore.

"I'll get it." Gethsemane pulled it open. "'Lo, Inspector."

Inspector Sutton's squat frame filled the doorway. His frown melded into the crags in his face as he glared at the apartment's occupants. "Brown. Why am I not surprised to find you here?"

"Because misery loves company and I get off on beating you to the punch. Please, come in."

Sutton grunted and pushed past her. He stopped in front of Verna. "Miss Cunningham, I'd like to speak with you concerning the death of Ty Lismore. At the station."

Frankie slipped an arm around Verna and pulled her close.

"You, too, Grennan," Sutton added.

"Do I need my solicitor?" Verna asked.

"You tell me, Miss Cunningham," Sutton said. "Right now, you're just cooperating with me in my investigation into a suspicious death. Right now, you're not under arrest. Right now."

"Let me get my purse," Verna said.

They waited as Verna disappeared in the direction of Frankie's bedroom. She reappeared, purse in hand.

Sutton ushered them out. "You," he said to Gethsemane, "stay here."

"This isn't my apartment, Inspector."

"Apologies, Brown, that was guard speak. Let me translate. Stay the hell out of my way."

Gethsemane called after them as they started down the hall. "How's Sunny, Inspector?"

Sutton stopped short. He answered without turning. "If you and Miss Markham don't stop aggravating me, I'll charge you both with interfering with a garda investigation and lock you both in the same cell. Then you can ask after her well-being yourself."

Sutton, Frankie, and Verna continued toward Erasmus Hall's main entrance. Verna called out as they reached the main door. "Gethsemane, would you please remind my sister to pick up her prescription? It's ready at the pharmacy."

Gethsemane stepped back into Frankie's apartment and closed the door. Prescription ready at the pharmacy? What did that mean? Dunmullach hadn't had a pharmacy since theirs blew up in an explosion nearly a year ago. So why...

She circled Frankie's living room. She placed the Tullamore D.E.W. back in the liquor cabinet and Frankie's used glass in the kitchen sink. Nothing else seemed out of place. Shelves packed with neat rows of records. Record player on its stand. A biography of John Coltrane on the coffee table. She moved into the bedroom. Everything in place there, too. Bed made, closet doors closed, dresser drawers shut. Comb and brush lined up with mathematical neatness on top, a few coins in a trinket tray.

She turned to go when she spotted fabric lying in a crumpled heap behind the bedroom door. She picked up a woman's cardigan, navy blue with yellow trim. Verna had worn it to the pub a few weeks ago. Why was this the only thing in the room not put away? Had it fallen from a hook or hanger?

Gethsemane pushed the bedroom door closed to see behind it. She kicked it before she spotted it—a pharmacy bag.

The label read, "Ballytuam Pharmacy, Cunningham, Vivian, dextroamphetamine 10mg."

Vivian's prescription, the one Verna asked her to remind Vivian to pick up. Except it was already picked up. By Verna. Gethsemane stared at the bag, trying to remember something. She reached in and pulled out an amber bottle filled with capsules of indistinct colors. The pub. These were the same pills that had spilled from Vivian's purse at the Mad Rabbit. The same ones she'd confused with Ty's Evoxil. Why did Verna have her sister's medication? And why alert her? Was she asking for help covering for her sister? Or was she throwing her sister under the bus?"

"Dextroamphetamine for ADHD." Gethsemane said aloud. "Dextroamphetamine, which sounds a lot like amphetamine. This is one of those times being related to a doctor comes in handy." She pulled out her phone and dialed her brother, Zebulon.

"Sis?" Sleep, concern, and a hint of annoyance commingled in her younger brother's muffled voice.

"How'd you know it was me?"

"Caller ID." The annoyance gained prominence. "Are you all right?"

"I'm fine, little brother."

"Then why—" Annoyance trounced both sleep and concern.

"Do you have any idea how late it is? You don't call someone at this hour unless you're dying, about to be wheeled into surgery, or need bail money."

She winced. She'd forgotten the five-hour time difference between Cork County and Washington, D.C. Which meant it was—she checked her watch—one o'clock in the morning where her brother was. "Sorry, I forgot. It's light here until almost ten. I can call back in a couple of hours."

"And wake me up again. At," she heard noises she assumed were from Zebulon checking his own watch, "at three a.m.?"

"I'm scarlet, Zeb. You're not on call, are you?"

"Not tonight, no." A heavy sighed filled Gethsemane's ear. "I figured I'd get some sleep tonight."

"I'm sorry. You can pay me back by texting me football memes or photos from your dermatology textbook."

"You know I love you, Sis, and during daylight hours, I love chatting with you, but—"

"I have a medical question."

"Someone's bleeding, seizing, complaining of chest pain, unconscious, missing a major body part?"

"Someone's dead."

Silence. "Oh." She heard shuffling. "I'm awake. What's your question?"

"Is dextroamphetamine used for anything except ADHD?"

"It treats narcolepsy. It's not really prescribed for anything else, these days. I assume you mean what is it legally used for."

"Would they show up on a drug test for amphetamines?"

"Yes, because they are amphetamines."

"How about PCP? Would they make a test positive for PCP?"

"What are you up to over there? Are you sure you're okay?"

"I'm fine. You didn't answer my question."

"No, amphetamines would not show up as phencyclidine on

a tox screen. What's going on?"

"A man died a couple of days ago. He had amphetamines and PCP in his system. No one's sure where he got the drugs." She turned Vivian's pill bottle over in her hand. "At least, not the PCP."

"Do you live in Cork County or Midsomer County?" Zeb shared her love of the long-running crime show and its fictional locale with a body count higher than most major urban centers.

"Dunmullach would do DCI Barnaby proud. Are you sure amphetamines and PCP don't cross react?"

"Yes, I'm sure. That's knowledge based on fifty-gazillion shifts in the emergency department."

"Damn," she muttered.

"Aren't you going to ask me what does cross react with phencyclidine?"

"What does cross react with phencyclidine?"

"Hang on." She heard her brother moving around. He returned to the call a moment later. "Had to grab my tablet. PCP, PCP...Here we go. Tramadol, dextromethorphan, alprazolam, clonazepam, carvedilol, diphenhydramine, doxylamine, ibuprofen, and naproxen."

"I recognize ibuprofen and naproxen. What are the rest of those? Use regular-people names."

"Tramadol is Ultram, a pain med. Diphenhydramine is Benadryl, doxylamine is Unisom. Dextromethorphan is Robitussin or Delsym—"

"Wait, Robitussin or Delsym? Those are cough meds, right?" Ty had been taking medicines for his cough. "Do they contain the same ingredients as Evoxil? Or Benylin?"

"Never heard of them. Are they brand names? Regular-people names, I mean?"

"I think so. Evoxil's an antibiotic. A doctor prescribed it and the Benylin for someone with a horrid cough."

"Let me check. Evoxil—that's a U.K. brand name for levofloxacin, an antibiotic, like you said. It's Levaquin over here. Used to treat pneumonia, among other infections. Benylin— that's a U.K. brand name for dextromethorphan. Robitussin or Delsym over here. Yeah, same ingredients."

"And dextromethorphan can show up as PCP on a drug screen."

"And can cause hallucinations in high enough doses. It's available over the counter, but sales are restricted and the packaging, at least over here, includes labeling warning parents about the dangers of kids overdosing on the stuff. Speaking of hallucinations, levofloxacin can cause them, too. It's not a common side effect but it happens often enough to be reported."

"If you combined Evoxil and Benylin in large enough doses you'd probably be lucky if the only thing you saw were pink elephants." Especially if you added a few capsules of your sister's ADHD meds to mix.

"What's all this got to do with someone dying? Are you thinking they had an allergic reaction?"

"A, um, lethal reaction. Hey, thanks, Zeb, and I'm sorry I woke you up."

"You're not mixed up in anything you shouldn't be, are you? Jackson told us about the situation you two landed in when he visited you a while ago."

The "situation" she and her brother-in-law had landed in had included art fraud, antiquities, theft, murder, and—almost— a go-directly-to-jail card for Jackson. "No, nothing like that." Neither art nor antiquities had anything to do with this. "I know someone who knows someone who knew the dead man, is all. He, um, fell off a high platform. The garda—the police—think he may have been under the influence of amphetamines and phencyclidine and may have been hallucinating when he died. I'm just trying to gather information for my friend's sake." True enough.

"Sis?"

"Yes, little brother?"

"Be careful."

Call ended, Gethsemane clutched the pill bottle. She'd bet a Stradivarius that the amphetamines in Ty's system came from Vivian's supply. But how did they get from her bottle into Ty? His flask? He drank alcohol before he died; the coroner found evidence of it. And the empty flask pointed to that being the source of the alcohol. Easy enough to doctor it up. Verna could have hidden her disgust for the man who ruined her life long enough to pretend to join him in a drink, long enough to slip powder she'd emptied out of capsules earlier into the wide mouth of the tarnished silver container. Had she emptied the capsules out on her own? Or had her sister helped her? Or acted alone? Verna getting her hands on Ty's flask was conjecture. She'd seen the flask in Vivian's hand. Vivian bragged about swiping it. Maybe she'd added something more than spit to its contents.

Sunny had access to the flask, of course, but not to the amphetamines. And she didn't peg Sunny as the type to ruin her own wedding by killing her groom. The bellman who'd returned the flask to Ty after he left it in the inn's bar? How big of a tip would you have to give him to get him to drug a guest for you? And who, other than the Cunninghams, would do it?

Gethsemane held the bottle up to the light. They really did look like Ty's Evoxil. Someone could have swapped the capsules in the bottle. Harder to do. You'd need access to both medicines and Ty would most likely only take the capsules the way they'd been prescribed. Probably not effective for inducing hallucinations. Lacing the alcohol in the flask with dextroamphetamine made the most sense and made one or both of the Cunningham sisters the most likely culprits.

Gethsemane scrolled through her contacts until she found Niall's number. Her finger hovered over the "call" icon.

"Shite." The dextroamphetamine pointed to one other person. She put down the phone and looked around. Frankie's closet, Frankie's dresser, Frankie's room. She found the pills in Frankie's room. Verna was Frankie's girlfriend and her things were at his place, giving him easy access. Verna wouldn't know if he went into her bag and took her sister's pills. At least, she could claim she didn't know. Frankie getting access to Ty's flask was trickier, but the guards probably wouldn't consider that a crucial detail. And Frankie admitted he hated Ty, too. The pills implicated him as much as the Cunningham sisters. Maybe Vivian wasn't the one Verna was throwing under the bus.

Gethsemane shoved the pill bottle in her pocket. She wouldn't go to Niall. His friendship didn't mean he'd stopped being a garda. She couldn't expect, nor could she ask, him to conceal evidence just because it pointed in a direction she didn't want it to. She couldn't get to Verna. No chance of Sutton letting her go before morning. Which meant the other Cunningham sister might have some time on her hands. Maybe Vivian could explain how the same medication prescribed to treat her ADHD had ended up in Ty.

Eighteen

Sometimes, culinary ineptitude paid dividends. Gethsemane didn't count cooking as one of her talents and avoided it as much as feasible. She often dined at Sweeney's Inn for breakfast on weekends, often enough that she considered herself a regular—as did the front desk clerk who waved her by without question as she headed for Vivian Cunningham's room.

She raised her hand to knock. The door swung open and Vivian, clad in one of the inn's signature plush terry robes, collided with her as she stepped into the hall.

Behind Vivian, inside the room, Brian sat up in the bed.

Vivian stumbled over an apology as she pulled the door closed, forcing Gethsemane back into the hall. She left the door open enough to keep from locking herself out. Enough for Gethsemane to see the large, intricate, multi-colored tattoo that covered Brian's torso, from his collarbones to where his waist disappeared beneath bedsheets.

"I can explain," Vivian said.

"Don't. What you do and who you do it with isn't my business. I thought you'd want to know your sister and Frankie were taken down to the Garda station a while ago. The coroner found drugs, amphetamines, in Ty Lismore's system and now thinks his death may not have been suicide. And I think these," she pulled the pill bottle from her pocket and shoved it at

Vivian, "are yours."

Vivian's eyes widened. She looked ill. She opened and closed her mouth a few times before managing, "Oh, jaysus. Please, let me get dressed."

She slipped back into the room and closed the door. Gethsemane pressed her ear against it but the historic hotel's thick wood dampened sound. She leaned against the wall and waited.

Several moments passed. The door opened and Brian, fully dressed, brushed past without making eye contact and hurried down the hall.

"Come in," Vivian said.

Gethsemane took the offered chair and waited until Vivian settled into the one opposite.

"What's happened to Verna?" Vivian asked.

"Inspector Sutton, of the Dunmullach Garda homicide unit, suspects your sister of involvement in the death of Ty Lismore."

"He arrested her?"

"No, not yet, anyway. Sutton," Gethsemane made air quotes, "'invited' her to come to the station for questioning. Sutton's invited me to the station for questioning before. It means he thinks Verna's guilty, he just doesn't have enough evidence to make an arrest. Yet."

"Frankie got the same invitation?"

Gethsemane nodded.

"Then Inspector Sutton must suspect him, as well. He hated Ty."

"Not as much as Verna did."

"Almost as much. Because of what Ty was putting Verna through, the way he made her suffer."

"You hated Ty for the same reason, didn't you? Hated him for a lot longer than Frankie hated him. You also hated him for killing your brother. And you're the one with the amphetamine prescription."

"Does Inspector Sutton know about that?"

"He will after I tell him. Which would be approximately fifteen seconds after I told him you stole Ty's flask. Good luck convincing him that spit was the only thing you added to it. And, in case you're thinking of losing your pills down the toilet, pharmacies keep records."

"You'd really turn me in?"

"Before I'd let you pin this on Frankie? In a heartbeat. Frankie's my friend. You're his girlfriend's sister."

Vivian sank back into her chair. "Please, don't. I swear I didn't drug Ty. I gave the flask to Mal to give back to him with nothing more in it than spit and whiskey. I had nothing to do with Ty's death. Neither did Verna."

"Nor did Frankie. So help me out and give me some idea of who else might have hated Ty as much as you and your sister." Gethsemane jerked her head toward the unmade bed. "What about Brian?"

"Brian? He didn't hate Ty. They were friends, had been for years. Brian maybe got frustrated with Ty sometimes—fed up with his thoughtlessness and recklessness—but he didn't hate him."

"How long have you and Brian been, whatever?"

"Hooking up? Isn't that what you Yanks call it?" Vivian grinned. "Since his first week in Dunmullach. Not smart, I know. Purely physical. You must admit, he's a fine bit of stuff."

"Would Verna approve of her sister hooking up with a long-time friend of the man who ruined her life and ended her brother's?"

"Of course, she wouldn't. Which is why I have no intention of telling her. Just because we're sisters doesn't mean we share everything. It's not as if Brian and I are truly, madly, deeply. As soon as he leaves Dunmullach, it's over."

"Brian, by your own assessment, is Ty's friend."

"He's not Ty. He's not cruel, nor selfish." Vivian shrugged. "A wee bit vain. With good reason. He's very pretty."

No argument on that. Handsome and impeccably dressed, she understood why Vivian was drawn to him. She just questioned her decision to give in to the urge. Was there more to it than physical attraction? Did Brian have something on Vivian, or did Vivian have something on Brian? Something that would point suspicion away from Frankie and the Cunninghams? She looked around the room, as if some object might explain Vivian's behavior or, at least, provide an opening to dig deeper. A stray sock, gray with an intricate geometric pattern, lay forlorn beneath the bed. She remembered the sigil. And something else.

"Brian's impressively inked," she said.

"Isn't his tattoo gorgeous? It wraps around to his back. Countless hours spent in the tattooist's chair. It's not finished yet."

"Where'd he have it done? New Orleans?"

Vivian blinked. "New Orleans? Why New Orleans?"

"That's where he, Theophilus, Ty, and Verna met Agnes." Gethsemane shrugged. "I thought the tattoo might be related."

"Brian never mentioned New Orleans."

"Did Verna?"

"Why do you ask?" Vivian's eyes narrowed. "Why should she or Brian mention it? Or anyone else?"

"Because I get the impression something happened there, something that none of the involved parties wants to talk about. Maybe whatever happened caused someone to hate Ty as much as you and Verna hated him. Maybe enough to load him up with hallucinogens and leave him on top of a lighthouse."

"You think one of those three, Theophilus, Agnes, or Brian, might be responsible for what happened to Ty? Or all of them?

Maybe they're in it together?"

Gethsemane shrugged. "Depends on what happened in New Orleans. If anything did. No one will talk about it. Too bad. I bet Inspector Sutton would be interested."

Vivian relaxed into a smile as if she'd just been thrown the last life preserver from a sinking ship. "I can ask Verna. She'd tell me, I'm sure, if I explain why it matters."

"So, where did Brian get his tattoos? Or, where does he get them, since you say he's not finished?"

"New York, Japan, and London. A trio of artists collaborates. Brian sends them rough sketches and they turn his ideas into the finished design."

Gethsemane showed Vivian the photo of the sigil on her phone. "Is this one of Brian's sketches? Is this design part of his tattoo?"

Vivian studied the photo. "No, I don't think so. I don't recognize it. It doesn't look like anything Brian would have inked. It's too crude. His design is so vibrant and life-like, you'd swear it was about to jump from his skin. You should see the dragon on his back. It looks like it could breathe real fire." She handed Gethsemane's phone back. "Where'd you get that?"

"Father Tim found it. The original sketch, I mean. He'd like to return it to its owner, if he can figure out who that is."

"Have you asked Theo? He has a bit of ink."

Vivian's phone rang. She picked it up from the bedside table. She read the screen but made no move to answer it. "It's Verna."

The ringing stopped. Vivian remained by the bed.

Gethsemane took the hint. Time to go. "I'll see if Theo is in."

"Two-fourteen. Top of stairs." Vivian didn't move to show her out.

"I'll see myself out." She turned at the door. "I don't see any need to tell Inspector Sutton about your prescription right now. But you will let me know what Verna says about New Orleans, won't you?"

"I will, yeah."

Gethsemane had been in Cork County long enough to recognize slang for "when hell freezes over." She narrowed her eyes at Vivian. "Because if I have to choose between friends and friends of friends, I choose Frankie."

She caught Theophilus going into his room.

"Just out for a walk," he said. "Felt like the walls were closing in on me."

"How's Agnes?"

"In tatters. None of us realized Aggie had a glad eye for Ty. We figured the occasional ride is all it was. She kept her true feelings well hid. Not that I blame her. Sunny's as mad as a box of frogs. Imagine what she'd have done to poor Aggie if she'd known she was pining away for her fella."

"What would she have done? Violence?"

"Not the physical kind, no. Sunny prefers head games. She'll ring your boss and tell him you're cheating on your timecard or call your spouse and tell her you weren't really at the football match with the fellas when you claimed you were. She's a cute hoor, always manages to engineer things to her advantage by playing one side against the other, sweet-talking some gack with more ego than sense, and, if all that fails, playing the money card. She'll get Daddy to drop a hint that a donation won't be made if sweetie doesn't get her way or have Mummy vote thumbs down when the club's electing new members. That sort of thing. She wouldn't resort to physical violence, though. Might ruin her manicure or spill blood on her designer dress."

"You, Agnes, Brian, and Ty sound as if you were a pretty tight crew."

"We were tight. We'd been together since last year of uni. Verna, too, until her blow up with Ty."

"You mean until Ty stood her up at the altar."

"Yeah. Gobshite move on Ty's part. Couldn't believe he did that. You find a bure who'll stick with you after you've shot her brother, you hang on to her. You don't leave her for a header, no matter how rich the header is."

"Ty left Verna for Sunny? I thought—"

"There were others in between, each one richer and more high-maintenance than the last. Ty had some grand plan for marrying into wealth. 'Trading up,' he called it."

Gethsemane shook her head. "I don't get it. Ty Lismore was a lousy excuse for a human being. Yet, you lot genuinely liked him. Y'all seem like decent, sane people. What kind of hold did Ty have over you?"

"Not a hold over, a bond with. After what we went through—" His jaw worked. He held Gethsemane's gaze for three seconds. Five. Then he turned away and fit his room key into the lock.

Gethsemane put a hand on his arm. "Theo, please. Tell me what happened. It might explain Ty's death."

Theophilus stared at the floor.

"New Orleans, right? Something happened in New Orleans. Something bad. What was it? Tell me, Theo."

He raised his head and opened his mouth as if to speak.

"You're out late this evening, Gethsemane." Rosalie appeared at the head of the stairs. "Are you and Theo planning a party?"

Damn Rosalie. Gethsemane swore a silent blue streak that would have made a sailor blush.

Theophilus dropped his head and opened the door to his

room. "I think I'll have a lie-down. I've been with Aggie this whole time and I don't mind telling you I'm knackered." He slipped inside before Gethsemane could protest. She heard the deadbolt turn.

"Oh, dear," Rosalie said. "Hope I didn't spoil things."

Gethsemane spun on the bridesmaid. "What are you? A witch? Conjure woman? Sorceress? Magician?"

"Is something wrong?"

"You. You're wrong. You show up at odd times, usually inopportune ones, you give cryptic warnings, try to talk me into a tarot card reading, and pretend you don't recognize occult symbols, when, clearly, you do." *And*, Gethsemane added to herself, *you set off my warning bells.* "What are you? And why are you here?"

"I'm Rosalie Baraquin, one of Sunny Markham's maids of honor."

"Yeah, I've heard all that. Skip the press release. Who are you, really? You're from New Orleans, Agnes told me. But you're not part of that gang—"

"Gang." Rosalie made a noise. "Interesting word choice."

"Gang, group, crew, squad, unit, bunch. I meant Ty, Theophilus, Brian, Agnes, and Verna."

"I know who you meant. And gang was the appropriate label. It implies criminality."

"Criminality. They committed some sort of crime in New Orleans?"

"I didn't say that. And just because I hail from the area around New Orleans doesn't mean I know everyone who passes through the city. It's a big place."

"But you know more than you're telling."

"Does any of this concern you?"

"Damn it, it concerns my friend. My good friend who's already had his heart broken and his life nearly ruined by one woman with secrets. I'm not going to stand around and watch that happen with a second woman."

"Everyone should be lucky enough to have a friend as fiercely devoted as you. What's the verse? John fifteen-thirteen? Greater love hath no man than this, that a man lay down his life for his friends."

"I don't know if that's supposed to be a compliment or a threat. I do know you're being coy."

Rosalie said nothing.

"At least tell me how you know Ty? Agnes said you introduced him to Sunny."

"I know them both from New York. Another big place with lots of people. People come to New York from all over. You never know who you'll run into. A girl from Louisiana might meet a guy from Dublin in New York."

"Did you have a secret thing for Ty, too?"

"Lord, no. I have better taste in men than Agnes and Sunny. My relationship with Ty was strictly professional. We were both in finance."

"And your relationship with Sunny? How did you meet her?"

"Sunny Markham's not the only one from old money. We struck up an acquaintance at a mutual distant cousin's debutante ball."

"And you thought she'd be perfect for Ty."

"I thought they deserved each other. You might say, it was in the cards. Speaking of which, my offer of a reading still stands."

"No, thanks, maybe some other lifetime."

"Then I'll bid you goodnight. All this drama's exhausting." She swept past Gethsemane.

Gethsemane called down the hall after her. "What do you know about that sigil I showed you in the church yard?"

Rosalie spoke over her shoulder as she stepped into her room. "I know enough to leave it alone."

"Is it meant to warn you about someone? Or to warn someone about you?"

The thunk of the deadbolt was her only answer.

Nineteen

"A crime." Gethsemane tossed her purse onto the couch. She plopped down next to it and pulled up an internet browser on her phone. "Ty committed a crime in New Orleans and the rest of that crew is covering for him."

Eamon materialized next to her. "Welcome home. What are you on about?"

"Something Rosalie Baraquin said when I ran into her at Sweeney's Inn. She made a joke about criminality. Which got me thinking, what if Ty Lismore committed some crime when he was in New Orleans with Verna and the rest of that bunch covered for him?"

"That makes no sense."

Gethsemane frowned at the ghost. "You've got a better idea about why they get so weird whenever anyone mentions the Big Easy?"

"Yeah. Another one of them, one who's still living, committed a crime and Ty Lismore covered for them. Probably for a price, seeing as Lismore was a heartless wanker."

"Okay, I give it to you. That is a better idea. But which one? Theophilus, Brian, Agnes, or..." She couldn't bring herself to say it.

Eamon finished the thought. "Or Verna. That would explain why she stood by him after her brother's death, chose him over her family. She couldn't hold a death against him if he didn't hold one against her."

"A death? You think she killed someone?" Gethsemane set her phone down. "Hard to picture Verna killing someone. Except Ty. But only because it's hard to picture anyone not killing Ty. I'm surprised he lasted as long as he did. But if she did kill someone, why would the others cover for her, especially after she left the group? Ty was the eye of that hurricane. He was the one who wielded a strange, irresistible influence over others. If they were going to cover for anyone, it would be Ty."

Eamon pointed at her phone and levitated it to eye level. "What are you googling?"

"Googling?" Gethsemane stared in surprise. "When did you learn that word?"

"Just because I'm dead, doesn't mean I'm brain dead. I listen and read and study. If I'm going to be around for the rest of eternity, I may as well learn something new."

Gethsemane grabbed the phone. "I'm googling 'New Orleans,' 'unsolved,' 'crime,' and—what year do you think they graduated from college? Theophilus said they met during their last year at university."

"They're all what, early- to mid-thirties? They'd have graduated in the early aughts."

"Don't 'spose you could pop into someone's room and take a peek at their ID."

Eamon vanished.

"Kidding," Gethsemane called.

He rematerialized. "Just google '2000-2007.'"

She typed the years into her phone's browser. A list of links filled the screen. "Six hundred thousand hits. It's under a million, anyway."

"Scrolling through all that may take you awhile." Eamon's amused green aura matched his grin.

"You're the one with eternity on your hands." She cleared the browser in frustration.

"Why don't you try it again with some of that lot's names?"

"Another good idea. Score two for the ghost." She typed. "Who should I try first?"

"Lismore."

She shook her head.

"Nishi."

"Nothing relevant."

"Derringer."

"Plenty of guns, but, no."

"Haywood."

"Bupkis."

"Cunningham."

She hesitated, then typed *Cunningham, Verna, Vivian*. She held her breath and hit enter.

"Well?"

"Nothing there." Did she feel more relieved or confused?

Eamon's aura transformed to a surprised brown flecked with puzzled sienna. "That's all of them. Maybe we're on the wrong track."

"Or maybe not."

"Not on the wrong track or not all of them?"

"Both." She typed again. *Baraquin*. Rosalie claimed she didn't know Ty in New Orleans. But that didn't mean she told the truth.

"Baraquin," Eamon read over her shoulder. "That's the other bridesmaid."

"The strange one. The stranger one."

"Anything?"

"No unsolved crimes, but…" Gethsemane clicked on one of the links. "A list of Creole family names pops up. Baraquin is Creole." Gethsemane read some of the other names. "Badet,

Bajoliere, Barthelemy, Bastien, Arige, Arnaud—"

"Fabulous restaurant," Eamon interrupted.

"Try to stay on topic. Anglade, Archer, hey!"

"Hey is a name?"

"No, hey, is an interjection, as in 'hey, Amotte's on the list.' Malcolm spells his without the 'e' but it's close. Think he's Creole? I did detect a hint of Louisiana under the practiced accent."

"Think he knew any of them back then?"

"I got the impression he didn't know any of them until Sunny hired him to photograph her wedding. No one's mentioned knowing him before that. And let's face it, the only ones who've concealed their past connections are the Cunningham sisters." She let the phone fall to the couch and covered her eyes with her palms.

"It's been a long day," Eamon said. "You can't do much more this evening. Why don't you turn in? I'll pop over to Sweeney's and see if I can suss out any secrets."

Gethsemane peeked at him from beneath a palm. "Since when do you 'pop' anywhere? I thought you 'translocated'?"

"Pop, translocate." Eamon winked. "I guess I'm spending too much time listening to your American English. It's beginning to rub off on me."

Beethoven's "Fifth" woke her at three a.m. She fumbled her phone to her ear. "Zeb?"

"Frankie."

"Frankie?" She hauled herself up in bed. "What's happened? What's wrong?"

"Nothing's happened, at least nothing new. I'm just calling to ask you a favor. Would you bring my car 'round to the garda station? If we wait for one of the uniforms to drive us home, we'll be here until supper. I'd ask Niall, but," he sighed, "at the end of the day, he's still a guard."

"You're still at the station?"

"Yeah, Sutton finished with us around midnight. Then he managed to drag the paperwork out for a few hours, out of spite, I'm sure."

"But I thought—" Verna had called Vivian hours ago; she'd assumed to tell Vivian that Sutton had released them and ask for a ride home. But if they were still there...Why had Verna called her sister?

"Thought what?"

"Nothing. Typical Sutton, I shouldn't be surprised." She wasn't surprised, not at Sutton, anyway. "Still keep an extra key to your apartment under the statue in the garden?"

"Yeah. You'll be okay going to St. Brennan's on your bike this time of morning?"

Eamon materialized at the end of her bed. "You're fecking kidding, right? You're not really going anywhere at three o'clock in the morning?"

"Don't worry about me," she said to Frankie and Eamon. "I'm your man."

"Thanks," Frankie said. "I know this is asking a lot. I owe you. Verna and I both do."

"Everyone should have a friend they can call for a ride home at three o'clock in the morning. And Frankie?"

"Yeah?"

"I am your friend."

She ended the call, then waggled her fingers at Eamon. "Vanish, please. I need to get dressed."

"You're actually going to fetch Grennan and his bure? At this hour? You're going to ride your bike to the school, drive to the station, drive back to the school, then ride your bike back up here? Nobody's that good of a friend."

"I am." She threw back her covers. "Frankie needs me. And in that wee span of time between the garda station and Erasmus Hall, I'm going to confront Verna with our theory about New Orleans."

"There's a method to the madness," Eamon said.

"And I'm not worried about riding from here to school and back because you're coming with me. If any boo-hags jump out of the bushes, you'll blast 'em with an energy orb or two."

"That's not funny. I'm not sure an orb would stop a boo-hag."

"Good thing it's only humans I'm worried about, then. We know the orbs will stop them. Now will you please leave so I can get dressed? Before Frankie and Verna find another way home."

Twenty

It was closer to four when she, Frankie, and Verna pulled away from the garda station. She drove. Frankie and Verna, exhausted from their marathon interrogation, sat in the back seat. She watched them in the rearview mirror, the glow from instrument dials and the satnav system illuminating the car's interior. Frankie held Verna's hand in both of his. She rested her head on his shoulder.

Gethsemane forced aside the guilt pangs that niggled the back of her mind. She had to do this. Frankie's happiness, and possibly his freedom, hung in the balance.

"I took Vivian's prescription to her, Verna, like you asked."

Verna sat forward in the seat. "You took it to her? You didn't just tell her it was ready?" She glanced at Frankie, who'd sat forward as well. "Er, I mean, thank you. That was out of your way. You needn't have gone to so much trouble."

"No trouble. Vivian and I got to chatting."

"About what?" Verna leaned back.

Gethsemane's eyes met hers in the mirror. "About tattoos. Did you know Brian has one covering his entire torso?"

"No, I didn't," Verna said. "He only had a small one on his shoulder when I knew him at uni."

"How does Vivian know about Brian's tattoo?" Frankie asked. "It doesn't show."

"Oh, Brian was there. In Vivian's room."

Verna looked at Frankie but said nothing. Frankie looked out the window.

"Viv always had a thing for fellas with tattoos," Verna said.

"Did you talk about anything else?" Frankie asked, his gaze fixed on his reflection in the glass.

"I asked Vivian about New Orleans."

"I don't think she's been there," Verna said.

"No, but you've been there. That's where you, Ty, Theo, and Brian met Agnes."

"Is there some point to this, Gethsemane?" Frankie asked. "She's admitted knowing them."

"I mention it because I ran into Theo at the inn. Sunny must have rented a block of rooms for the wedding party. Anyway, Theo and I got to chatting, too. About New Orleans. About the time you all spent down there."

Gethsemane and Verna locked eyes in the mirror again.

"Why are you doing this to me?" Verna asked. "I just want to be happy. Is that wrong of me? After all Ty put me through, don't I deserve that?"

"Watch the bloody road," Frankie said, "before you crash us into a tree."

Gethsemane concentrated on driving. Then, "Theo started to tell me about something that happened in New Orleans. Something bad, I think."

"You think," Frankie said.

"Well, Rosalie Baraquin interrupted us before he could tell me what happened." She drove for a moment before adding, "She thought whatever happened might be criminal."

"Rosalie wasn't there," Verna said.

"No, but she's a good guesser." Or something.

Frankie pulled away from Verna and crammed himself into the opposite corner of the seat. "Jaysus, Vern, for feck's sake, just tell us what the bloody hell happened in New Orleans. I'm sick of the lies."

"I'm not lying to you, Frankie." Verna grabbed for his hand. "I just—"

Frankie evaded her grasp. "What. Happened?"

Verna covered her face and let out a sob. She spoke without raising her head. "It wasn't only me. It was all of us." She sobbed again. "We killed a man." She lowered her hands and glared at Gethsemane. "Are you satisfied now? I said it. We—Ty, Theo, Brian, Agnes, and I—killed a man in New Orleans."

"Stop the car." Frankie raised his voice. "Stop. The. Car. Now."

Gethsemane pulled over and put the car in park.

Frankie turned to Verna. "What do you mean, you killed a man?"

"It was an accident, Frankie, I swear."

"What did you do?"

Verna looked back and forth between Frankie and Gethsemane, then looked down at her hands. "It was an accident. We'd been drinking, a lot. Me, Ty, Theo, Brian, Agnes, and Jared."

"Jared?" The name slipped out before Gethsemane could stop herself. "Who's Jared?"

"Jared Ely. He is—was—Agnes's boyfriend."

Her boyfriend, the "guy she was with" whose name she claimed not to remember. Gethsemane bit her lip. Interruptions risked derailing the story.

"Was her boyfriend," Frankie said. "Past tense. What happened to Jared?"

Verna's voice trembled when she spoke. "L-like I said, we'd been drinking. We were ossified, the lot of us. Someone suggested—I suggested—we drive up to Lake Pontchartrain. Jared didn't want to go. We, the rest of us, talked him into it."

She fell silent.

"Go on," Frankie said.

"You can guess what happened."

"I want to hear it from you. All of it."

Verna hung her head. She said nothing for a full minute, then spoke barely above a whisper. Gethsemane strained to hear her. "We never made it to the lake. We had no idea how to get there. We were too fluthered to stop somewhere for a map or to ask for directions. We took a wrong turn somewhere and..."

"And?"

"And the car ended up in a bayou. In the water." She took a deep breath before continuing. "Ty got out first. He left the rest of us to fend for ourselves. Brian and Theo helped Agnes and me. Broken glass caught Theo in the face. That's how he got the scar. But he and Brian made it out, too. Jared didn't. He couldn't swim."

"That's it?" Frankie asked. "The whole story?"

"Not quite the whole story," Verna said. "When the rescue squad and the police came, we told them Jared had been driving."

"You lied?"

"Ty was the driver. He convinced us to say Jared had been behind the wheel."

"You lied."

"What good would have come from telling anyone that Ty was the driver? Jared was dead. He couldn't be charged with anything. If we'd told the truth, that Ty was driving, he'd have been arrested, prosecuted, sent to prison for years. His life would have been ruined. All of his plans—"

"Jared Ely's life didn't exactly turn out the way he'd planned, did it?" Frankie asked. "But I guess he was in no position to complain about your fabricated version of events."

"Frankie, please."

Frankie uncrumpled himself from the corner and leaned forward around the driver's seat to speak to Gethsemane. "Would you please drop me at the Mad Rabbit then take Miss Cunningham back to her apartment? You can keep the car until tomorrow."

Verna pleaded. "Frankie, listen to me, please."

"What are you waiting for?" he asked Gethsemane. "Drive."

"Frankie." Verna grabbed his arm.

He shook her off. "Drive!" he shouted at Gethsemane. "Have you gone deaf? Drive. The. Damn. Car."

Gethsemane snapped her attention back to the vehicle and eased back onto the road.

"Please, Frankie," Verna said. "Let's go back to your place. We can talk about this—"

"Talk about what? Talk about how a bunch of ossified gits drove a man into the water and left him to drown? Talk about how they blamed the whole thing on him so his family would remember him as a drunken driver who nearly killed five people and was responsible for his own death? Is that what you want to talk about, Verna? Drop me at the Rabbit," he said to Gethsemane.

"Frankie, please." Verna grabbed his arm again. "I need you."

Frankie pushed her away. "I need a drink."

Verna turned on Gethsemane. "This is your fault. You couldn't leave it alone. You had to push and push and keep pushing, until—"

"Shut yer gob." Frankie snarled the words. "You lied to me, Verna. You lied to me. Me, the man you claimed you—" He turned away from her. "And now you're blaming Sissy for your lies? I guess I shouldn't be surprised. You've had years of practice blaming your sins on others."

"Frankie..." Verna's voice trailed off and she dissolved into tears.

"Why don't I take her to the Inn?" Gethsemane said. "Her sister can look after her. Then I'll drive you home."

"Then you'll drive me to the pub."

Gethsemane, for one of the few times in her life, did as she was told.

She drove first to Sweeney's Inn where the doorman helped extract a still-crying Verna from the back seat and promised to see she got to her sister's room. Then she drove Frankie to the Mad Rabbit.

"It's four o'clock," she looked at her watch, "five o'clock in the morning, Frankie. The pub doesn't open until ten thirty. Let me take you home."

"Don't worry, I have an in with the barman."

"Frankie, c'mon—"

"Would you lay off? You're not my wife and you're not my ma. You're—" He opened the rear passenger door. "Just let me out and drive away."

"All right, Frankie. I'm sorry."

"Sorry for what?" He climbed out of the car. "For not lying to me?" He slammed the door and stood watching, arms crossed, as she pulled away from the curb.

She waited until she reached the end of the street to look back. Frankie leaned against the pub's wall, head in hands. From the way his shoulders shook, she knew he was crying.

Twenty-One

"It's all bollixed." Gethsemane dumped a fourth spoonful of sugar into her coffee mug then slid the sugar bowl across the kitchen table.

"May I dilute that syrup for you?" Eamon pointed at the coffee pot, which rose and tipped, steaming black liquid into the cup. "And I think you mean banjaxed."

"Bollixed, banjaxed, all effed up. Whatever. Frankie's in tatters, which is not what I intended." She rested her forehead on her hands.

"He just found out his mot's been lying to him more than not, she played an integral part in a drunk driving death, and she helped frame an innocent man, the victim, to protect that gobshite, Ty Lismore. What did you expect, that he'd dance a jig in the village square?"

"Of course not. I knew he'd take it hard. Verna was the first woman since Yseult he's been romantically involved with. But I didn't think he'd start drinking again." Frankie drank legendary amounts of alcohol when she first met him. He'd cut down in recent months, but now... "I wanted to help Frankie, not trigger his downfall."

"Don't get ahead of yourself. He's hardly lying plastered in the gutter. And being done up for a murder he didn't commit for the second time in as many months wouldn't do much for his mental well-being. From what you described, the Cunningham sisters were closing ranks and blood is thicker than whatever Verna felt for Grennan. They'd marked him for sacrifice. Now they've got someone else to shift suspicion to. You might want to warn Agnes to be wide."

"Maybe Agnes did it. Drugged Ty, I mean. Jared was her boyfriend."

"Whose loss she mourned by shagging the man who killed him. By the way, when are you going to share this information with the guards? Not that I'm a fan of helping them do their job, but it's not like you to hold out this long. You don't have to go to Sutton direct, you can tell O'Reilly and let him be the bearer of incriminating tidings."

"I know, I know. Concealing information about a potential crime is a crime. At least, I think it is over here. But I didn't want to say anything to put the cross hairs on Frankie. I'll tell Niall everything. Just as soon as I talk to Vivian about Agnes. Don't look at me that way."

"What way? The 'are you not the full shilling' way? Or the 'why in the name of all that's holy would you tell Vivian the time of day' way?"

"You said it yourself, Irish. The Cunningham sisters won't hesitate to point the finger at someone else to save themselves. I can't trust Verna to bring up Agnes's reason for hating Ty since it implicates her in a cover-up. But if I put a bug in Vivian's ear, I bet she'll think of a way to drop a hint. You should have seen her face light up earlier when I suggested others might have had motive to hasten his demise."

"You're going to frame Agnes?" Eamon glowed a horrified aubergine.

"No, I am not going to frame Agnes. Why would you say such a thing?"

"Drop the indignation and listen to yourself. You all but

admitted that you were going to suggest that suspect A—the one with means as well as motive, given she's the only one with a prescription for the drug found in Lismore and she's the only one you know for a fact had his flask in her possession, by the way—manufacture evidence to put the guards on the scent of suspect B—who was in a long-term relationship with Lismore and seemed genuinely traumatized by his death. What's gotten into you, darlin'?"

"Lack of sleep. Caffeine deficiency." She crossed her arms on the table and lay her head down. "Utter desperation." The fabric of her sleeve muffled her voice. "Some part of me still wants to salvage Frankie and Verna's relationship."

"It's not your job to salvage their relationship and, before you say anything, no, you did not submarine it. Verna did that when she chose to lie."

"But maybe they can repair things. People have survived rough patches. 'The course of true love never did run smooth.' So sayeth the Bard."

"Should you try to salvage a relationship with a murderer? Or an accessory to murder? Even if you accept Jared's death as an accident, slipping amphetamines to a man who's already on meds that tend to cause hallucinations, then luring him to the top of a lighthouse where a noose just happens to be ready and waiting, is murder. Even the disagreeable Inspector Sutton would agree with me on that. If he could see and hear me. Grennan and Verna may work things out. They may not. But withholding information from the gardaí isn't going to help."

"All right, you win. Almost."

"Why do I not like the way that sounds?"

"I promise I will call Niall—after I talk to Brian one more time."

"Because?"

"Because he may be able to tell me if Agnes had the

opportunity to grab some of Vivian's dextroamphetamine tablets."

"And if she did, who do you think would have given her that opportunity? The man who's riding the pills' owner."

"Good point. I'll try to talk to Theophilus. As far as I can tell, he's not sleeping with anyone."

Sweeney's lobby sat empty when Gethsemane arrived. A small sign at the front desk advised visitors, in elegant script, to "Ring for Service." Gethsemane considered this a DIY mission, so she ignored the advice.

She got as far as the foot of the stairs leading to the second floor.

"Sissy."

Her heart leapt to her throat, blocking the curse word trying to make its way out. A few deep breaths assured her she still lived. Niall walked up behind her.

"Jaysus, Niall, are you trying to put the heart crossways in me?"

"Five points for decent use of Irish idiom. Minus ten points for planning to confront a murder suspect on your own and minus infinity for withholding information pertinent to an active garda investigation."

"Minus infinity doesn't exist. How'd you know I was here?"

"I got a text. Can't tell who from." He held his phone for her to see the jumble of numbers that appeared where the sender's phone number usually displayed. "It's not a working phone number. But the message, 'Sissy,' 'snooping,' 'Sweeney's,' was enough for me to suss what you were up to. So I high-tailed it over here."

A text from a non-existent number? Had Eamon figured out how to communicate by smart phone? A lesson learned from his time trapped on an SD card? She'd heard reports of people receiving spectral texts, but—No time to worry about that now.

"How long," Niall asked, "am I going to have to wait for you to tell me what you're—"

"Whisht." Gethsemane held a finger to her lips and pushed Niall around a corner as a door opened mid-hallway. Malcolm backed out of the room into the hall, followed by Vivian's head and shoulders. He bent to kiss her.

Gethsemane and Niall ducked out of sight as Malcolm broke the kiss and turned to go. When they poked their heads around the corner again, Malcolm had gone and the door had closed.

"Didn't expect that pairing," Niall said. "Thought he had the glad eye for Sunny Markham."

"Malcolm manages Sunny like a lion tamer manages big cats in a Vegas show. No romance involved. But I'm surprised, too. I thought Vivian was with Brian. At least, she was yesterday. I caught him in her room."

"Maybe they were swapping recipes."

"Maybe I'll be elected Queen of All That Surrounds Me tomorrow."

"Vivian's a modern woman. Where's your feminist spirit? You're not turning into a prude, are you?"

"No, I am not turning into a prude. I don't care if Vivian is at it with two guys or ten. It's not my business. Now that I think of it, she started panting after Malcolm the day he introduced himself in the pub and she noticed his tattoos." Maybe her offer to help Mal carry his gear to the lighthouse had been more than an opportunity to snag Ty's flask. Maybe grabbing the flask had been an added benefit. "I guess she wasn't kidding about having a thing for ink. By the way, didn't you fix dinner for Vivian a couple of weeks ago?"

"I may have whipped up a little something once or twice."

"Do you have any tattoos?"

Niall blushed. "One. A small one. A cat. Well-hidden."

Gethsemane suppressed a grin. "As long as a dinner or two doesn't cloud your objectivity."

"Objectivity about what? You still haven't told me anything."

"Here's the one-hundred-forty-character version: Way back in the day, Ty did something, something terrible." She hesitated.

Niall frowned. "Go on."

"He drove Agnes's boyfriend, Jared Ely, into a bayou and left him to drown."

"Murdered him, you mean."

"Displayed depraved indifference to human life, at a minimum."

"Giving Agnes excellent reason to want Ty dead." Niall's frown deepened. "But why wait 'til now to get even with him? 'Back in the day' is American for a helluva long time ago. So why now? Why here? Surely, Agnes had opportunity to do away with Ty before now."

"Because revenge is a dish best served cold?"

"Only in the movies. Why seek revenge at all and risk spending the rest of her life in prison? Why not tell the police that Lismore murdered her boyfriend? I'm no expert on U.S. law, but I'm pretty sure a halfway competent prosecutor could make a murder charge stick to a man who left another to drown."

Gethsemane thought of some notorious cases where what seemed like a sure conviction turned into an acquittal. "People were in the vehicle with Ty. They helped him cover up what he did."

"Cover up what he did? Cover up his crime, you mean. Who helped him? You know, don't you?"

She nodded. "Agnes. Agnes helped Ty cover up her

boyfriend's death. She couldn't go to the police."

"Brilliant." Niall closed his eyes and massaged the bridge of his nose. "You said 'some' people. Who else was in the vehicle?"

"Brian, Theo—" She couldn't bring herself to add Verna to the list.

Niall noticed her pause. "You're holding something back."

"I am?'

"Coy doesn't become you. You're no starry-eyed ingenue. I've known you long enough to know when you're holding back. Who else was in the car?"

"Before I answer, not telling the police about a death isn't the same as murder, is it? Legally, I mean. If all you did was keep your mouth shut, is that a crime?"

"You're asking if lying to law enforcement is a crime."

"Isn't not saying anything to the police akin to pleading the Fifth?"

"That's a question for a U.S. Constitutional law expert, not a lowly Irish garda."

"You're not a lowly anything. Here's an easier question. Let's assume not telling the police about a murder you witnessed is a crime. It's not murder, so there's a statute of limitations, right? I mean, after a while, you wouldn't be able to prosecute the person for not coming forward. Right?"

"Probably not. And, to save you the trouble of asking, yes, something that happened in an American bayou would be out of my jurisdiction. I wouldn't arrest anyone unless there was a warrant in the jurisdiction where the crime occurred and they asked us to detain the person. Which is a call someone much higher up the food chain than an Inspector would have to make." He took off his hat and adjusted its band. He spoke without looking at Gethsemane, his voice a few decibels lower than it had been. "An Inspector could, however, make the decision to arrest someone within his jurisdiction for interfering with a Garda investigation." He replaced his hat on his head and locked eyes with Gethsemane. "Am I wrong in guessing one of the people in that vehicle bears the initials V.C.?"

Resistance was futile. "Verna. Verna was also in the vehicle."

"And the reason you didn't want to tell me about her is because her involvement in Ty's coverup implicates her in Ty's death." He leaned his face closer to Gethsemane's, the brim of his hat grazing her forehead. "Give me the rest of it."

"Vivian takes dextroamphetamines for ADHD. I found a bottle of Vivian's pills in Verna's possession." No need to mention Frankie's bedroom. "I also caught Vivian with Ty's flask."

"Shite, Sissy, when were you planning to share all this with Sutton?"

"With Sutton? Three days after hell froze over. I planned to tell you the whole story right after I talked to Theo to find out if Agnes had any opportunity to swipe some of Vivian's ADHD meds."

"To point suspicion away from the Cunningham sisters toward Agnes. Why talk to Derringer, in particular?"

"Because it occurred to me that Agnes's best opportunity might have been Brian. He has—had—all-access to Vivian and her room. If he and Agnes were working together to avenge Jared's death or get out from under Ty's thumb or for any one of probably a dozen as-yet-unknown reasons to want Ty Lismore dead, he could have helped himself to enough amphetamines to send Ty, literally, over the edge."

"All right, we'll chat with Derringer. Notice I said, 'we,' as in you and me together."

"Well, I wasn't going to ask you to wait in the lobby." She nodded toward the stairs. "Let's go."

"That's my line."

"Try to keep up." She dashed up to the second-floor landing.

"I can still arrest you, you know," Niall said as he trotted up after her.

"For what? I'm not interfering. Well, I am but you sanctioned it."

"For criminal smart-alecky-ness."

"Theo's in two-fourteen, if I remember correct—" She stopped short.

"What's wrong?" Niall asked, narrowly avoiding colliding with her.

"The door." She pointed to the room she'd stopped in front of. The door stood ajar. "Two-oh-eight."

"Do you know whose room this is?"

"No, but I think most of the wedding party is on this hallway."

Niall stepped in front of her and lowered his voice to a whisper. "Let me."

She matched his volume. "Why don't I let you? Meanwhile, I'll think of an excuse in case we barge in on a guy in the shower."

"I don't hear water running. And in all the hotel rooms you stayed in during your travels and touring, how many doors did you forget to pull shut?"

"None." She crept after him.

He stopped short, causing her to smash her nose against his back. "Will you wait until I've made sure—"

She cut him off. "No. This isn't some American cop show. You don't even carry a gun."

Niall rolled his eyes and they entered.

This room was larger than Vivian's. A short hallway, home to a closet and a built-in minibar, separated the sleeping area from the entrance. Niall froze at the end of the hall. Gethsemane put a hand on his shoulder and tried to peer around him. He threw out an arm to keep her from advancing farther.

Then she saw what made him freeze.

Brian Nishi lay face down on the bed, shirtless. The dragon tattoo Vivian had admired coiled up from his waist to his shoulder. Brilliant orange-red flames burst from the dragon's mouth and scorched across Brian's upper back. Vivian had been right. The tattoo did look alive. Unlike Brian.

Standing over him, syringe in hand, Verna Cunningham looked as if she wished she was dead, too.

Twenty-Two

"I—I can explain," Verna stammered. "This isn't what it looks like. I found him like this, I swear." The tip of the long hypodermic needle attached to the syringe gleamed red.

Niall raised one hand in a "stop" gesture. He kept the other arm between Gethsemane and the sleeping area. "Put the syringe down, Verna."

"I didn't do this, Niall. You have to believe me."

"Put the syringe down and we'll talk about it."

"I wanted to talk to Brian about, about—things. I wanted to tell him," she glanced at Gethsemane, "that people knew about New Orleans. I found him lying on the bed like this with the needle stuck in his neck." She stared at the syringe and needle as if they had just appeared in her hand. "I—I touched him to see if—to check for a pulse. I must have pulled—I didn't kill him, I swear I didn't."

"I want to help you, Verna," Niall spoke in a calm, reassuring tone, "but I can't talk to you while you have that—" He nodded at the syringe. "—in your hand. Put it down. Set it on the floor or the bed and come here to me. C'mon now."

Verna noticed Gethsemane. She changed her grip on the syringe and held it like a knife, needle pointing toward the pair. "You—" She spoke through clenched teeth, with narrowed eyes. "—you're behind this. You set me up. You've been out to get me ever since I told you how I felt about Frankie. You're trying to ruin things between us. You don't want me to be happy."

"Verna!" Niall brought her attention back to him. "Put the syringe down and come away from there. Do it now." He stepped forward.

Verna slashed at him with the needle. He jumped back, bumping Gethsemane against the wall.

Verna raised the syringe over her head and, with a screech a banshee would envy, rushed them. Niall pushed Gethsemane down, she pulled him on top of her, and Verna ran past them into the hall.

Niall and Gethsemane disentangled themselves and clambered upright.

"Are you okay?" he asked.

"Peachy. You?"

"Fine," he answered as he ran after Verna.

Gethsemane ran after him.

Several heads protruded into the hall from doorways, but there was no sign of Verna.

"Which way did she go?" Niall asked the onlookers.

Several pointed to the stairs. Niall bounded down them two at a time.

Gethsemane examined the faces framed in doorways. Sunny, silent for once, gaped from a room at the far end of the hall. Malcolm stared from the room opposite, as did Rosalie from the room next door to his. Two faces she didn't see: Agnes and Theophilus.

Inspector Sutton stared down at Vivian Cunningham from her right. Niall stared down at her from her left. She hunched in an armchair in her hotel room, eyes red, cheeks damp with tears. She twined and untwined her fingers.

"For the tenth time," she said, "for the fifteenth, for the fiftieth, I. Don't. Know. I don't know where Verna went. I only know she didn't do what you're accusing her of. She didn't kill Brian. She couldn't have. She wouldn't have. My sister's no killer."

"Not counting Jared Ely," Sutton said.

Gethsemane had told him about Jared Ely's death and the cover-up. In the excitement of putting out an alert for Verna, he'd neglected to eat her head off for holding out on him. She kept quiet and hoped he wouldn't remember.

"Verna did not kill that man. She wasn't driving, Ty was."

"Verna didn't save him, either. And she covered for Ty," Sutton said, "Ruined the dead man's reputation, dishonored his memory. And she did it for years. How did Ty repay her? By abandoning her. So when she saw her chance to get revenge she stole some of your pills—or did you give them to her?—slipped them to Ty, waited until he was high as a kite, then goaded him into putting a noose around his neck and jumping off a catwalk."

"No, no, no, no, no." Vivian punctuated each denial with a fist pounded against the chair. "That's not how it happened. Not at all."

"How did it happen, Vivian?" Niall asked.

"Niall," she pleaded up at him, "you know me. Help me."

"The best way, the only way, to help your sister right now is for you to tell the truth," he said.

"I am telling the truth!" She pounded the chair again. Fresh tears welled in her eyes. "Why won't anyone believe me?"

"Brown and O'Reilly found your sister standing over a dead man with the presumptive murder weapon in her hand. She attacked them."

"She was scared. She panicked." She turned to Gethsemane. "Please, Gethsemane, please listen to me. Verna didn't do this."

"If your sister didn't do it," Sutton asked, "then who did?"

"Has anyone seen Agnes? Or Theophilus?" Gethsemane asked.

Sutton glared at her.

"Just asking," she said.

"Yes, yes, she's right." Vivian sat up in her chair. "Find Agnes and Theo. I bet one of them did it. Or they're in it together."

"Or the two of them are in it with your sister," Sutton said. "We'll find Verna first, then worry about the other two."

"Would Verna go to Frankie Grennan for help?" Niall asked.

"I called Frankie's apartment," Gethsemane said. "No answer."

"Which doesn't mean he's not there," Sutton said. "They could be lying low."

"Frankie was pretty furious with her when I dropped them off this morning." She told them about the confrontation in the car after Sutton released them. "They parted on non-speaking terms."

"Where'd you drop them?" Sutton asked.

"Verna, here, Frankie, the Rabbit."

"The Rabbit doesn't open until half ten," Niall said.

"I know. Frankie didn't care. He demanded I let him out of the car and leave. I left him standing on the corner."

"He could be anywhere," Sutton said.

"Not anywhere very far from the village." Gethsemane held up his car keys. "I've got his car."

"Wouldn't do Verna much good to run to him, then," Sutton said.

"My sister is not trying to flee the village," Vivian said. "She's not some dangerous fugitive, stop talking about her like she is. She didn't kill anyone."

"We'll ask her about that when we find her, and we will find her. We'll find the others, too, Derringer and Miss Haywood. As for you, Vivian Cunningham," Sutton motioned to two uniformed gardaí who'd appeared at the door, "they'll escort you to the station to answer some questions in an official capacity. And, in case you're wondering, you are not obliged to say anything unless you wish to do so, but whatever you say will be taken down in writing and may be given in evidence."

One of the gardaí turned back to the door as noise in the hall grew louder.

"What's the commotion?" Sutton asked.

"It's that American, sir," the garda said. "The header."

Sutton gave Gethsemane the side eye. "You'll have to be more specific, lad."

"The one that was going to marry the stiff."

"Jaysus, Mary, and Joseph." Sutton pressed a hand to his forehead. "Not now." The noise grew louder. "Bolt the fecking door, McGillicuddy, don't let her in."

Too late, the garda tried to push the door shut. Sunny burst through like a rocket, slamming the door open with an arm, right into McGillicuddy's face.

"Ow!" The garda grabbed his nose.

"Inspector Sutton!" Sunny stomped into the room and confronted the inspector, her unblemished complexion a few inches from his craggy one. No hint of little-girl-sweetness accompanied her words. "I demand you tell me what's going on."

"What's going on, Miss Markham, is that I'm trying to conduct a murder investigation."

"Mur-*ders*, Inspector. Plural. First my dear—" A catch arose in her voice as if summoned. "—dear Ty. Now his best friend and member of my wedding party." The quaver disappeared as quickly as it had come. "What are you doing to find this, this…"

"Fiend?" Gethsemane offered.

"Wedding wrecker!" Sunny stomped her foot.

Vivian curled her lip and narrowed her eyes. She tried to rise out of her chair but a garda's hand pushed her back down. "Wedding wrecker?" She spat words at Sunny. "Is that all you care about, you horrid little shite? Your wedding? Two people you allegedly cared about are dead, two more haven't been seen, and you're worried about your wedding? What's the matter? Can't get your deposit back from the caterer?"

"You shut up, you cow." Sunny lunged for Vivian but Sutton blocked her. She struggled to reach Vivian around the inspector's burly chest. "You're behind this, you and that pathetic sad sack sister of yours. She couldn't stand seeing Ty with me so she killed him. You helped her, you codependent loon. Why'd you two kill Brian? Did he find out what you did to Ty? Threaten to turn you in? Or did Brian decide to move on to something better than you? Maybe you're as crazy jealous as she is, so you killed him rather than lose him."

Vivian screamed and tried to launch herself from her chair. McGillicuddy and the other uniformed garda grabbed her. Sunny tried to push past Inspector Sutton.

"That's enough of that, Ms. Markham." Sutton held up a hand.

Sunny pushed against his chest. "Will you get out of my way, you ignorant ox?"

Sutton took a deep breath and made a noise that sounded like a bull getting ready to charge. "You're under arrest."

"Arrest?" Surprise, apparently genuine, transformed Sunny's features from furious cat to indignant owl. "For what?"

"Assaulting a guard." He grabbed her arm. She kicked his shin.

Niall leapt forward and grabbed her. She bit him.

He pulled away from her and sucked the base of his thumb. "Are you completely gone in the head, woman?"

Before Sunny could respond, a coverlet sailed from behind her and landed on her head. Gethsemane pulled the coverlet down over the irate influencer, then spun her around, entangling her in the quilted fabric. She pushed her toward the uniforms, who uncovered enough of her to handcuff her wrists. Muffled curses emanated from the bundle.

"How much trouble am I in?" Gethsemane asked Niall and Sutton.

"For assisting a garda in distress?" Niall said. "None."

"None from me, either," Sutton agreed. "Never thought I'd say this in this lifetime, but I owe you one." He turned to the uniforms. "Take Miss Markham down to the station, book her on whatever charges you can make stick. O'Reilly and I'll handle Miss Cunningham. He pulled Vivian up from her chair.

"Please, Gethsemane," she said as Sutton led her from the room, "Please find Verna. She didn't do this. I know she didn't. Please, find her."

Twenty-Three

Gethsemane drummed her fingers on the dashboard of Frankie's car. She drummed them on the steering wheel. She pounded on the steering wheel. "Damn it, Frankie, where are you?"

She'd cruised the streets of Dunmullach searching for her friend. Murphy, the Rabbit's barman, confirmed Frankie had stopped in around the time the pub opened and stayed long enough to have a few drinks. No one answered at his apartment and his neighbors hadn't seen him. She'd even tried church, but Father Tim denied seeing Frankie in the building or on the grounds.

Gethsemane scanned the area as she drove from St. Brennan's to the village square and back. Without warning, Eamon materialized in the middle of the road leading up to the school. Gethsemane slammed on the brakes. The car skidded through Eamon, stopping with its hood in the ghost's midsection. A charge buzzed through the car and into Gethsemane. She yelped and let go of the steering wheel.

Eamon stepped out of the car's front end. He brushed his hands against his pants as if wiping away dust. Gethsemane rolled down the window. "Are you nuts? Appearing in the middle of the road like that? I hit you."

"As I'm incorporeal, you didn't hit me, you drove through

me. And you did no damage, darlin'. Although a half-ton of metal plowing through my middle gave me quite a buzz."

"Skip the spectral semantics and tell me what you're doing here. I'm trying to find Frankie."

"I found him for you. Halfway up the road to Golgotha."

Gethsemane smacked her forehead. "His rose garden, of course. I'm an idiot."

"It's eejit, and no, you're not. You're a good friend. So go be a good friend. Drive safe." He vanished.

Gethsemane raced toward Carnock. The gnarled trees and dense underbrush that usually filled her with dread as she climbed the hill sped by in a harmless blur as she rushed to intercept Frankie. She spotted him at the hill's crest.

She rolled down the car window. "Frankie, are you all right?"

He kept walking. "In what sense do you mean 'all right'? If you mean am I still amongst the living, yes, I'm all right. If you mean, am I suffering from alcohol poisoning?" He held up a bottle three-quarters full with whiskey. "Not yet, but I'm working on it. If you mean, is that comical look on my face because my insides have been kicked out, no, I am not all right."

"You can still quote *Casablanca*." They shared a love of classic films, especially the Humphrey Bogart masterpiece. "I take that as a good sign."

"Technically, it was a paraphrase."

"You're still snarky. Encouraging."

He stopped walking. "Will you leave me alone?"

Gethsemane stopped the car, blocking the path. "No. No, I won't leave you alone because you're my friend and you're hurting and I'm worried about you. And because no one can find Verna."

Puzzlement creased Frankie's forehead. "Why should anyone be looking for Vern?"

"Well..." Gethsemane let out a deep breath. "After Niall and I found her standing over Brian Nishi's dead body, she tried to stab us with a hypodermic needle and ran away. The guards want to ask her some questions about the deaths of Brian and Ty."

"Jaysus, Mary, and—You're coddin' me, right? Please tell me you're coddin' me."

She shook her head. "Sorry. You haven't seen her have you? We thought she might try to contact you. Sutton, optimist that he is, thought you might try to help her escape."

"After the way we left things? I'm the last person she'd turn to for help."

Given how angry Verna had been when she accused her of sabotaging her relationship with Frankie, Gethsemane had doubts about the accuracy of Frankie's assertion. But expressing her doubts right now probably wouldn't help the situation. She opened the passenger door. "Get in."

Frankie climbed into the car. "I don't want to go home."

"I'm not taking you to the pub."

He pointed toward the remains of St. Dymphna's. "Verna might have gone up to the garden."

Gethsemane drove up to the campus and parked on the side road where Frankie had parked before. They both walked to the garden. Roses bloomed even more beautiful than before. But no Verna.

Frankie fiddled with an arbor, pinching a few spent blooms from a climber. "Do you believe she did it? Verna, I mean. Killed Brian."

Gethsemane considered. "I don't know."

"You're one of the few people in my life who's never lied to me, Gethsemane." Frankie spoke without looking at her. "Don't start now."

"Honest, Frankie, I don't know. I do think she drugged Ty,

with or without Vivian's help. Most likely with. I think she agreed to meet Ty at the lighthouse because he terrified her. The thought of losing you because of what he might reveal terrified her. Removing Ty would remove the threat to her chance at happiness, a chance she thought she'd never get again until she met you. So she emptied the contents of her sister's dextroamphetamine capsules, met Ty at Carrick Point, shared a drink from his flask—a toast to old times or something—then slipped the amphetamines into the remainder of the flask's contents, knowing he'd eventually finish them. She probably figured he'd die of an overdose. I doubt she knew the combination of amphetamines, dextromethorphan, and levofloxacin would interact and cause hallucinations. I believe Ty put the rope around his own neck and jumped because he hallucinated something, lord knows what. I don't think he meant to kill himself. I don't know if inducing hallucinations that lead a man to hang himself meets the legal definition of murder. But Brian?" Gethsemane shook her head. "Why kill Brian? He was no threat to her or Vivian. He shared equal guilt for covering up Jared's death. He could hardly run to the authorities and dime her out. He was hooking up with her sister—"

"Seriously?"

"By mutual consent and with enthusiasm, I gathered, spurred by Vivian's tattoo fetish. That was no reason to kill him. And to kill him in such a direct manner—a syringe full of whatever to the neck. Close-range and personal. Not quite the same as slipping drugs in a guy's flask then beating it while chemistry plays its hand. It *is* possible she could have gone into Brian's room, just like Niall and I did, and found him already dead. I don't know Frankie, I really don't know."

"Everything's such a bloody mess." He sat on a bench and ran his hands through his hair. "It was lovely for a while, it really was. But the lies. I just can't get past the lies."

"I'm really sorry, Frankie, I am. I wish I had some magic spell that could turn the clock back two weeks and keep all this from ever happening. But I doubt even Father Tim's grimoires contain any incantations powerful enough to do that."

"Mostly because magic's not real."

Gethsemane bit her tongue.

Frankie scuffed his shoe in the dirt. "Maybe I should just give up women. My track record..."

"Don't say that Frankie." She sat next to him. "Not every woman on the planet is like Yseult and Verna. Give the rest of female humanity a chance."

A grin softened Frankie's expression. "Listen to you, undercover romantic. I haven't exactly noticed you out there giving male humanity a chance."

She blushed and shrugged. "That's not where I am at this point in my life. But just because I'm feeling monk-ish doesn't mean you should be."

"Do as you say, not as you do? Or don't do." He nudged her shoulder.

"Something like that." She rose and held out a hand. "So where can I take you? Not home, not the pub, Sutton's people are crawling all over the village."

He grabbed her hand and pulled himself up. "How about Our Lady? A cup of Father Tim's Bewley's will set things right."

"Frankie, it's tea."

"A cup of tea always sets things right."

Twenty-Four

Father Tim welcomed Gethsemane and Frankie into the rectory's kitchen. He concurred with Frankie's assessment of Bewley's restorative powers as he poured around the table. "My oul' wan used to say, 'when the world is going to hell in a handbasket, stop and wet the leaves.' Tea helps you gain perspective."

Gethsemane spooned sugar into her teacup as steam wafted up from the reddish liquid and surrounded her with robust, malty comfort. "Tim, in the midst of the apocalypse, if the world was literally going to hell, I believe you'd offer the four horsemen a cuppa."

Frankie sipped his tea without joining the banter.

Gethsemane laid a hand on his arm. "We'll find her Frankie." As she withdrew her hand, she brushed against papers stacked near the edge of the table. "Sorry, Tim." She bent to scoop them up.

"Don't worry about those. Just research I'm doing for my lecture on economic, racial, and ethnic disparities in application of the death penalty I'm preparing for the Dumullach Ethical Society next month." He set the papers aside. "Why don't you try calling Verna again, Frankie?"

"What's the point, Father? She'll see it's my number and ignore the call. She doesn't want to speak to me. Can't say I blame her, the way I reacted."

"The news came at you out of left field," Gethsemane said. "You handled it better than most."

"I've an idea." Tim handed his phone to Frankie. "Why don't you call her using my number? She wouldn't recognize that." He excused himself. "I need to go check on—"

Loud clanging and thumping emanated from somewhere below the kitchen.

"Jaysus," Frankie said. "What was that?"

"Sounds like the old boiler kicking over," Tim said.

"It's July." Gethsemane frowned. "Why would the boiler be on in July?"

"Don't know," Tim answered. "July or December, that one shouldn't be on at all. Haven't used it to heat the place since renovations five years ago when we had a furnace installed."

"You don't have ghosts in the basement, do you, Father?" Frankie forced a laugh.

"No, I don't," Tim answered, not laughing at all.

Gethsemane and Frankie followed him to the basement steps. They halted at the landing as more clanging and thumping reverberated off the walls of the narrow stairwell.

"There are three of us," Gethsemane encouraged.

They crept downstairs, single file. Gethsemane recited baseball stats in her head. Father Tim mouthed a prayer. Silent Frankie wore a grim expression. The stairs opened into a dank, mildewed, unfinished room. Jumbles of buckets, brooms, old candlesticks, and sagging boxes lined the walls.

Frankie hefted one of the candlesticks. "Brass." He handed another to Gethsemane.

"The boiler room's that way." Tim led them past the stacks of junk.

The hum of machinery grew louder as they approached the boiler room. A heavy steel door fitted with an ancient lock guarded the room's entrance. A small porthole cut into the door's upper third provided the only visualization of the interior.

Gethsemane stood on tiptoe. She glimpsed white fumes. Off balance, she lowered herself to her flat feet. "Should there be smoke?" she asked. She touched the scar on her forehead, chilled by the memory of fire at St. Dymphna's.

Tim peered through the porthole. "Those are exhaust fumes. And no, they shouldn't be in there." He grabbed Frankie's hand as the latter reached for the door's handle. "No, don't. I can't vouch for the ventilation in this area. You could gas us all."

Gethsemane jumped to get another glimpse inside. "Hey, I think there's someone in there." She pounded on the door.

Tim cupped his hands around the porthole and pressed his face against the glass. "You're right. Someone's in there."

Tim tried the door handle. It didn't move. Frankie tried it. Nothing. They pushed, pulled, jiggled, and tugged at it together.

"It's jammed," Tim said.

The men pounded and kicked at the door. Frankie smashed at the lock with the candlestick. The stick bent. The lock held fast. Frankie slammed the end of the candlestick against the porthole, only to drop it as the impact of the brass against glass as thick as the door caused a kick back forceful enough to leave him doubled over in pain, hands tucked into armpits.

Gethsemane spied Tim's phone protruding from Frankie's pocket. She grabbed it. "What's Verna's phone number?

Frankie recited it from memory. Gethsemane punched digits, then held her breath, hoping she was wrong. One second, two seconds, three seconds. The call connected. A musical ringtone, a tinny rendition of "Put on a Happy Face," played. She heard the notes, clear and distinct, in the ear she held pressed against the phone. Her other ear picked up a faint echo from someplace near. Very near. She lowered the phone. Music was still audible. She pivoted toward the boiler room. She felt sick.

The tinny notes of "Put on a Happy Face," almost imperceptible through steel and over pounding, played from inside the boiler room.

Twenty-Five

Gethsemane sat on a bench in the church cloister, her arm around Frankie. She watched as Scene of Crime gardaí wheeled a stretcher burdened with a covered body toward an ambulance. Frankie did not watch. Father Tim laid a hand on Frankie's shoulder and said a prayer. In the distance, Sutton and Niall conferred with a woman wearing a fire brigade jacket.

Niall broke away. "They've given the all-clear to go back into the rectory, Father." He laid a hand on Frankie's other shoulder. "I'm really sorry."

Frankie shook priest, guard, and Gethsemane off and walked into the churchyard. He sank down next to a statue and buried his face against his knees.

Niall cleared his throat. "Sutton, uh, thinks it's—"

Gethsemane cut him off. "Don't say suicide. You know it wasn't."

"I said, 'Sutton thinks.'" Niall looked over his shoulder at his colleague. "Only he doesn't really. He's not thick. The violent deaths of three people involved in the cover up of a fourth death. That's too much to explain away, even for him."

"So why even suggest suicide?"

"Because," Niall said, "'Verna Cunningham contributed to the death of Ty Lismore and murdered Brian Nishi, then killed herself out of remorse or to avoid prosecution' sounds better to the Superintendent than 'we have a serial revenge killer on the loose in Dunmullach and we can't locate either of the two most likely suspects."

"Agnes and Theo," Gethsemane said.

Niall nodded.

"Where's Vivian? Someone needs to tell her about her sister."

"Still at the station. Sutton will notify her."

"In a gentle and sensitive manner, no doubt."

"Give the man some credit. Informing family members of the deaths of loved ones is, unfortunately, part of his job."

"Any idea how someone got into the basement?" Tim asked. "No one came through the upstairs. I'd have seen them."

"Jimmied the lock on the basement door. Which doesn't prove Verna didn't do it. Wood's nearly rotten. A baby could've yanked it off. And the lock on the boiler room door could have been jammed from the inside or out. The machine was connected to a timer that turned it on."

"Do you really think Verna was a small electronics expert?" Gethsemane said. "That she rigged a timer to turn on a boiler."

Niall's back straightened with indignation. "I didn't say I thought—"

Gethsemane held up a hand.

A commotion at the edge of the yard drew everyone's attention. Two women, anemic and reedy, and a rotund man, as ruddy as his companions were pale, argued with the uniformed gardaí positioned as barricades between the crime scene and the rest of the village. They gesticulated and cast increasingly unpleasant glances toward Father Tim.

"Oh, heaven have mercy, not now." The priest sighed. "The divil himself is less of a pain in my—" He crossed himself.

"Who are they?" Gethsemane asked.

"Folks looking to get arrested." Niall headed over to offer

the uniforms reinforcement. His arrival prompted angry glances in Tim's direction from the women and a wave from the man.

"Who are they?" Gethsemane repeated.

"They're the president, vice president, and secretary of the Dunmullach Ethical Society, come to discuss my lecture. Meaning criticize it before they've even heard it. I forgot we had a meeting."

Gethsemane snapped her fingers as the Ethical Society members, with final displeased looks at Tim, yielded to the gardaí and departed. "Your lecture! Tim, that's it."

"That's what?"

"The death penalty. Don't you see?"

"I'm afraid I don't."

"Call it a side effect of being from the U.S. Death penalty cases are always in the news. The three deaths we've had here— Ty, Brian, and—" She cast a glance at Frankie as the ambulance pulled away with its tragic cargo. "Verna. Hanging, lethal injection, and the gas chamber. They're all methods of execution."

Gethsemane and Tim stared at each other for a moment as the impact of what she'd said sank in.

They yelled simultaneously, "Inspector Sutton!"

He frowned, then excused himself from the fire brigade woman and strode toward the cloister. Niall hurried to catch up with him. Frankie looked up from his grief but stayed put by the statue.

"Why is it, Brown," Sutton began, "that whenever you get that gleam in your eye, I regret quitting smoking?"

"At least she's not Sunny Markham putting on a holy show." Niall elbowed his colleague in the ribs.

"What do you want?" Sutton asked.

"To find Agnes Haywood and Theophilus Derringer before it's too late."

"Before they make it to an airport and onto a plane out of the country? Yes, I—"

"No. Before the executioner carries out their sentences. They're not murderers, Inspector Sutton, they're the next victims."

Sutton worked a muscle in his jaw that allowed a grudging, "Go on."

"Ty was hanged, Brian was executed by lethal injection, Verna died in a gas chamber. Someone's decided that crew escaped punishment for their roles in Jared Ely's death for long enough and now they're pronouncing sentence. Agnes and Theo were both in the car the night Jared drowned. They both put the blame on Jared and they both covered it up."

"They've been weighed in the balance and found wanting," Tim said.

Sutton patted his pockets as if looking for cigarettes. "Damn."

"You don't believe me," Gethsemane said.

"I do believe you. That's why I want a cigarette."

"Who in the village, besides Agnes and Theophilus knew what happened in New Orleans?" Niall asked.

Good question. Sunny? Would Ty have told her? Would she have cared if he had? Rosalie? "Rosalie's from New Orleans, or somewhere around that area. She might have heard about Jared's death in the local media." Or read about it in her tarot cards.

"Hearing about a death is a far cry from murdering those you hold responsible for it," Tim said.

"We need to know more about Jared Ely," Gethsemane said.

"If you're right," Sutton said, "and I grant that you probably are, Derringer and Miss Haywood don't have time for us to do a deep dive on Ely. No one's seen them since we found Nishi's body. They haven't answered their phones nor tried to contact anyone." He smoothed a hand over his thinning hair. "We may be too late as it is."

"Which of the two is most likely to, you know—" Gethsemane made a slicing motion across her throat, "—first?"

"Most likely to get it, you mean?" Frankie joined the group. "Theophilus Derringer. He'd be next on the list."

Sutton frowned at him. "You know that how?"

"Speaking as a man who has a shite track record with women. Whoever's doing this is someone close to Ely, someone who loved him, would do anything—even kill—for him. A blood relative."

"Like Vivian and Verna," Gethsemane said. "Blood's thicker than everything. Those two would have sacrificed anyone to save each other."

Frankie swallowed hard before continuing. "This person, this executioner, he or she is sending a message. They'd save the best—or the worst, depending on how you look at it—for last."

"Agnes is the worst?"

"Absolutely. She was Ely's girlfriend. She should have chosen him over a bunch of maggots she'd just met at a bar. But instead, she chose them. Her choice cost Ely his life. Then, to add insult, she starts shagging the fella who killed him. Betrayal upon betrayal. Agnes Haywood will die last."

"Unless we find her first," Sutton said. He turned to the other gardaí and motioned for them to gather around.

Niall spoke to Gethsemane. "Do us a favor? See if you can find some connection between Rosalie Baraquin and Jared Ely. I don't know the New Orleans area, but if it's anything like Dunmullach, most folks are related somewhere back. Text me if you find anything."

"And let us know if you locate Agnes and Theophilus," Father Tim said. "I'll pray for their safe recovery."

"Thanks, Father." Niall shook his hand. "We need all the help we can get." He nodded goodbyes and joined his fellow gardaí.

"When all else fails," Gethsemane said, "turn to the internet. Ely and Baraquin are both Creole names. Let's hope Creoles are proponents of online genealogy."

Twenty-Six

"I know the fire brigade deemed it safe to go back to the rectory, but I feel more comfortable waiting a bit longer." Father Tim snapped on the lights in the sacristy. "We can use the computer in the robing room."

"This is where you write your sermons, Father?" Frankie asked.

"I mostly write them at the library." Tim powered up a PC set atop a writing desk and logged in. "This comes in handy for looking busy when the head of the altar guild and head of the flower guild want me to mediate one of their endless disputes."

Gethsemane's phone rang out Beethoven's "Fifth." "Niall? You what?" A sickening knot tightened in the pit of her stomach and she sank to a chair. She felt as if all the vitality had been sucked from her. "Oh. I'll tell them."

Frankie sat in a chair next to her. "Which one?"

"Theophilus. Shot."

"God rest his soul." Father Tim made the sign of the cross.

"Firing squad," Frankie said. "What's left?"

"Beheading, electrocution, burning at the stake. Poor Agnes."

"Beheading and burning weren't much used in America, were they?" Frankie asked.

"I don't think they were used at all," Gethsemane said. "Not officially, anyway. Hanging and shooting were the most common methods of execution until the advent of alternating current."

"Then I vote for electrocution." Frankie grimaced. "You know what I mean."

"It's not that easy to electrocute someone, is it?" Gethsemane asked. "It's not like spare electric chairs are lying around. An electrocution would require a set up and technical know-how."

"Our executioner has had all day, at a minimum, to set things up," Frankie said. "If he or she found someplace to hide the works, they could have set things up in advance in secret. And as we saw with the boiler room..." Frankie's voice caught. Gethsemane squeezed his shoulder. He patted her hand and continued. "The boiler room, he or she has technical know-how."

"Hey, now we're sucking diesel." Father Tim clapped his hands. Gethsemane and Frankie gathered around him. He opened a website with a jubilant click of the mouse. "'The Louisiana Creole Family Database, the most comprehensive online French and Black Creole genealogy collection available without a subscription.' At least, that's how they describe themselves."

"There's a search box." Gethsemane tapped the screen. 'Find family connections.' Type in Ely and Baraquin."

"Zero hits," Tim said after a moment.

"Search for Jared's obituary. It might list some extended family members." The familiar "da-da-da-dum" trilled from Gethsemane's phone. A text from Saoirse.

Miss, I'm not supposed 2 know about sigil but I do
Showed Colm and twins
Feargus told me about deal with devil website

"Why does Feargus Toibin know about 'deal with the devil'

websites?" Gethsemane said aloud.

Frankie scanned the computer screen over Tim's shoulder. "Because he's a teenaged boy. Teen boys are repositories of information both horrific and shocking."

Gethsemane rolled her eyes and muttered about chatting with his mother. The text continued.

No sigils. Lots of tat2s

Several screengrabs showing tattoos followed. Gethsemane scrolled through them. She stopped at the twelfth. "Try Amott. Add an 'e' to the end."

Tim and Frankie looked up from the computer.

"Try Amott," Gethsemane repeated. "In that Creole genealogy database, search for a connection between Amott and Ely. Spell Amott with an 'e' at the end."

Father Tim typed. "Looks like Amottes have been marrying Ely's for centuries."

"Malcolm Amott is related to Jared Ely." Gethsemane held her phone so the men could see. "This tattoo, the human hand grasping the monstrous claw hand. I've seen it before. On Malcolm Amott's arm. He keeps it covered but," she remembered remarking on his tattoos at the pub, "once he rolled up his sleeves high enough for part of it to show. He wears this tattoo."

"Given your outburst regarding Feargus Toibin's web surfing habits," Frankie said, "I'm going to assume this tattoo is often worn by—"

"People who've made deals with the devil."

"Come look at this." Tim beckoned them back to the computer. "I found Jared's obituary. It ran in the *Times-Picayune*."

Frankie whispered to Gethsemane, "What's a picayune?"

She shrugged. "A small, furry, swamp animal? How do I know?" She addressed Tim. "Can you pull up the obituary?"

Tim clicked the link. A grainy photograph of a stunning young man with large dark eyes and a mop of curls filled the screen. His birth and death dates, printed below his photo, revealed a too-short span between them.

"Look at Jared's middle name," Gethsemane said. "It's his mother's maiden name—Amotte. Jared Amotte Ely."

"A blood relative of Malcolm Amott."

"Who intends to claim Agnes's blood as payback for Jared's death." Gethsemane texted the information to Niall as promised. "They'll never find them in time. We have no idea where to look for her."

"Look no further." Rosalie stepped into view of the robing room. "The answer you seek is in your own backyard."

"Oh, for—" Gethsemane closed her eyes and counted to three. "We've no time for your cryptic nonsense, Rosalie." *And I've no time for you, either, Tchaikovsky*, she added silently as "Pathetique" welled up in her head.

"No nonsense, I promise. I read the cards today. They predicted death."

"Really, which one? We've had four."

"A fifth. The last. Not yet happened but approaching."

"Perhaps you could give us some specifics, Miss Baraquin," Father Tim said.

Frankie gaped, his eyes wide with incredulity. "You're not listening to any of this woo-woo foolishness, are you, Father?"

"Miss Baraquin's trying to help," he said.

"Enter Baraquin and Landreneau in your search box, Father." She spelled the name. "It's Malcolm's middle name. He shared it with my great-grandmother."

"You're related to Malcolm?" Gethsemane asked.

"New Orleans is a big place, Gethsemane," Rosalie said, "but it's not that big. Mal and I are cousins. Mal and Jared were cousins but Mal treated him more like a little brother. Jared's parents raised Mal after his mother died."

"You knew it was him?" Frankie asked. "Behind the murders?"

"Not until I read the cards today. Malcolm is—guarded. He's able to keep things from me, able to shield himself."

"A perk of selling your soul to the devil, no doubt." Gethsemane fought the urge to fly at Rosalie and shake the whole story out of her. "Bet you learn all sorts of things in exchange for eternal damnation."

"If only you knew." Rosalie wiped at tears. "You knew I was lying when I said I didn't recognize that sigil."

Gethsemane nodded. "Too many similarities between it and your pictograph message and your tattoo for me to believe you had no idea what it was, despite your protests. That and your reaction to it."

Rosalie continued. "I knew it was meant for me. My...business associate...letting me know it was time to settle accounts. A reminder, like the note he sent to me at Sweeney's."

"Why would your 'business associate' deliver the sigil to Father Tim, instead of directly to you?"

"One, to put the Church on notice—"

"Tim did say something about professional courtesy."

"Two, as a joke at my expense, a hint that I'd better hurry and make my final confession and receive Last Rites. He knew the priest would connect the sigil to me. Father Tim's gained a reputation in some circles because of his occult collection. His late brother's skill as an exorcist was infamous. Or legendary, depending on whose side you were on." Bitterness filled her laugh. "My associate hadn't counted on you."

"I suspected Malcolm planted it to throw suspicion your way, or maybe to warn you off. He figured the similarity to one of your tattoos would be noticed. The similarity isn't coincidental, is it?"

"No." Rosalie pushed up her sleeve and exposed the tattoo. "This sigil is the spell I used to..." Her voice trailed off.

"Wait a minute, wait a minute," Frankie sputtered. "Are you telling us you actually sold your soul to the devil? And the devil came to Dunmullach to collect it?"

"Frankie's a skeptic," Gethsemane said.

"And you're not? Seriously, Sissy?"

Gethsemane held a finger to her lips. "Frankie, you know that old saying about 'speak of the...?' Maybe you could not mention his name."

Rosalie hung her head. "It's true, Frankie. I made a Faustian bargain. Something Mal and I have in common. Guess you could call it a family tradition. I have the tattoo to prove it. It's like Mal's but better hidden." She pushed her sleeve up farther and raised her arm. A small tattoo of a human hand clasped in a demonic handshake with a clawed monstrosity lay tucked near her armpit.

"Why, in the name of all that's holy, child, would you do such a dreadful thing?" Father Tim asked.

"It seemed like a good idea at the time. Of course, it wasn't worth it in the end. It never is, is it? But when you're so full of hate and anger that you can hardly breathe, you don't think things through to their logical conclusion. I've regretted making the deal ever since the ink dried."

"Ink?" Frankie sneered. "Not blood? You didn't sign your deal with the devil in blood?"

"That's an old wives' tale." Rosalie raised her arm higher and pointed at the handshake tattoo. "Ink's just fine."

"What was the deal?" Frankie asked. "What did you want that was so terrible or so wonderful that your soul seemed a fair price to pay?"

"You ask almost as many questions as your friend." Rosalie jerked her head toward Gethsemane.

"She's a bad influence," Frankie said. "She's also taught me not to be easily put off. What did you do? Did it have anything to do with Ty?"

"Hardly. Ty Lismore wasn't worth the time of day to me, let alone my soul. I'll spare you the gory details of my contract because they're none of your business, but since you won't be put off," Rosalie paused for emphasis, "I will tell you that what happened occurred a long time ago, on the River Road. Cousin Mal knew about it. It's what gave him the idea to make the same deal to avenge Jared's death." Another bitter laugh. "I guess I'm a bad influence, too."

Frankie started to speak but Gethsemane stopped him with a hand on his arm. "Did Mal turn to you for help?" she asked Rosalie. "As the one person who could understand what he was going through?"

"And not judge him because she'd done the same? Yeah. Mal asked me to introduce him to Sunny. He wanted to offer her his skill as a photographer. What better way to get her to eat from your hand than to make her look good on social media? No deal with the devil required."

"I thought Sunny's mother introduced her to Mal after seeing one of his shows."

"She did. I got Mrs. Markham the ticket to the show. I earned a...contract extension by agreeing to help Mal. I figured a degree of separation in the introductions would keep my name out of it. Sunny's mother is a respected art collector. I met her when I worked in a gallery. And Mal really is a brilliant artist. He specializes in video installations. He does all of the work, lighting, and everything himself."

"Meaning he has the technical know-how to set up his executions."

"Twisted performance art," Rosalie said. "Brilliant right? But brilliance doesn't pay the rent or buy groceries. Mal wasn't shy about admitting he needed paying work. Sunny paid. A lot. In advance."

"Sunny's money was the icing, wasn't it?" Gethsemane said. "What he really wanted was access to the people he blamed for killing Jared."

"He didn't come right out and say so...but I knew."

"A man willing to put up with Sunny Markham's brand of melodrama," Frankie said, "to get revenge on her fiancé, is a dedicated man. I almost admire him."

"Mal doesn't mind Sunny," Rosalie said. "He has a way with her, you've seen it."

"More icing? The ego boost of managing the unmanageable?" Gethsemane asked.

"Mal appreciates Sunny's ability to control others by creating chaos."

"She came by her talent without having to sell her soul."

"You can't sell what you don't have. She was born without one." Rosalie crossed herself. "Sorry, Father."

"Don't apologize," Tim said. "But do tell us how Malcolm knew the truth about Jared's death."

"Jared bragged to Mal about his New York girlfriend and his plans to hang out with 'the Brits' for the week. For all of his airs, Jared was a River Road hick, easily impressed. His name was the only thing high class about him."

"Mal didn't know Agnes?"

"He never met her. He was on assignment for a travel magazine, had been out of the country for almost two years, somewhere between the Galapagos and Fiji, when Jared and she got together."

"How did he know the truth about the accident?"

"Mal never believed Jared was the driver. He used to rage about Jared being blamed. Wanted the police to investigate the other people in the car. He knew Agnes's name; Jared told him that much." Rosalie shrugged. "Once he tracked Agnes down, I guess it wasn't hard for him to find out who she hung with."

Gethsemane gripped Rosalie's arms and held her face an inch away. "Where has Mal taken Agnes, Rosalie? No more 'mysterious Creole conjure woman' routine. Agnes is running out of time. Where are they?"

Rosalie wriggled free. "They're here."

"Not amused, Rosalie." Gethsemane grabbed her arm.

"Can you think of a better place for the devil's minion to commit murder than in a house of God?" She wrenched out of Gethsemane's grip.

Frankie ran from the sacristy. He returned in a moment. "The narthex and nave are empty."

"How could Mal electrocute anyone in the church? People are in and out all the time. They'd have seen him rigging up whatever he plans to use to do the, the deed." Gethsemane shuddered at the thought of a killing machine being hidden somewhere waiting for its victim. "Unless his plan was to stick her hand in the holy water font and toss in an iron? And people would see him dragging her in to the church. I'm guessing she's not cooperating with the man who's trying to kill her."

"The baptistry."

Everyone turned to look at Father Tim.

"The old baptistry in the subbasement. He could use the baptismal pool."

"He knows it's there, he's seen it," Gethsemane said. "He mentioned it when he talked about scouting photo shoot locations. Too gothic for Sunny."

"But not for murder," Father Tim said.

"He found a way in through a side entrance. One without a lot of foot traffic. The baptismal pool. It was used for immersions?"

The priest nodded.

"Then Agnes would fit."

"The pool would be dry, surely," Frankie said.

Gethsemane reddened. "I told him about the stream that runs under here, about how it provided water for the pool. Mal's resourceful. He's had time to find access to the stream."

Twenty-Seven

Tim led the procession through the undercroft, past the basement level, to the subbasement. Bare overhead bulbs cast a mournful glow over dust-covered cardboard boxes and surplus religious paraphernalia. The items here looked as if they'd been neglected even longer than those in the rectory's basement.

"This was the baptistry's narthex," Tim explained. "These bulbs," he pointed at the overhead lights, "are a modern addition. They're not kept burning, as a rule."

"Someone's here," Gethsemane said.

"Yes," a voice, a hint of Louisiana audible under its polished veneer, called out from the dim recess of a back room. "Please join me. Executions need witnesses."

"It's Mal."

"The baptistry's that way." Tim led them into the semi-darkness.

Gethsemane called out, "Is Agnes with you?"

"Of course." Malcolm's reply gave her goosebumps. "She's the guest of honor."

"Did anyone think to call the guards?" Father Tim whispered.

"I forgot," Gethsemane whispered back.

Frankie pulled his phone from his pocket.

"And," Malcolm added, as if sensing Frankie's action, "if

any of you are thinking of phoning for help, Agnes will be dead before the police, excuse me, the gardaí, get here."

Frankie tucked his phone back in his pocket. Gethsemane pulled it out again and mouthed, *Text anyway.*

They kept walking toward Malcolm's voice. It brought them to an octagonal chamber cluttered with more church surplus and discards. More overhead bulbs illuminated the remains of faded, damaged frescoes, partially visible between cardboard box towers, depicting the life of John the Baptist. Three stone steps led from the center of the room down to a piscina—a baptismal pool that should have been dry after two centuries of disuse. Instead, water filled it to its brim. Puddles formed at its edge where water lapped over the sides. Agnes, up to her neck in water, sat in its middle. Duct tape covered her mouth and bound her hands. Her eyes pleaded for salvation. Malcolm stood over her, bright camera monolight in hand. The light's electric cord trailed off into the gloom behind him.

"Pull up a box, ladies and gentlemen, make yourselves comfortable." Malcolm's apparent calm made his words seem even more malevolent. "Father, if you wish to administer last rites, I don't mind waiting. I don't think Miss Haywood is Roman Catholic, but given the circumstances, I'm sure you'll overlook technicalities."

"Stop this," Tim demanded. "How dare you profane this sacred space, desecrate God's holy church?"

"Be careful up there on your high horse, Father. It may hurt when you fall. Our Lady of Perpetual Sorrows will hardly be the first holy place to serve as witness to death. Ask Thomas Becket."

"This is sacrilege!"

"This is justice!" Malcolm's eyes flashed as fury contorted his features. "Justice for Jared, whose only 'crime' was choosing a faithless, rotten woman." He spat at Agnes.

Agnes made noises behind her duct tape and tried to move away from her tormentor. Gethsemane strained to see what kept Agnes in the pool—something wrapped around her legs.

Malcolm noticed her stare. "It's a weight. An anchor, specifically. The condemned is usually strapped into the electric chair with a leather belt, but an anchor seemed more practical."

"Agnes doesn't deserve to die for being a lousy girlfriend," Gethsemane said.

"Let's ask Frankie." Malcolm turned his malicious grin on the math teacher. "He's had more than one man's fair share of lousy life partners. What's a just punishment for betraying the trust of the man who loves you?"

"How do you know about—" Gethsemane caught herself before she said Yseult's name.

"Heartbreak and despair? A rosy little bird told me, didn't you Cousin Rosalie? When she warned me you were snooping around, asking about New Orleans and what happened there. I admire you for wanting to protect your friend. If others had been as loyal as you they wouldn't be dead now." Malcolm turned back to Frankie. "How about it? What's the best way to deal with cheating hearts?"

"A restraining order and suing for custody of the dog," Frankie said. "Not this."

"You're too soft-hearted, my man. For what it's worth, Verna did love you. Although, she wouldn't have hesitated to feed you to the wolves to save herself and her sister."

Frankie tensed and leaned toward the piscina. Gethsemane squeezed his arm and willed him to wait.

"This isn't justice," she said. "It's murder. Common murder."

"Not murder." Malcolm raised the monolight above his head. The bright beam hit the water, illuminating it as if lightening had flashed. Agnes's jaw quivered as she tried to scream behind her gag. Tears streamed, rippling the surface of the font's water where they dripped from her chin. "Justice." Malcolm drew his arm back.

"Retribution!" Gethsemane shouted. "Cheap, tawdry, two-bit revenge. Straight out of a bad movie."

Mal remained still. Agnes tried to scream again.

Gethsemane stepped forward. "Being a shite girlfriend is heartbreaking. It is not a crime. And, even if it was, it wouldn't warrant the death penalty."

"And Jared? Did he deserve a death sentence?" Malcolm lowered the light as he spoke. As the beam arced toward the floor, it flashed over Frankie. The math teacher crept up behind Malcolm.

Gethsemane kept talking. "Jared's death was an accident."

"An accident? Is that what they call driving under the influence where you come from? Everyone in that car was blind drunk. Lismore had as much business behind the wheel as a duck has wearing a wig. But that didn't stop ol' Ty, did it? He got drunk, got in the driver's seat, and drove into a bayou. He saved himself and left Jared to drown. Not even brave enough to admit what he'd done. Instead, the coward put the blame on poor, dead Jared, the man he killed. That's no accident."

"Granted, it probably qualifies as vehicular homicide. On Ty's part, not Agnes's. She's an accessory, at best. Turn her over to the authorities and let them dispense real justice."

"Hah!" Malcolm sneered. "Dispense justice? You mean let them do nothing. Let them tell Jared's mother that it's been too long to prosecute anyone for the death of her only son. Let them tell his father that there's not enough evidence, that their case load's too heavy. Let them tell Jared's family that Jared isn't important enough to be bothered with." He raised the light.

Gethsemane threw up her hands. "No, don't!"

"Why the hell not?"

"B-because," she stammered as she tried to think of a reason. Any reason. She forced herself to ignore Frankie as, behind Malcolm, he picked up a brass candlestick. Stall, stall, stall. "Because the one thing I can't figure out is how *you* figured out what happened that night. Sure, you knew Agnes's name but not the others'. Maybe sussing out who her friends were after you met her wasn't difficult, but they weren't talking. They'd all agreed to keep mum about that night. How'd you know? Some kind of occult trick? Did Cousin Rosalie read the answer in the tarot cards?"

Malcolm's mocking laugh angered more than frightened her. "Now who sounds like a bad movie? You've been spending too much time with the spooks, m'dear. My method of deduction was quite mundane. Taking photos of Sunny meant taking photos of Ty and their friends, or hangers-on, or entourage, or whatever you want to call them. All part of the social media strategy of curating their image. Not that they minded being photographed. Except for Theophilus, they were as vain as the happy couple. You'd be surprised at how open people are with the man behind the camera. Maybe not as open as they are with their hairdressers and bartenders, but I bet they tell me more than they tell their priest. Isn't that right, Father?" he called to Tim.

"Please, I beg you," Tim said, "stop this madness. Let Agnes go."

Gethsemane sensed Malcolm's mood shift. She redirected him. "Tell us the rest."

"Pact or no, people have a hard time keeping secrets, especially when they're guilty ones. Sharing our burdens is human nature. I'd hoped to get Agnes talking, but she turned out to have more of a backbone than I'd anticipated. I'd admire her if I didn't hate her. Brian Nishi turned out to be the weak link. He gossips. Excuse me, gossiped, past tense. Dead men tell no tales. Drunk men, however, do. Brian and I bonded over tattoo art and I plied him with liquor. He let enough details slip for me to piece together his involvement and get a pretty good idea of that of the others. But it wasn't until I'd seduced him that he let the whole story out."

"Seduced?" Surprised crept into her voice. "But I thought—I mean, what about Vivian?"

"You're shocked," Mal said. "How charmingly conventional. Sunny and Ty's crew is a broad-minded bunch. And the damned's gotta do what the damned's gotta do. I scored a bit of luck there. Turns out Brian talked in his sleep. He suffered from full-blown somniloquy—monologues, dialogs, the gamut. I don't know what position the National Sleep Foundation takes, but I'm convinced his vow of secrecy about Jared's death triggered his sleep-talking disorder. The strain of covering up a murder during the day led him to talk about it at night. And I lay beside him, taking it all in. He didn't realize he talked in his sleep. Even if he had, I'd no fear he'd admit to the others that he'd blabbed."

"You never let on that you and Brian had a relationship."

"It ended before we turned up in Dunmullach. Brian had a serious girlfriend who was not broad-minded enough to tolerate being cheated on and I had my own reasons for not wanting to go public, so we kept things hush-hush. Besides, it wasn't a relationship. It was a fling that I ended once it had served its purpose."

"Your purpose being to find more names to add to your hit list."

"I'd already planned a send-off for Agnes. I blame her for Jared's death more than anyone, even Ty. If he'd never met her..." Malcolm closed his eyes for a second.

Frankie raised the candlestick, started to swing—

Malcolm opened his eyes and shifted his weight, moving out of Frankie's target zone. Frankie pulled back. Gethsemane held her breath and locked her gaze on Malcolm.

Malcolm continued. "If Jared had never met Agnes, he'd be with me still. Agnes was always going to die. But I knew she hadn't acted alone. Why should she die alone? Once I got the full story from Brian, I decided that since Agnes, Ty, Brian, Theo, and Verna had all hung together, they should all hang together. Metaphorically speaking. Ty's the only one who actually hanged."

Realization dawned. "Coming to Dunmullach for this pre-wedding photoshoot was actually your idea, wasn't it? So you could get at Verna. Ty talked Sunny into coming with some nonsense about the scenery complementing her hair, but you talked Ty into it, didn't you?"

Mal winked. "You're really getting the hang of this detective stuff. Not that I had to twist Ty's arm. I'm not the only one who wanted to get at Verna."

"Your hook up with Vivian. Also part of your plot against Verna?"

"Mostly. Say ninety percent? Ten percent was just for me. Vivian's...enthusiasm...is alluring. Initially, I envisioned using one Cunningham sister to target the other. But once I discovered how unguarded Vivian was around her ADHD meds..."

"You stole dextroamphetamine capsules from Vivian to put in Ty's booze." Gethsemane tried not to look at Frankie, arms raised, candlestick ready, behind Mal. He shook and sweat beaded his forehead despite the cool of the basement.

"Seemed fitting. Her sister protected the man who stole my cousin's life. Next you'll want to know how I slipped them to Ty. Since we've got to get this show going, I'll save you the trouble of asking. Vivian handed the flask to me after her spitball stunt and asked me to return it to Ty. She'll be disappointed to learn that I dumped the flask and refilled it with fresh stock. I don't know how spit alters the taste of whiskey and I needed Ty to drink the stuff." Mal shifted position again. Frankie aborted his blow.

Did she imagine a gleam in Mal's eye? Did he know Frankie was behind him? Was he messing with them? "Did you know how the dextroamphetamine would interact with the meds Ty was taking for his respiratory illness?"

"No idea. But I knew they'd interact with the alcohol. I spiked it with enough speed to send Ty zooming to the moon. Then I swung by the bar and gave him back his flask like the straight up guy I am." Sarcasm ran so thick in Mal's voice; Gethsemane marveled he didn't choke on it. "Ty was in no hurry to get back to his blushing bride-to-be so I knew he planned to slip out and find a place to get drunk, someplace Sunny wouldn't catch him. Ty's a sloppy drunk and Sunny hates sloppy."

"Someplace isolated, where he could meet Verna without fear of Sunny catching him. Did Vivian tell you or did you guess?" She willed Frankie to hurry up and swing already.

"I guessed. Ty was as predictable as he was cruel. He practically foamed at the mouth at the thought of getting back into Verna's head."

"What if Ty had OD'd on that amphetamine-booze cocktail you served him?"

Mal shrugged. "It would have been that much easier to get him over the railing."

"What if Verna shared Ty's flask? Weren't you afraid—"

Malcolm waved the question away. His raised arm threw off Frankie's aim. "That was a chance I was willing to take. I trusted that Verna Cunningham had enough hard-won sense not to indulge in mind- or mood-altering substances in the presence of Ty Lismore. I was right. She declined his offer of a drink as well as his advances."

"You were there?" There *was* a gleam in Ty's eye.

Gethsemane forced herself to keep her eyes on his face. *Damn it, Frankie, screw mathematical precision—swing!*

"Of course. I wanted to see Lismore die. I waited until Verna left and Ty got drunk, then I climbed up to the walk and whispered terrifying things in the dark. With his mind turned to susceptible mush by that chemical stew he'd ingested, convincing him there was only one way to save himself was pathetically easy. He grabbed the noose from my hand." Ty pantomimed a hanging. Frankie repositioned himself and took aim.

Gethsemane fought to keep the anxiety out of her voice. She wanted to yell to Frankie, "Do it now!" Instead she asked Malcolm, "Why not kill Verna then and be done with both of them?"

"You might as well ask Dame Christie why she didn't put all of the murderers in *And Then There Were None* in a ferry and sink it, to be done with all of them at once. Where's the fun in that?"

"Fun? You think this is fun? Killing people one by one—"

"Don't forget directing suspicion to the Cunningham sisters. I enjoyed that, too."

Nausea rose from the pit of Gethsemane's stomach. "How can you call serial murder fun?"

"Serial retribution. It was at least as much fun as Jared had, drowning alone, trapped in a slowly sinking truck, clawing at his seatbelt, pounding on windows, holding his breath until his lungs threatened to explode, understanding with his last moments of consciousness that people he trusted, the woman he loved, the person who put him in that water had saved themselves and left him behind to die. It was at least that much fun.

A sickening thwack, the sound of metal on bone, echoed off the baptistry walls. For a full ten seconds, the room held its breath. The world froze.

Then Malcolm turned, his slow movement an agony to watch. Frankie stood behind him, brass candlestick gripped like a major league batter swinging for a home run. Anger, annoyance, and hate played across Malcolm's face. He smiled reminiscent of a vicious schoolboy the second before he swatted a harmless ladybug.

"Pathetique" warned Gethsemane the second before it happened. She couldn't yell his name fast enough. "Frankie!"

Malcolm's arm shot out and hit Frankie hard across the face. The math teacher flew backward and slammed into a stack of boxes. The uppermost box tipped and altar candles rained down on his head as blood rained down from his nose. The candlestick clattered to the floor and bounced into the piscina. Agnes tried to dodge away from it but the anchor kept her from moving more than a few inches.

"That wasn't very nice," Malcolm said.

"Neither was hitting Frankie." Gethsemane rushed to her downed friend. "I think you broke his nose."

"I might have killed him." He watched as Father Tim searched through boxes. The priest uncovered a bundle of purificators and tore it open. He held one of the linen cloths against Frankie's nose. Malcolm sighed. "I'll be generous and mark this down to attempted self-defense. I won't prosecute."

"Won't prosecute?" Gethsemane scowled. "Who the hell appointed you D.A., judge, and jury?"

Malcolm shrugged and pushed up his sleeve. He aimed his light at his tattooed devil's handshake, the mark of his Faustian deal.

"And why are you still standing?" she added with a shudder. "We all heard that candlestick make contact with your skull. They probably heard it all the way in Cork. You're not even bleeding."

Father Tim replaced Frankie's saturated purificator with a clean one.

Malcolm touched his head where the blow landed then held up his hand and wiggled his bloodless fingers. "Now that, ladies and gentlemen, is what we who are damned to hell call an occult trick."

Rosalie leaned her head back against a wall. She spoke without looking at the others. "Some of those tattoos gracing my cousin's arms are more than mere body art. They're sigils used as protection spells, part of the deal my cousin made with the devil. He won't die until he has his revenge. Agnes is still alive, therefore, so is my cousin. If you let him kill Agnes and then hit him..."

Agnes squirmed and splashed and tried to get out of the pool.

"Of course," Rosalie leaned away from the wall, "we can't let that happen." She pulled a brass bishop's crozier from the shadows. "Forgive me, Father, for I have sinned."

"Cousin Rosalie," Malcolm tightened his grip on the monolight, "what are you doing?"

Rosalie offered Gethsemane a rueful smile. "That tarot card reading I told you about, the one that predicted approaching death? The death it predicted—is mine." She raised the crozier and jammed its end into an electrical socket. Sparks flew, then the baptistry went dark.

"The lights!" Gethsemane reached out in the pitch black of the room. Her hand landed on Frankie's head. He groaned.

"Rosalie blew a fuse." Father Tim's voice sounded nearby.

"Agnes?" Gethsemane called out. "Agnes, make some noise. Please."

Splashing sounded from the direction of the piscina.

"Rosalie?" Gethsemane waited. "Rosalie, are you there?"

Rosalie didn't answer.

Gethsemane hesitated. She lowered her voice. "Mal?"

She jumped at a scrape and hiss near her ear. Father Tim's face appeared in the light of an altar candle. He handed it to Gethsemane and lit another.

She held hers aloft. Frankie lay next to her, blood-soaked purificator pressed against his nose. Father Tim knelt opposite. He also held his candle up and scanned the room.

Shadow and light flickered across the piscina. Agnes struggled against the duct tape. Beyond her a form lay crumpled next to a bishop's crozier.

Tim blew Gethsemane's candle out. "You don't want to see that."

She faced the opposite direction and Tim re-lit her candle. "Where's Mal?"

"Gone." Tim went to Agnes's aid.

Twenty-Eight

Frankie waved the EMT away. "The bleeding's stopped. I'm fine. I don't want transport to hospital." He shifted on the ambulance seat. "Could you make this thing any less comfortable?"

The EMT stripped off her rubber gloves and threw them on the ambulance floor. "This is why I prefer unconscious patients." She eyed Gethsemane with pity. "Let me know if he changes his mind."

"Frankie," Gethsemane said, "your nose is broken. It's going to heal crooked."

"A bump mid-nose adds character. Don't fuss."

They fell silent as Scene of Crime gardaí wheeled a stretcher through the church yard for the second time that day. Gethsemane slipped an arm around Frankie's shoulders.

Niall's voice came from behind them. "Poor Rosalie. Her overloading the circuit killed power to the whole church, including Mal's camera light. Saved Agnes from electrocution but at such a price. Any idea why she sacrificed herself? She and Agnes weren't close."

"Rosalie had her demons," Gethsemane said. "Literally, it seems. How's Agnes?"

"Being treated for shock but grateful to be alive."

"What happens to her now? Will you arrest her?"

"Arrest her for what?" Niall asked.

"For covering up a murder, what else?"

"I'm afraid, my sweet justice warrior—" He held up a hand to stop her protest. "I mean that sincerely. I'm afraid this may be one of those times when not all who have it coming, get what's due them. Even if New Orleans wasn't out of my jurisdiction, which it is, there may no longer be a crime with which to charge Agnes. Remember our earlier conversation, when you hesitated to tell me about Verna being in the car with the others for fear I'd arrest her? I did a bit of research on American law. You were right. Statutes of limitations may apply to concealing evidence of a murder and obstruction of justice. Since Agnes hardly qualifies as a most wanted criminal, I doubt there'd be much impetus to extradite her, even if the statutes haven't expired."

"So, unless she returns to New Orleans on her own..."

Niall slipped an arm around Gethsemane and hugged her. "I know a fella with the N.O.P.D. We met on an ITAC CEPOL CPD course in Dublin."

"A what in Dublin?"

"A continuing professional education course focusing on law enforcement cooperation and information exchange at the Garda College. This fella and I keep in touch. I'll give him a heads up on the situation."

"But I shouldn't hold my breath. Unless Agnes turns herself in, she'll end up like Yseult."

"A fugitive on the run from theft and fraud charges? Not exactly a pleasant outcome."

"Better than near electrocution. Agnes will have to live with the trauma of that experience. So I guess she's not getting off with no punishment."

"She'll also be looking over her shoulder for Mal. Something tells me he's not the sort to leave a job unfinished."

"Speaking of the devil, any idea where Mal is?"

"Not yet." Niall adjusted his hat. "No sign of him on the

church yard, at the inn, or in the pub. Sutton's put an all-points out for the train and bus station and the Cork airport. We've also got patrols out on the roads. We'll catch him."

Niall excused himself as Sutton beckoned from the ambulance where a sodden Agnes huddled under a blanket on a stretcher as EMTs attached monitors and started an IV. Father Tim bowed his head in prayer near the foot of the stretcher.

"Don't count on it," Gethsemane said.

"Count on what?" Frankie said.

"Catching Mal."

"Malcolm Amott can go straight to hell."

"He will. Eventually."

Frankie climbed down from the back of the ambulance. "Time to go."

"Go where?"

"I dunno. Anywhere. Away from here. For a walk." He started for the church gate. "Come with me? I could use a friend."

Gethsemane linked her arm through his and they walked toward the village square.

Eamon materialized when they came even with the post office. He walked by Gethsemane's other side. "You know they've not a chance in hell of finding Amott? Literally, not a chance in hell."

She answered without thinking. "Yeah, I know."

"Sissy?" Frankie said.

She swore under her breath. She'd forgotten Frankie could neither see nor hear ghosts. And, truth be told, she'd forgotten Eamon was a ghost. "What, Frankie?"

"Who are you talking to?"

"Oops. Sorry." Eamon laughed, not sounding sorry at all, and dematerialized.

"Who am I talking to? Besides you?"

Frankie stopped. "Sissy, I'm the one who got smacked in the head, but you're the one not making sense. You were just talking to yourself."

"Not exactly."

"Then who were you talking to?"

She tugged his arm and started walking again. "That, my friend, is a long, strange story. How about you come up to the cottage with me, I'll fix you a cup of tea, and tell it?"

"I'm going to hear this story and think you're a header, aren't I?"

"Probably. But you'll still like me because we're friends."

An ambulance drove past. The EMT who'd failed to convince Frankie to go to the hospital leaned from the window and waved at them. They paused to look back at the sun setting over Our Lady of Perpetual Sorrows. In the yard, gardaí and EMTs and a solitary priest busied themselves restoring order from chaos.

"Frankie," Gethsemane said.

"Yes?"

"Don't call me Sissy."

Twenty-Nine

Tick. Tick. Tick. Tick.

Gethsemane stood in the center of Carraigfaire Cottage's music room with her eyes closed and listened as the metronome atop the piano marked a beat.

Tick. Tick. Tick. Tick.

No other sounds intruded. No Tchaikovsky in her head. No shrieking social media influencers. No threatening gardaí. No pleading, no begging, no crying, no lies. Only the low-pitched, slow, echoing tick of the metronome. For the first time in days, she felt at peace.

A deep breath drew air to the bottom of her lungs. She exhaled fully, feeling the anxiety and tension and fear and worry that had consumed her, since the first notes of "Pathétique" had warned her of the dangers to come, flow from her body like bad humors escaping after a long illness. Her next breath carried with it the freshness of soap overlaid with the aromas of leather, cedar, and pepper.

She held a finger to her lips. "Ssh. Don't say anything."

She opened her eyes to Eamon seated at the piano. "Now you may speak."

"Are you all right?" Eamon asked.

"At this moment, I'm all right. I'm all right for the first time since I heard the names Ty Lismore and Sunny Markham. At this moment, no one is being murdered, no one is being accused of murder, no one is being lied to, no one is lying to anyone, and no one is having their heart ripped out and stomped on by someone they loved and trusted. This moment is perfect. With my luck, five minutes from now a corpse may turn up on the front porch. But not right now. Right now is good."

Eamon turned to the piano. He silenced the metronome with a glance and began to play. His fingers disappeared into the keys as he drew the quick, bright notes of Beethoven's "Piano Sonata No. 9 in E Major, Op. 14 No. 1" from the instrument. The music surrounded Gethsemane with joy and replaced the darkness of the past few days with a lightness that almost overwhelmed her.

"Thank you for that," she said as the notes died away. "I needed it."

"How long has it been since you've picked up your violin?" Eamon nodded at her Vuillaume in its case on a stand.

"Too long." Preoccupied with murder, she'd neglected her music over the summer, and she realized, felt the worse for it. She raised her violin into position and eased into the first movement of Beethoven's "Violin Sonata No. 9 in A Major, Op. 47." Her opening adagio gave way to an intense presto as Eamon joined her on the piano, their two instruments combining to create a virtuosic performance that transformed her last, lingering shreds of grief into an indescribable feeling of rapture.

The movement ended and she collapsed onto the piano bench next to Eamon. "I haven't felt this good in—when have I felt this good?"

"Too bad you can't package some of this feeling and share it with your mate, Frankie."

"Frankie." An arrow of sadness pierced her joy. "Saying I'm worried about him is an understatement. For the second time in his life, love's hauled off and kicked him in the teeth. Plus, he's been suspected of murdering the ex-lover of a woman he loved for the second time in less than six months and he watched one of those women die a horrible death, unable to save her even though she was only a few feet away. Then I tell him I live in a haunted house and see dead people and oh, by the way, the man who murdered his girlfriend is in league with the devil, literally." She plucked the opening measures of the third movement, "Scherzo. Pizzicato ostinato," of Tchaikovsky's "Symphony No. 4 in F Minor, Op 36." "He's started drinking again. Heavy drinking, I mean."

"He's got a god-awful road ahead of him."

"What if I can't save him?"

"What if you're just there for him?"

Something scuffled at the front door. Gethsemane gasped with a start that sent the Villaume sliding from her hands.

Eamon's well-aimed, pointed finger saved it from tragedy. "Careful." He levitated the priceless instrument back into its case.

"Did you hear that?" She stood and rushed to the cottage's entry.

"Not so fast." Eamon materialized between her and the door. "Allow me." He vanished.

A moment later, the door swung open. Eamon stood on the threshold. An envelope levitated in front of him.

Gethsemane grabbed it. "Did you see who left it?"

"Nope. Not a soul in sight. I went all the way to the foot of Carrick Point Road."

The thin envelope weighed no more than a single sheet of paper. Gethsemane's title and last name, "Dr. Brown," marched in block print across the center front. No other writing, nor marks, nor stamps were present. She held it up to the light.

"It'd be much easier to read if you opened it," Eamon said. A letter opener appeared.

She slit the top and unfolded the contents.

A line drawn rendition of Malcolm Amott's devil's handshake tattoo filled most of the sheet. Below that, the printed words:

Until next time.

Gethsemane gave into an urge she seldom yielded to. She sobbed.

Thirty

Gethsemane answered the door a few mornings later to find Agnes on Carraigfaire Cottage's porch, tote bag slung over a shoulder, roll-aboard at her feet.

"Agnes, you're out of the hospital. How are you?"

"Alive," Agnes said, "for the time being, anyway."

She swung the door wide. "Come in."

Agnes chuckled without mirth. "Are you sure you want a known criminal in your home?"

"Agnes, I—"

"It's okay. I know what I've done. I know what I am. Thanks for the invitation but I'm not staying. I didn't want to leave Dunmullach without saying thank you and goodbye. And to ask you to give my thanks to Frankie and Father Tim."

"Where are you going? Back to New York?"

"Back to Sunny's home turf?" Agnes shook her head. "No, thanks."

"Back to New Orleans?"

"Back to the scene of the crime to 'fess up and throw myself on the mercy of the justice system? What's the word they use over here? Fecking? Are you fecking kidding?"

"It's more like 'feckin.' Drop the 'g.' Add 'eejit' after for the full effect. 'Cop on, ya feckin' eejit, what'd I be doin' that fer?'"

Eamon's voice sounded in Gethsemane's ear. "Not bad,

darlin'. The brogue's improved."

"The answer's no. I'm not going to go back and turn myself in. Agnes Haywood is not a do-the-right-thing type of girl. I'm going to take a page from Sunny's book—" Agnes laughed. "As if Sunny Markham ever read a book. I'm going to take a post from Sunny's feed and look after me. You don't know what to say."

"Um, good luck with that?"

Agnes sighed and her shoulders slumped as if a great weight had just landed on her. The tote bag slid to the ground.

"Are you sure you don't want to come inside?" Gethsemane asked.

"I'm sure." Agnes shook herself and hoisted her bag. "The real reason I'm not going back to New York or New Orleans— aside from not wanting to risk serving a lengthy prison term in a Louisiana prison—is that those are the first two places Mal will look for me."

"You really think Mal will—"

"Come after me? I heard what Rosalie said in the baptistry. That Mal's deal with the devil means he lives until I die. And I heard the hatred in Mal's voice. Yes, I know he will come after me. If he catches me, well, a Louisiana prison would look like heaven in comparison. So, hi ho, hi ho, it's on the run I go."

"You should go to Father Tim. Ask him to—"

"Pray for my miserable soul? Ask God's forgiveness on my behalf? Do you believe everyone deserves forgiveness, Gethsemane?"

She thought for a moment. "I believe everyone deserves a chance at redemption."

"You're a better person than I am. How could I redeem myself for leaving Jared to die? Mal will never forgive me. Mal will kill me if he finds me and he's got an eternity to spend looking for me. I intend to drag the search out as long as possible."

"Good luck with that. I mean it."

"You could do me a favor." Agnes rolled her suitcase toward Gethsemane. "Donate the case and its contents to a local thrift shop."

"Won't you need clothes? Unless you're planning to hide out from Mal at a nudist colony."

Agnes patted her tote bag. "I'm only traveling with what I can carry in here. I'll buy anything else I need when I get to...wherever I'm going. I need to stay six steps ahead of Mal, which means I need to travel light." She pushed the case closer to Gethsemane. "They're quality clothes. They'd earn at least a few bucks for a charity."

"A few Euros." Gethsemane rolled the case inside. "I'll take it."

"Thank you," Agnes said. "For everything. For saving my life, unworthy as it is."

"Everyone's worth saving."

"Even Ty? Sunny?"

As much as she'd disliked Ty and couldn't stand Sunny, she didn't wish either of them dead. "Even Ty and Sunny."

"Even Mal?"

Malcolm Amott, motivated to kill out of pain and anguish over the unpunished death of a cousin who'd been like a brother to him. "Even Mal." Especially Mal. "But I don't think he wants saving."

"No, he wants retribution. Unholy retribution. He's waited all these years, he can continue to wait."

"How will you get by? Moneywise, I mean."

"When I said I was in finance, I meant I'm an expert financial planner. I have money saved. And Rosalie left me a little something. I received a letter from her addressed to me at Sweeney's Inn yesterday. She'd mailed it before—before what happened at the church." Agnes shifted her bag to her other shoulder and offered Gethsemane her hand. "My flight leaves Cork airport in a couple of hours. I have to go."

"Take care of yourself, Agnes."

"Thank you. And say a prayer for me, if you're so inclined. Every little bit helps. Bye."

Gethsemane watched as Agnes disappeared around the bend in the road leading to Carrick Point.

Eamon materialized next to her, glowing a worried saffron. "You'd do well to take care of yourself, darlin'. Mal's the vengeful type. You bollixed his plan. I doubt he's best pleased with you. He's got an eternity to nurse the grudge."

"Forever's a long time to hold a grudge."

"He's up to the challenge. Be careful. You're my friend and I'm in no hurry to see you end up the way I am. There's a limit to my watching over you. I mean, I'd offer to take a bullet for you, but—" He passed his hand through the wall. "I'm afraid it's a bit late for that."

Gethsemane tip-toed to kiss his cheek. A charge zipped from her head to her fingertips as her lips passed through what would have been his skin.

Eamon's aura dimmed a bit, then brightened. "That tickled."

"Thanks, Irish, for having my back. I don't show my appreciation as often as I should but I'm glad you chose to stick around."

"Aww, shucks."

"My brogue's better than your cowboy accent."

"All joking aside, will you go see our favorite priest and ask him for a talisman or a blessing or a spell or something to keep Malcolm Amott from darkening our door?"

"I will, I promise. This afternoon."

"I'm not coddin', Gethsemane. The wanker sent you a note promising to return."

"I promise. What do you want me to do? Pinky swear?"

"Will you also promise to stay away from dead bodies, dangerous supernatural forces, and murderers?"

If only. "I don't go looking for those things, Irish." She shot the front door's deadbolt. "They find me."

"I mean it about Father Tim."

"I mean it about going this afternoon. I have a couple of stops to make first."

Thirty-One

Gethsemane rang the old-fashioned bell perched on the marble top of Sweeney's Inn's front desk and waited for the smartly uniformed desk clerk to appear.

"How may I help you?" the young man asked.

"I'm here to see Vivian Cunningham. Would you ring her room and see if she's in?"

The clerk hesitated. He fiddled with a pen and wouldn't look at Gethsemane.

"Vivian Cunningham," she repeated. "She's in—"

"Miss Cunningham checked out."

"Checked out? When?"

"Last night, ma'am."

"Did she say where she was going?"

"She didn't say, ma'am. But I believe the ambulance took her to hospital."

"She left by ambulance?"

"Yes, Ma'am."

Gethsemane sighed. Sweeney's Inn took discretion seriously. "Would you please just tell me what happened? I'm not a reporter nor a process server. I'm not going to broadcast the news nor where I got it all over town."

The clerk chewed his lower lip.

"Please." Gethsemane leaned her elbows on the desk and

lowered her voice. "Miss Cunningham's sister was my friend's girlfriend. Frankie Grennan, do you know him? I'm going to see him later and I'm sure he'd be very concerned about Miss Vivian's well-being."

The clerk hesitated once more, then leaned in toward Gethsemane. He spoke in hushed tones. "Miss Cunningham came down to the lobby late last night, said she couldn't sleep and wanted to know if she could sit by the fireplace and if someone could bring her some paracetamol. Apparently, Miss Markham had the same problem because she came down to the lobby a few minutes after Miss Cunningham got here." He paused.

"Go on," Gethsemane encouraged.

"Miss Markham saw Miss Cunningham sitting by the fire, keeping herself to herself, by the way. She saw Miss Cunningham sitting and she went over to her. She lit into Miss Cunningham, calling her names and accusing her of ruining her wedding."

"What did Miss Cunningham do?"

"Nothing, at first. Just tried to ignore Miss Markham. But after a moment or two of non-stop having her head ate off, Miss Cunningham stood up and punched Miss Markham in the mouth."

Gethsemane's mouth fell open. She echoed the clerk. "She punched Miss Markham?"

"Yes, ma'am. And that's when the holy show began. A real knockdown, drag out."

Gethsemane surveyed the lobby. No disarray. Nothing broken or bent. Everything in its immaculate place.

"We cleaned up." The clerk sounded indignant.

"Then what?" Gethsemane asked. "How'd the fight end?"

"We called the guards and they came and broke things up. Between you and me, I'd declare Miss Cunningham the winner.

No knockout, but I'd award points for technique and form."

"The guards came and..."

"The guards broke up the fight, but Miss Cunningham wouldn't stop screaming. Wailing. Calling for her sister, over and over and over. Terrifying to watch. The guards couldn't calm her, so they sent for an ambulance."

"Poor Vivian."

"We all heard what happened to her sister, gossip in this village being what it is. The anguish of losing her sister that way must have pushed her over the edge. Sorry. Miss Markham hasn't checked out yet. I can ring her, if you like. Not sure if she'll see you, though. She refuses to leave her room until the swelling in her face goes down. She won't let anyone in except housekeeping and room service."

"No, thank you," Gethsemane said. "And thank you for the information."

The trip to Carnock, with its menacing trees and threatening brambles, felt as desolate as always. However, this time concern for what she'd find when she crested the hill kept her anxiety at bay. She reached the old asylum and headed straight for the rear of the building, not heeding the weeds and rubbish as she made her way to the low stone walls covered with her namesake rose. She poked her head into the entry way and scanned past the lush blossoms to the garden's back wall. He sat on the bench in the corner, knees drawn to his chest, bottle of whiskey beside him.

"Frankie," she said.

He didn't look at her. "I don't want any lectures on how I shouldn't be moping, I shouldn't be drinking, I shouldn't be hiding away in a corner, or how soon I'll get over it."

"How about I just sit next to you and not say anything."

He raised his head. "That'd be all right."

He moved the bottle and she sank down next to him on the bench. He rested his head on her shoulder and they sat, surrounded by sweetly perfumed beauty in the middle of decay.

Photo by Peter Larsen

ALEXIA GORDON

A writer since childhood, Alexia Gordon won her first writing prize in the 6th grade. She continued writing through college but put literary endeavors on hold to finish medical school and Family Medicine residency training. She established her medical career then returned to writing fiction.

Raised in the southeast, schooled in the northeast, she relocated to the west where she completed Southern Methodist University's Writer's Path program. She admits Texas brisket is as good as Carolina pulled pork. She practices medicine in North Chicago, IL. She enjoys the symphony, art collecting, embroidery, and ghost stories.

The Gethsemane Brown Mystery Series
by Alexia Gordon

Henery Press Mystery Books

And finally, before you go...
Here are a few other mysteries
you might enjoy:

PILLOW STALK

Diane Vallere

A Madison Night Mystery (#1)

Interior Decorator Madison Night might look like a throwback to the sixties, but as business owner and landlord, she proves that independent women can have it all. But when a killer targets women dressed in her signature style—estate sale vintage to play up her resemblance to fave actress Doris Day—what makes her unique might make her dead.

The local detective connects the new crime to a twenty-year old cold case, and Madison's long-trusted contractor emerges as the leading suspect. As the body count piles up, Madison uncovers a Soviet spy, a campaign to destroy all Doris Day movies, and six minutes of film that will change her life forever.

Available at booksellers nationwide and online

Visit www.henerypress.com for details

PUMPKINS IN PARADISE

Kathi Daley

A Tj Jensen Mystery (#1)

Between volunteering for the annual pumpkin festival and coaching her girls to the state soccer finals, high school teacher Tj Jensen finds her good friend Zachary Collins dead in his favorite chair.

When the handsome new deputy closes the case without so much as a "why" or "how," Tj turns her attention from chili cook-offs and pumpkin carving to complex puzzles, prophetic riddles, and a decades-old secret she seems destined to unravel.

Available at booksellers nationwide and online

Visit www.henerypress.com for details

CPSIA information can be obtained
at www.ICGtesting.com
Printed in the USA
LVHW081910300821
696475LV00010B/122/J

9 781635 115185